"I've never <thank-you for my son."

Jenna stood motionless at Ward's words, scarcely able to breathe from the lethargy that suddenly invaded her limbs. She moistened her lips. "There's no need," she murmured, flustered.

"There's every need." The quiet intensity of his voice stunned her. "I don't know how I'd have made it through this past year without him. And I'm beginning to wonder how I ever got along without you." There was something faintly alarming in his last statement, but for the life of her, she couldn't think what it was. All she could do was stare at him, at the oddly humble expression in his eyes. "Thank you, Jenna. From the bottom of my heart, thank you."

Dear Reader,

A Family Affair, Sandra James's first Superromance, has long been a favorite of editors and readers alike. "A keeper!" our readers enthusiastically told us when this title first appeared on the stands.

After a distinguished string of Superromance hits, readers still recall with fondness this heartwarming story of a surrogate mother who finally finds happiness creating a blended family with the little boy she can't help but remember and the father she'll never forget. We've been delighted to keep this Oregon author and mother of three busy writing for us. Eight more of Sandy's Superromance novels have been equally well received, each exhibiting the author's hallmark warm, emotional tone and family-oriented plots.

We're excited about the Superromance lineup for the months ahead—a wealth of involving stories featuring memorable characters, heightened emotions and complex tensions. Don't miss the enjoyment and satisfaction you've told us you cherish in these contemporary tales of modern life and love!

Marsha Zinberg
Senior Editor, Superromance

Sandra James

A FAMILY AFFAIR

Harlequin Books

TORONTO • NEW YORK • LONDON
AMSTERDAM • PARIS • SYDNEY • HAMBURG
STOCKHOLM • ATHENS • TOKYO • MILAN

A FAMILY AFFAIR © 1986 by Sandra Kleinschmit
Original Harlequin Superromance edition
published in March 1986.

FASHION A WHOLE NEW YOU edition
published in September 1991.

ISBN 0-373-15157-8

All rights reserved. Except for use in any review, the reproduction or
utilization of this work in whole or in part in any form by any electronic,
mechanical or other means, now known or hereafter invented,
including xerography, photocopying and recording, or in any
information storage or retrieval system, is forbidden without the
permission of the publisher, Harlequin Enterprises Limited, 225
Duncan Mill Road, Don Mills, Ontario, Canada M3B 3K9.

All the characters in this book have no existence outside the
imagination of the author and have no relation whatsoever to
anyone bearing the same name or names. They are not even
distantly inspired by any individual known or unknown to the
author, and all incidents are pure invention.

® are Trademarks registered in the United States Patent and
Trademark Office and in other countries.

Printed in U.S.A.

CHAPTER ONE

THE STILLNESS of the night was broken only by the quiet murmur of the sea. Gently undulating waves lapped the Gulf Coast shoreline. Soft as a sigh, a salt-tanged breeze wrapped its way around the solitary figure roaming the sandy stretch of beach.

There was a sensual fullness to the tall and graceful form, from the curve of rounded breasts beneath the pale blue cotton top, to the coltish legs clad in dark blue slacks. The woman ceased her restless prowling and slowly closed her eyes, lifting her face to the sable canopy that stretched endlessly above. Hundreds of diamond-bright stars wove a meandering pathway through the night-dark sky. The moonlight shone down on her profile, etching in silver the small straight nose, the full mobile mouth, the wavy hair that flowed like silk halfway down the proud lines of her back.

To a casual observer, she might have appeared much like the serene moonlit Texas night of which she was so much a part. But only the moon, the stars and the sky were there to bear witness to the turmoil in her mind—and her heart.

No, there was little comfort to be found in the solitude of the night for Jenna Bradford. And for the third night in a row, she was very much afraid she would find sleep just as elusive.

A sudden burst of wind sent her long black hair whipping around her face. Eyes that were normally a vivid shade of green turned dark with uncertainty as she opened them and lifted a slender hand to brush the wayward strands from her face. Wrapping her arms around herself to ward off the sudden chill, she retraced her steps with a long-legged stride that soon carried her to the rear of a long string of apartment buildings dotting the shoreline. Once on the flag-stoned terrace, however, she made no move to enter her home. Instead she settled herself on a lounge chair and gazed out at the glasslike surface of the Gulf.

Jenna smiled a little ruefully as she pulled a blanket over her shoulders. Neil would have a fit if he could see her now. Her late-night excursions would have to stop once they were married; he would never stand for it. Perhaps Neil was a bit overprotective, but he had compensating qualities, she hastened to remind herself. He was concise and articulate, not only in his manner of speaking but in his way of thinking, as well. She suspected this stemmed from his years in law school. With his oftentimes serious, intent look, she occasionally teased him that he reminded her of a wise old bird. A pair of owlish glasses was all that was needed to complete the picture. Yet, even though she admired his sound reasoning and judicious nature, she was beginning to wonder if he wasn't rather... ambitious.

And somehow, Jenna wasn't quite sure how she felt about that.

But now was a time for joy, a time to love and be loved, a time every little girl dreams of. She should have been deliriously happy, she told herself for what seemed the thousandth time that day. Well, perhaps not deliriously so, since that wasn't her style. But certainly she had every reason to be thankful.

Again her eyes grew troubled as she gazed at the luminescent moon riding high in the sky. *Thankful*. It was, perhaps, an odd word to describe a woman who was to be married to a successful Houston attorney in six weeks' time.

Prewedding jitters. Could that possibly be what this vague uneasiness about her future husband could be? She breathed an uneasy sigh. She wasn't sure, and a twinge of guilt shot through her. Neil, her wedding, her future with him, should have filled her thoughts to the exclusion of all else. Instead the past few days had found her looking over her shoulder, unable to escape the specter of the past.

No, it wasn't Neil who dwelled in her thoughts so much as... Robbie. *Robbie*. Again she felt that elusive tug on her heart, like a fish caught on a hook and struggling to be free.

It was hard to believe the evening three days prior had started so innocently. Jenna shook her head. Her feelings, capped tightly in storage for nearly four years, had suddenly escaped, like a burst of steam from a kettle, and now she was being forced to deal with them. The only problem was how. Her heart gave her only one choice, but her mind urged caution. Three days of searching and she still wasn't sure. But was her choice the right one? For her? For him? For all concerned?

Her doubts had started Monday night, just a few days after she'd stopped working. It had been ages since she'd taken a vacation, and with so many details to be taken care of before the wedding, she had decided to take a short leave of absence from her nursing job in the Galveston Hospital Emergency Room. She and her mother had spent the day in Houston shopping for a wedding gown, and when her mother had headed home late in the afternoon, Jenna had met Neil for an early dinner. Later, when the nose of his car pointed toward Galveston, she glanced over in surprise as he exited the highway for a suburb twenty-five miles from the city. He drove straight to the heart of a residential district, finally pulling over to the curb on a wide, tree-lined street.

"Well, what do you think?" With the characteristic energy that was almost his trademark, Neil was at the car door and opening it for her before she had a chance to turn in her seat.

Out on the sidewalk, Jenna could only stare at the large Cape Cod-style house in front of her. Dense foliage edged the house before giving way to a velvety green lawn that stretched to the curb. Tendrils of ivy hugged the base of the huge oak tree in the middle of the front yard, lending a homey ambience that she found immensely appealing.

"Why are we stopping here, Neil?" she asked curiously as he pulled her toward the house. "I thought you were taking me home."

A slight breeze ruffled his thick brown hair, and he grinned openly at her. "How would you feel about calling this place home?" Pulling her toward the front door, he laced his fingers through hers.

Stunned, Jenna turned slightly to stare over his shoulder. Her gaze encompassed the house and surrounding expanse of lawn before she turned her tentative look on him.

"Well, don't you have anything to say?"

A niggling feeling of suspicion traced its way up her spine. "Neil," she began, "are you trying to tell me—"

"I bought this place?" he finished for her, smiling. "Not exactly, but I think we should think seriously about it. Even the location is perfect—halfway between Houston and Galveston. It's no more than a thirty-minute drive to work for either of us." He grabbed her hand and pulled her along behind him. "Come on, I'll give you the grand tour."

Jenna was speechless as he produced a key and led her through the house, exclaiming delightedly over the extensive use of wood and brick throughout, the polished oak and parquet floors, the crisp starched curtains hanging at the windows. When they were standing in what Neil informed her was the master bedroom, he wrapped an arm around her and tipped her face up to his. "Tell me the truth now. Do you like it?"

"I—I love it," she told him breathlessly. "But I had no idea—"

"I know." His mouth curved in a self-satisfied smile. "I wanted to surprise you. You don't mind, do you?"

"Mind! How could I mind living in this lovely home?" Her fingers traced his cleanly shaven jaw. "You're a treasure, Neil. You know that, don't you?"

He laughed and pressed a kiss in the palm of her hand before his eyes roamed around the room. "You're the one who's a treasure. I wish I'd found you years ago. Long before I ever met Anna." He shook his head. "Marrying her was the worst mistake of my life. Thank God the marriage lasted only two years."

Jenna smiled. "Marrying her was probably the *only* mistake you've ever made in your life," she teased gently. "And you did find the perfect woman eventually."

"A woman after my own heart," he said, looking down at her. "Just as dependable, efficient, stable and practical—"

"As you are," Jenna finished, laughing. "I've never been much of a believer in the theory that opposites attract."

Neil drew her body firmly against his. "We are a lot alike, you know. Anna used to prattle on incessantly. I think your reserve was one of the first things that attracted me to you."

"I didn't think you even noticed," she recalled dryly. "The night we met you were too busy talking about the job offers you'd had and which one you were going to accept."

His smile was a little sheepish. "What can I say? I was fresh out of law school and I guess it went to my head."

On reflection, she could see why. Neil had worked hard for his law degree. His parents had farmed a small piece of land in west Texas that had seen drought after drought for many a year, and his childhood hadn't been the easiest. After a stint in the military, Neil had been nearly twenty-six before he'd been able to scrape up enough money even to begin college. But despite juggling his classes with a full-time job, he had graduated from law school with honors. As a result, he'd had offers from several prestigious law firms. He had finally accepted a position as legal counsel for Citizens for Texas, a watchdog land conservation group that had become a force to be reckoned with during the past two years.

"You told me once you thought I was rather stand-offish," she remembered suddenly.

"You do come across that way at times," he said, raising an eyebrow. "You're not shy, just rather conservative. Not that there's anything wrong with that." A rare twinkle appeared in his eyes. "But I certainly never thought I'd have an Amazon in my bed."

She smiled in spite of herself. "You may never have one in your bed if you keep this up," she warned him with mock severity. Neil was usually so serious and businesslike; she enjoyed the few times he teased her. But the fact that she didn't wear her heart on her sleeve was no indication that her feelings weren't as strong as the next person's. And as for her height, she *was* tall for a woman—five-nine in her bare feet. Secretly she was glad she didn't have the large bone-structure that sometimes went hand in hand with such height in a woman. As a child, she'd hated towering over her schoolmates, boys and girls alike. It wasn't until Jenna was thirteen, when her mother finally convinced her to throw back her shoulders and make the most of her slender gracefulness, that she'd gotten over her self-consciousness. And, she had to admit, it was certainly no liability for a nurse to have a strong back.

She lifted her hands to Neil's shoulders and glanced up at him. "When Mother and I were shopping today, I found the most fantastic wedding dress at Neiman-Marcus." Touching her lips gently to his, she smiled up at him. "You should see it, Neil—yards and yards of ivory satin and lace, a high Victorian neckline..."

A half smile tipped his lips. "Are you trying to tell me I'm marrying an old-fashioned girl?"

"I thought I was marrying an old-fashioned guy," she retorted pertly.

"You are." Gently he untangled her arms from around his neck. "Come on, I'll show you the rest."

There were four bedrooms upstairs, a country-sized kitchen, very spacious living room and a small den downstairs. Though the house was old, it had obviously received a great deal of tender loving care.

"Has it been on the market long?" she asked as they stepped into the dining room. Her voice bounced off the walls of the empty room.

Neil shook his head. "The owner was transferred out of state. I don't think it will take long to sell once it goes into multiple listing. Mark Henderson tipped me off about it."

"Mark?" She glanced over in surprise. A big, sandy-haired man with a booming voice, he was an acquaintance of Neil's. "I thought he was an insurance salesman."

Neil nodded. "He's taken up real estate on the side." Blue eyes alight, he clasped both her hands in his. "Well, what do you think? Should we buy it?"

Jenna frowned. "What about the price?" she asked cautiously. "You're not a struggling young attorney anymore, but can we afford it?"

A faint line appeared between his eyebrows. "You said it yourself, Jenna. I'm not a struggling young attorney. Do you think I'd even consider it if I thought it was beyond our reach?"

It was, she decided, a silly question, after all. Neil was perhaps the most organized person she had ever known, always planning ahead. Her smile reappeared. "Does that mean no more peanut butter sandwiches for lunch?"

He seemed to relax. "No more peanut butter sandwiches," he assured her, then kissed her briefly on the mouth. "The owners are eager to sell and they're asking less than market value. I think we could make this place a home, Jenna." Slipping an arm around her narrow waist, he walked her into the living room, glanced sideways at her and said lightly, "I can see it already—coming home from the office into your arms, the smell of fresh-baked bread drifting through from the kitchen, the pitter-patter of little feet upstairs...."

"Whoa!" Jenna wrinkled her nose at him. "I might be a little old-fashioned, but homemade bread? Not unless you'd like a few broken teeth. Yeast and I just don't get along. And as far as the pitter-patter of little feet..." She shook her head. "There's no hurry, remember? We've already decided to put that off for a while."

"I know. But I've been thinking." He gave a shrug. "We've got money in the bank and we're financially able to support a child. Why wait?"

Jenna stared up at him for a few seconds before gently pulling away from his arms. "But we already agreed," she protested. "We were going to wait at least a year."

Neil frowned. "What's the matter, Jenna? I thought you liked children."

She half turned away from him, aware of the displeasure in his tone. "I do," she said earnestly, then hesitated. "But there's plenty of time...."

"*This* is the perfect time." Neil's face softened as he caught her by the shoulders and turned her to face him. "And *you* are perfect in every way for me, Jenna. You'll be a perfect wife, a perfect mother." He bent to take her lips in a brief kiss. "That's why I'd like to buy this place. My apartment in Houston is no place to bring up a child. Here he or she will have room to run, room to grow."

Jenna grew suddenly stiff in his arms. "You want to buy this house because you think it's the perfect place to bring up a child? I thought you wanted it for *us.*"

The minute the words were out of her mouth she realized how selfish they sounded. But Neil didn't seem to notice.

"I do. For all of us. And now that I've been giving it some serious consideration, I like the idea of having a child right away. After all, I'm a man on his way up and I won't be at Citizens for Texas forever. And I have an idea being a family man could be a big plus for my career."

"A man on his way up . . ." Jenna could hardly believe what she was hearing. His tone was matter-of-fact, but laced with a touch of something she found oddly disturbing. "I thought you liked your job," she said slowly. "I thought you believed in what Citizens for Texas stands for. Environmental law is your specialty."

"That's not the point, Jenna." There was a slight tinge of exasperation in his voice. "The experience has been invaluable, but who says I have to be locked in to one organization for the rest of my life? In fact, I've been putting out a few feelers lately and it looks as if I might be in hot demand. We're going places, lady!" he said almost gleefully. "I have big plans, Jenna. Plans for me, plans for you, plans for *us.*" His blue eyes gleamed as he squeezed her waist and grinned down at her.

Jenna felt almost sick. There was nothing wrong with a little ambition. After all, Neil had had so little as a child and he'd come such a long way. But she couldn't shake the feeling that he was being greedy, that he wanted too much too soon. She had to struggle to find her voice. ''And those plans include starting a family right away?''

''The sooner the better. In fact, even six weeks is too long to wait.'' His expression changed as he bent to take her lips in a hungry kiss. ''I wish we were getting married tomorrow,'' he whispered against her mouth. ''And don't say you weren't warned—I don't intend to let you out of bed for an entire week after we're married.''

And that should accomplish what he wanted quite effectively, Jenna reflected with some resentment. Unable to feel her usual tingling response at his touch, she pulled away from him to gaze out the window. Darkness was settling, and pink and purple clouds hovered on the horizon. Love and family and children were what marriage was all about, so why was she feeling such a burning sense of betrayal? Neil was a strong-principled man, staunch and firm in his beliefs. He was close to his parents and two sisters, perhaps not as close as she was to her mother and father, but they kept in touch and spent many holidays together. And yet... here he was talking about making a home, having children and his *career* in the same breath.

She clenched her hands. She was overreacting, she told herself frantically. Putting too much into his words, looking beyond them. But that didn't explain her strange reaction to the mention of a baby so soon in their future.

Jenna's skin grew cold and clammy. Suddenly she knew what was behind this vague feeling of doubt she was experiencing, and it could be summed up in a word.

Robbie.

"Jenna, what's wrong?"

She could feel Neil's puzzled look on her face and shook her head quickly. There were some things better left unsaid and—God, but she hated to think it—forgotten. Buried in the past, where they belonged.

She forced a smile. "Nothing. Nothing at all."

And she went through the evening with a curious feeling of hope in her heart—hope that the matter would work itself out and things could go back to the way they were before. But it was a sense of blighted hope, as she soon discovered.

They had finally agreed to put off making a decision about the house and give it a little more thought, but again and again over the next three days she recalled his wish for a child, and soon the words hung over her like an oppressive shroud. He wanted a family right away. Regardless of Robbie, regardless of Neil's reasons, the idea shouldn't have bothered her so much. They had discussed children soon after their engagement six months ago, and she'd known the first time they'd touched on the subject that she was going to have to deal with it eventually. But now that the prospect was baldly staring her in the face, she was aware of a nagging restlessness inside her, and she wasn't sure why.

Still, she tried to delude herself. She even tried to picture herself as the mother of Neil's child. Would he or she have Neil's rich brown hair and her green eyes? Or would he have her dark hair and Neil's blue eyes? Or would their child be a carbon copy of him—or her?

But that was when the trouble really started, because no matter how many times she tried to envision herself with a baby in her arms—*Neil's* baby—all she could see was another.

She drew a deep, unsteady breath as she continued to gaze vacantly at the Gulf. There would come a day when she could remember Robbie without this hurting, empty ache inside, but when? *When?*

She couldn't hide things from Neil any more than she could continue to deceive herself, and the matter had finally come to a head a few hours ago. Neil had come for dinner, and it was after they had cleared the table that he drew her down beside him on the couch.

His fingers slid beneath her hair to knead the taut muscles of her shoulders. "Something's bothering you, Jenna," he remarked softly. "Tell me what's wrong."

Jenna sat silent for a long time, her fingers clasped tightly in her lap. For an instant she considered telling him the truth—"the whole truth, nothing but the truth." The phrase rang like a death sentence through her mind. Still, given the same set of circumstances again, she knew she'd have done exactly the same thing as she'd decided before. But would Neil understand? Would he forgive her? Yet what was there to forgive? She'd done nothing wrong; she had nothing to be ashamed of. She had given two people what they had desperately longed for, all they'd ever wanted in the world, and it was a gift more precious than gold.

She had once promised herself there would be no regrets, no dwelling on the past or on what might have been.

"You've been acting strangely ever since I showed you the house." Despite his soothing touch on the muscles of her shoulders, there was a trace of impatience in his voice. "I thought you liked it."

A sigh escaped her lips and she smiled weakly. "I love the house, Neil."

When she hesitated, he pressed on. "Then what is it?" His eyes on her averted profile, he frowned, and then comprehension suddenly dawned. "It's what I said about having a baby, isn't it?"

Jenna nodded, then hesitated. "I'm not sure we should rush into it right away," she said slowly. "It would be nice to have some time to ourselves for a while."

"We've known each other for two years already, Jenna," he reasoned calmly. "And we'd have almost another year even if you got pregnant right away."

She turned away from his eyes, unable to bear his piercingly direct regard. Somehow she realized she'd secretly been nursing the hope that his desire to have a baby so soon was perhaps a moment of whimsy, a fanciful notion. After all, they'd been standing in what he hoped to see as their home, looking into the future.

She shifted uneasily on the cushions. "Yes, that's true, but..." She stopped, unsure of what she wanted to say, unsure of what was driving her. She and Neil were about to start a life together. Why was she suddenly plagued by doubt and senseless fears? What was wrong with her?

"I don't think you realize how strongly I feel about this, Jenna," he told her with a hint of obstinacy. "So I'd like to have a baby. What's the problem?"

"That's all well and good, Neil," she said in a carefully neutral tone. "But you seem to be forgetting I have a voice in this, as well."

Neil drew back from her abruptly. "I'm not trying to force you into anything," he said coldly. "But I'm thirty-six years old. I want to have a family while I'm young enough to enjoy it. I want to be able to run and play with my children—I don't want to be resigned to sitting on the sidelines because I'm too damned old to have a little fun.''

Jenna prickled like a cat at his sharp tone. ''You're exaggerating,'' she countered swiftly. ''You're as fit as any twenty-year old—and you're making it sound as if you're about to fall over dead any day now!''

His mouth tightened angrily. ''I suppose it never occurred to you that not only would I like to be around for my children, but I'd like to be here to see my grandchildren, too!''

Her lips puckered with annoyance, she stared at him as he paced around the room. He was being completely unreasonable—wasn't he? How many couples did she know who elected to have a baby right after they were married? Surely not many. If it happened, more than likely the baby was on the way before they were married. If only he hadn't mentioned that a family could be a boon to his career. If only...

But suddenly she realized she was only making excuses. No matter what his reasons, she should have had no reservations about carrying Neil's baby, whether it was now or ten years from now. Creating a child together was the ultimate expression of love between a man and a woman, wasn't it? The thought of having Neil's child should have held no doubts, no uncertainties, but—God help her—it did. And she didn't know why.

She knew only that in some twisted, jumbled way deep in her soul it had something to do with Robbie. She closed her eyes as a feeling of hopelessness rose inside her.

''Well, don't you have anything to say?''

Jenna flinched at Neil's angry bark, opening her eyes to stare at him. His arms were crossed over his chest. She could see frustration warring with anger in his dark blue eyes, and something else, as well. The harsh and implacable look she detected on his face stunned her.

Her mind whirled giddily. She had the strangest sensation that she was seeing him for the first time... and he wasn't the earnest, thoughtful man she had come to know at all, but a stubborn one. Unyielding. She felt helpless, suddenly drained, suddenly... so very empty inside.

Slowly she shook her head, her eyes dark and cloudy as she looked at him. "I'm sorry, Neil," she said quietly. "But this is something I'll have to work out for myself."

A tense silence settled over the room. When Neil finally spoke, his voice was curiously flat and hollow sounding. "So this is where we stand. You go your way and I go mine." He paused. "Is this any way to start our marriage, Jenna?"

EVEN NOW, hours later, his words caused an empty ache and a feeling of frustration to well up inside her. Jenna stirred on the chair and glanced at the luminous dial of her watch. It was nearly midnight. She rose and stretched her cramped muscles. In the time that she had known Neil and they had started to date, they'd had the usual heated exchange every so often. But he had never—*never*—walked out on her. She was sorely tempted to call him....

As if on cue, the telephone rang. Jenna hurried to answer it, her voice rushed.

"Jenna. Were you asleep?"

Neil. "No. I was just outside...thinking." Her tone was carefully neutral as she eased into a chair. Was he still angry? Upset?

"Outside? You were outside at this time of night?"

She nearly laughed at his sharp tone, reminded of her earlier thoughts. "I'm fine, Neil," she said softly.

He surprised her by pressing no further. Instead he said in that brisk, no-nonsense way of his, "I had to talk to you, Jenna. I called to apologize." When he cleared his throat, she had the feeling that for once he was at a loss for words. But when she made no response, he went on. "You were right, Jenna. Having a baby is something we should decide together. When we make up our minds to go ahead with it, I want it to be something we both want. So..." He seemed to hesitate. "We'll put the idea on hold for a while until you make up your mind."

Jenna sat quietly through the brief speech. Perhaps she should have been relieved; she had won, hadn't she? He wasn't going to try to force something on her she didn't want or wasn't ready for. Neil had come through, after all.... As she had known he would? She *hadn't* known that, and the thought was jarring.

"I love you, Jenna."

Jenna opened her mouth—but nothing happened. Her throat constricted tightly against the words uttered so easily up until that moment. They simply refused to come, and it was several seconds before she finally found her voice. "I—I love you, too."

"Then I'm forgiven?"

Her fingers tightened on the receiver. "Y-yes."

He didn't seem to notice the almost imperceptible hesitation, and they went on to talk for several more minutes. But while she was on the phone with Neil, the hazy shroud of doubt that had plagued her these past few days at last began to slip away, and she finally felt able to see her way clear through the uncertainty, the shadow of the past....

Her thoughts were a strange mixture of hope and fear as she tumbled into bed that night. Later. Later she would sort out this jumble of emotions about Neil, but for now it would have to wait. Her marriage would have to wait. *Everything* would have to wait. And she could only hope that Neil would understand, because she had the feeling he would never have brought up the subject of a child if he'd known what it would trigger.

Because in the past few minutes Jenna had come to a very important decision and a startling realization about herself. She had once promised herself she would never look back, but she couldn't go on any longer as she had been—floundering in limbo, caught somewhere in time, trying to forget and never quite being able to, not wanting to go back and yet afraid to take that first step forward to sever all ties.

She was trapped and there was only one way out. In her mind there was no right, no wrong, no past and no future. There was only *now*....

And an overpowering need to see her son once more.

CHAPTER TWO

THE DECISION finally made, Jenna was left feeling oddly at peace with herself. She slept the sleep of the dead that night, awakening the next morning feeling far more refreshed and revitalized than she had all week. She had never been one to wallow in indecision for long; once her mind was made up, she wasted no time making clear her intentions. "Willful" was what her mother called her. She smiled a little as she showered and slipped into jeans and a pale yellow T-shirt. Her father wasn't one to mince words. "Pigheaded" was how he often referred to his daughter.

She made several quick calls to the florist and caterer. But once she sat down to address the wedding invitations she'd started a week earlier, her brief respite of peace began to shatter once more. She had to force herself to plod through the remainder of the guest list. It was well after lunch when she drove over to the post office, but once there, she stood before the big blue mailbox outside for a full minute before slowly dropping the bundles of envelopes inside. Without being consciously aware of it, she found herself at her parents' house a short time later.

She glanced up warily at the threatening purple storm clouds gathering overhead as she switched off the car engine. A gusty wind blowing in from the Gulf rattled the leaves of the huge cottonwood tree bordering the sidewalk as she hurried toward the white two-story house, wrapped on three sides by a wide porch. Jenna had come to live in this house when she was five years old, and even though she had been on her own since she'd finished her nurse's training, this was the one place in the world she would always think of as home.

A drenching sheet of rain began to fall just before she reached the shelter of the porch. Mindful of her wet feet, she ran around to the back entrance and slipped off her sandals.

"Whew! Just in time!" she muttered, stomping into the kitchen. She reached for a towel and smiled at her mother as she wiped the moisture from her face.

Marie Bradford looked worriedly from her daughter's rain-spattered cotton blouse to the moisture trickling freely down the windowpanes. "Oh, dear," she murmured, "your father will be dripping wet by the time he gets back."

"Dad's gotten lazy since he retired," Jenna said with a shake of her head. "I suppose he's out fishing again."

Her mother nodded. "I'll have to dig out the hot water bottle before he comes home. His circulation isn't what it used to be."

"Oh, come on, Mom," she said softly. Already she could feel herself relaxing, and her lips twitched as she held back a smile. "Can't you think of a better way to keep him warm?"

"Like what?"

"Like body heat, for instance," she murmured. "If it were my husband out there getting soaked to the bone, that's the first thing I'd recommend. And as a nurse, I can't think of a better remedy."

Marie Bradford turned to face her daughter with her hands planted squarely on her hips. "I know what you're trying to say, young lady, and I don't think I need to remind you that you and Neil are half our age!"

Jenna didn't miss the amused glitter in her mother's brown eyes. She sat back and eyed her as she bustled around the kitchen, wiping the counter and spooning fragrant grounds into the coffee maker. Her mother was in her mid-sixties, and if it hadn't been for the snowy white hair that she wore in a loose bun on her nape, she might have been taken for a woman twenty years younger. Her skin was smooth and free of wrinkles, her brown eyes snapping and vivacious.

"I hope Neil and I are as happy as you and Dad have been all these years," she said suddenly, last night's argument with Neil abruptly jumping into her thoughts. Her parents had been married for forty-five years, and she couldn't help but wonder—would her own marriage last that long?

There was a hint of wistfulness in her tone, and Marie looked at her in surprise. "I'm sure you will be," she said softly, moving to sit across from her daughter. "Dad and I were happy and content before you came to us, but there was something missing. I'll never forget how you looked the first time we ever saw you. You were so tall and straight, and you tried to look so brave—" She shook her head in remembrance. "But I could sense how lost and alone you were." Her eyes lifted to Jenna's and a soft smile lighted her face. "And I knew then how much joy you'd bring into our lives."

Jenna's thoughts drifted fleetingly backward. When she was four years old, her parents had been killed in a collision with a train. Miraculously she had emerged with barely a scratch. With no family other than an eighty-year-old great-aunt in Maine who was too old to be burdened with a small child, custody had been given over to the state. Her memories of that time were few: stark white walls, hard narrow cots, being shuffled from foster home to foster home for over a year. She had been too young to understand the whispered excuses...*too quiet, too withdrawn*...but old enough to understand the loss of warmth, the absence of love from her young life. Two people whom she had loved and depended on had been wrenched from her and there was no one to replace them. No one who willingly gave what her tender four-year-old self craved so desperately: a warm pair of arms to hold her, the solid strength of a shoulder to lay her head upon.

Not until Jerry and Marie Bradford had entered her life.

She smiled across at Marie, her heart filled with tender emotion for this unselfish woman who had given her so much. She reached across the table and squeezed her mother's hand. "And you brought love back into mine," she said softly. Their eyes met and held, but suddenly a troubled light entered Jenna's.

"Mom—" She traced an idle pattern on the tablecloth, trying to find the right words. "What you said before...were you trying to say that children have a way of bringing people together?"

Marie shrugged. "I suppose so. Some people—the *right* people." She paused. "Not that I think it's a way to cure a troubled marriage, but I know that my own marriage to your father wouldn't have been nearly as meaningful without you."

Jenna took a deep breath. "I suppose a lot of people feel that way. People like—like Megan and Ward

Garrison.'' Her fingers closed tightly around her coffee cup.

Marie regarded her steadily. ''There's nothing wrong with that, Jenna.''

''I never said there was,'' Jenna said quickly. She hesitated, then blurted out, ''Neil...he—he'd like to have a baby right away.''

For a long moment her mother's eyes remained riveted on Jenna's carefully controlled features before drifting to the white-knuckled grip of her hands around her cup. After all these years, there was still so much that Jenna held inside.... Marie offered a quiet statement. ''And that bothers you.''

There was a tight little silence. ''Yes and no,'' she finally admitted, her tone carefully neutral. Fingers that weren't entirely steady traced the rim of her coffee cup. ''We—Neil and I had decided to wait a while before we had a baby, but now he's changed his mind.'' She hesitated. ''And nothing would make me happier...eventually. But right now...right now it brings back so many memories, and I can't help but think of—'' She broke off, stung to the core by her suppressed pain.

''Robbie,'' her mother finished for her softly. Again her hand reached out to cover Jenna's.

She nodded slowly, drawing both strength and comfort from the touch of her mother's hand. ''Tomorrow I'm going to Plains City to see him, Mom,'' she said quietly. ''Even if they won't let me touch him or hold him.'' Her eyes seemed two huge pools of longing in her pale face. ''I have to do this, Mom. I *have* to.'' She looked across at her mother, somehow not surprised to see a kind of gentle comprehension reflected in the soft, brown depths. Instantly the years fell away....

IT WAS A NEWSPAPER article that had first caught Jenna's eye nearly five years earlier. "CHILDLESS COUPLE SEEKS SURROGATE MOTHER" was how the headline in the Houston newspaper had read. Since her adoptive mother had been unable to have children, Jenna was intrigued by the unique approach to the problem of infertility. On reading the story, she discovered that Megan and Ward Garrison, a couple who lived in northern Texas, were actively searching for a woman to bear Ward's child. Married for fifteen years and puzzled by Megan's inability to have a child in all that time, both had undergone a battery of tests several years earlier, only to find that Megan's fallopian tubes were blocked by scar tissue and she could never become pregnant.

Jenna was working as an office nurse for a physician with a family practice in Texas City at the time, and both the receptionist and the bookkeeper could talk about little else.

"You wouldn't catch me offering to have this guy's baby," Vera, the bookkeeper, declared later that morning. She flicked a disdainful finger at the newspaper. "My sister was sick for weeks on end when she was pregnant—and she looked like a cow from the time she was two months along!"

Marsha, the mother of a ten- and a six-year-old and infinitely more mature than Vera, held a different viewpoint. "Your sister also had twins," she pointed out. "And some women love being pregnant—"

"Not me!" snorted Vera.

Marsha had simply smiled and shaken her head. "Wait until you're married," she said with a smile. "You might feel fat and ugly and you might be so sick you feel like you could never hold your head up again, but the minute you hold that tiny bundle of life in your arms, it's all but forgotten."

Vera cast a wary eye at the older woman. "That might be," she sniffed a little indignantly, again waving a hand at the newspaper, "but if you ask me, this is a little weird. I'd say that any woman who volunteers for this is doing it strictly for the money!"

"I'm not sure," Marsha said thoughtfully. Her eyes skimmed over the article. "It says here that the man is an engineer, and I doubt if they make all that much money. And though it says all hospital and legal expenses will be taken care of, it doesn't specify how much the fee is."

"It would have to be one heck of a lot before I'd do it," Vera snorted.

Jenna and Marsha exchanged a glance that seemed to indicate Vera needn't worry about the possibility. Marsha glanced down again at the newspaper. "It also says that any woman applying will be tested physically *and* psychologically." She frowned, then said slowly, "I guess that makes sense. I suppose that they would want to make sure she really knew what she was getting into, and after all—" she shrugged "—if a person went to all that trouble and expense, I guess they'd want the mother to be reasonably intelligent."

"Good Lord." Vera looked disgusted. "Imagine having to *apply* to have a baby—just like applying for a job!"

"It wouldn't be easy giving up a baby," Jenna put in pensively. "I suppose if you looked at it in terms of a job right from the start, it might make it a little less traumatic when the time came to hand over the baby.''

''And that's not all,'' Marsha added. ''It says here that single women are preferred. Apparently both the couple and their lawyer seem to think a woman who's never had a baby wouldn't be as likely to have second thoughts about giving it up.''

''Well, they can count me out!'' Vera's voice rang out loudly. ''I might be single, healthy and intelligent, but there's no way I'd get involved in anything like this!''

There was a pause, and then two pairs of eyes simultaneously turned to Jenna.

''Don't look at me!'' She held up her hands and laughed. ''I tend to agree with Vera. It's a little too bizarre for me.'' The plight of these two people was rather sad; she felt a small stab of pity that they were so desperate for a child of their own, and the fact that they were willing to go to such lengths even made her admire them to a degree.

But beyond these thoughts, the realization of the heartache these two people were going through didn't hit home until several days later, when she walked in on her mother watching a local talk show that featured this same couple. More out of courtesy for her mother than any vested interest, she sat down to watch.

Seeing the actual faces of those two, instead of merely reading names in a newspaper, made the situation all the more real and all the more heartrending. Her first impression of Megan Garrison was that of a woman in intense pain. She was very blond, and small-boned and fragile-looking. Her husband, Ward, was as dark as she was fair, good-looking in a rough sort of way. There was something in the quiet tautness of his tone that caught Jenna's attention as they pleaded their cause, but it was his wife she responded to. She listened as they related how a previous attempt at locating a surrogate had ended in heartbreak: after carrying the baby to term, the woman had changed her mind at the last minute. And adoption was all but ruled out; the waiting list was seven years long at the least—they had been waiting years already.

Jenna's heart turned over in her chest as she heard the woman say, "I die a little inside with every day that goes by, and I see the hope that someday I may hold a child in my arms grow dimmer and dimmer. And hope is all I have—" Her voice broke tearfully, and long painful seconds ticked by before she was able to speak again. "Hope is all I may *ever* have."

The desperation, the fear, the despair, the realization that the woman had only this one small thread to cling to, touched something deep inside Jenna's soul. She longed to reach out and comfort Megan as her husband was doing, to wrap her arms around her and tell her that it was only a matter of time before her hope became a reality.

When it was over Jenna turned to her mother with a murmur of sympathy on her lips, only to find her doe-soft eyes swimming with unshed tears.

Jenna rushed to her side. "Mom, what is it?" Her tone was anxious as she pressed a handkerchief into her hand.

Marie attempted a watery smile. "I'm all right." She dabbed at her overflowing eyes and leaned her head back tiredly. Concerned, Jenna sat on the arm of the chair and searched her mother's face.

"I'm fine, really," Marie said again. She set aside the handkerchief and turned to Jenna with a sigh. "It's just that seeing that couple brought back so many memories." She lapsed into silence, but again her eyes grew red.

Jenna sat very still. She knew that she had been adopted because of her mother's fierce desire for a child, but for a moment she was almost stunned at her mother's heartfelt reaction to the plight of two people who were, after all, strangers. Instinctively she said, "You know exactly how that woman feels, don't you?"

"Oh, yes—*exactly*." Marie dashed at her eyes, and Jenna patiently handed the handkerchief back to her. "I wanted a child so badly I could taste it. Everywhere I looked—the grocery store, the drugstore, the doctor's office—there were mothers with children, mothers *about* to have a baby. And there I was, helpless, frustrated, hating myself for being jealous and wanting what they seemed to take for granted." A pained expression flitted across her face. "No one knows how worthless the inability to have a baby can make a woman feel—except perhaps a woman who's been through it herself." A pensive smile curved her lips as she looked up at Jenna. "But your father was wonderful through it all. He was the one who suggested adoption." She reached up a hand to cradle Jenna's cheek in her palm. "You'll never know how much of a blessing you were. Like a day of sunshine after a storm."

Jenna's throat felt raw. She tried to speak, but the sound refused to pass through her throat. She could only grip her mother's hand more tightly. Her eyes turned toward the television screen, where a newscaster's voice now droned on and on. She chastised herself for being the most insensitive clod ever to have been born. And yet these two people weren't the only ones involved.

"I hate to say this..." She hesitated. "But finding someone to bear a child for them seems so—so drastic." She slipped onto the carpet in front of the chair, laced her arms around her legs and rested her chin on her knees. "Another woman is going to have to give up nine months of her life for these people. How many women would be willing to do that?"

"Oh, Jenna." The raw emotion in Marie's tone brought Jenna's eyes to her mother's in a flash, and they were held there by a depth of intensity she'd never glimpsed before. "What are nine months compared to a lifetime of loneliness? Some women can go through life without a husband or child, but there are others who can never be fulfilled unless they can share their love with a husband and family. Women like Megan Garrison—and me." She paused, her eyes now shining luminously. "It would take a very special woman," she said softly. "A woman who isn't afraid to give all of herself." She shook her head, a wistful smile on her lips. "I can't imagine being able to give anything more precious than the gift of life."

The gift of life. Almost with a sense of awe Jenna absorbed the words. Her parents had taken her into their home and their hearts, freely bestowing all the warmth and love they were capable of giving. She knew, beyond a shadow of a doubt, that their love for her was no different from what they might have felt for a natural child, had they been able to have one. And during the past few minutes, somehow all the long lonely years her mother had struggled through were poignantly brought to life inside Jenna. She could feel the same intense longing, the empty ache inside, that both her mother and Megan Garrison lived with day after day. But there was one difference.

She rushed to find a pencil and pad. Her fingers shook as she scribbled down the name of the Garrisons' Dallas attorney. It might be too late, or they might not want her, but by heaven, she was going to try. Her heart fluttered almost painfully in her chest as she looked up at her mother with shining eyes, her heart bursting with emotion.

She, Jenna Bradford, was determined to have the child these two people wanted so desperately. For herself, for Megan Garrison—and for the woman before her, who had given her own life so much meaning. The woman who had taught her how precious love really was.

"JENNA." A gentle voice prodded her back to the present. "I understand what you're going through, but I have to ask this. How are the Garrisons going to feel about this? Have you talked to them yet?"

"No." She shook her head quickly, stilling the sudden pitter-patter of her heart that the words evoked. "I know we all agreed to make a clean break," she said quietly, looking straight at her mother. "But I think Megan will come around fairly quickly."

"And Ward?"

Jenna frowned. She took a sip of her coffee, grimacing at the cold, bitter taste. Carrying the cup to the sink, she emptied the contents, pondering the question while she poured a fresh cup. She had sympathized with Megan even before they had chosen her for a surrogate, but it had come as a surprise to find how much she really liked her when they had finally met face-to-face. Ward, on the other hand, was a different story. He was sweet, warm and tender with his wife, and though he was gracious enough the few times the three of them had been together, he wasn't nearly as easy to read as Megan who was much more vocal. In fact, one of the last times she had seen him had left her feeling rather shaken.

She'd been in her sixth month of pregnancy at the time. Ward was in Houston on business, and Megan had come along with him. She'd met with them briefly at their hotel, and Megan was absolutely delighted at feeling the baby's vigorous movements inside her.

"Come and feel this!" she'd beckoned to Ward. Wasting no time, she snatched one large hand in hers and guided it to Jenna's protruding tummy. "He's doing somersaults in there!"

Jenna had laughed a little self-consciously, but at the sight of that dark hand lying so intimately on her belly, she'd felt an odd tightening in her chest. It really brought home the fact that it was this man's child she was nurturing inside her, but before she had time to analyze the feeling, the baby moved. Ward's hazel eyes flitted to hers in surprise before an oddly shuttered expression came over them, and then he abruptly snatched away his hand. The incident had hurt for some unknown reason, and she was left feeling just a little bit wary.

She turned to face her mother. "I'm not sure how Ward will feel," she admitted. "I didn't do it for him, you know. I did it for Megan." She mulled a moment longer. "But I think if Megan agrees, he will, too."

Marie nodded, then smiled. "I already know what your father will say."

Jenna resumed her place at the table and shook her head fondly. "He'll boom and bluster the way he did when I told him what I was up to in the first place, and then he'll say in that gruff way he has—" she drew her brows together over her nose and stuck out her lower lip wrathfully "'—you'll do what you want, anyway!'"

They both ended up laughing at a time when they very much needed the release. "You obviously see through him just as I do." Marie laughed one last time, then looked at her daughter. "How long do you plan on staying?"

Jenna's smile drooped a little, but she kept it firmly in place. Surely Megan and Ward couldn't deny her if she was practically camped on their doorstep. She refused to think beyond that.

"As long as it takes, Mom," she responded with false lightness. "As long as it takes."

"Then that leaves just one person to contend with, doesn't it?"

Her mother's voice was so quiet Jenna almost suspected she knew. Her fingers tensed in her lap. She took a deep breath. "It's his problem if he doesn't understand, Mom. Because I'm going to do it, anyway."

Marie darted her a surprised look. "That doesn't sound like you, Jenna. Surely you and Neil aren't having problems already? Heavens, you're not even married yet!"

Jenna could tell the laugh she gave was forced. Suddenly her thoughts darted back to the time when she was a lanky thirteen-year-old and had just discovered that their neighbor, Darren Phillips—the boy who threw stones at her and boasted he was the better baseball player simply by virtue of his sex—wasn't such a disgusting creature, after all. A ghost of a smile tipped her lips. Intent on proving him wrong, she'd spent many an evening with her father pitching a ball to her and giving her tips on her stance and swing. She'd broken the kitchen window twice with some very nifty line drives. And then the day came when Darren had given her her first kiss and she'd decided it was time to shelve her ball and bat. She had breezed in from outside, dropped herself at the kitchen table and *promptly* asked her mother how a *woman* knew when she was in love.

She'd never forgotten her mother's reply: "If you ever have to ask yourself if you're in love," she said with a secretive smile, "then you're probably not."

Suddenly Jenna couldn't help but recall the moment last night when she hadn't been able to tell Neil she loved him.

Marie reached out a hand to cover Jenna's. "You're not having second thoughts, are you, dear?"

Her reply was a long time in coming. "Neil is everything a woman could possibly want in a man. He's mature, nice-looking, attentive, and he has a very good job...." Yes, he was a prize catch, according to her friends in E.R.

"That doesn't tell me much, Jenna. You say Neil is everything a woman could want in a man, but is he everything *you* want? You know I like Neil," Marie said slowly, "and I'll be more than happy to have him as a son-in-law, but we're talking about your happiness. And what you just said sounds strangely like an excuse." Her mother gave her a long, thoughtful look. "None of us needs excuses for loving, Jenna. Do you?"

Jenna looked down to where her hands rested in a white-knuckled grip in her lap. This time she didn't answer—though not because she didn't want to. She couldn't.

All of a sudden she didn't know.

THINGS DIDN'T FARE well at all with Neil that night. The changing expressions on his face would have been rather comical if the situation hadn't been quite so serious. Jenna could almost see the wheels turning in his head. At first he looked totally blank when she mentioned the term "surrogate mother." An extremely brief look of amazement came next, followed by disbelief and then what she really hadn't expected to see—a cold-faced fury. In fact, if the truth were known, she had been much more worried about Megan's and Ward's reaction than Neil's.

"Damn it, Jenna! How could you do something so harebrained, so foolhardy, so thoughtless?" Neil slammed his fist down on an end table and glared at her. "You, of all people!"

"Why, thank you. I'll take that as a compliment!" Her voice dripped icicles as she watched him pace around her living room. "It wasn't thoughtless, Neil," she countered harshly. "I knew exactly what I was getting into."

"And did you think about how you might feel five or ten years down the road? Did you ever think about how you're feeling *now*?"

When he threw her another furious glance, Jenna dug in her heels and prepared to do battle. Good Lord! Did he think she had gone into the arrangement blindly? Even if she had, the Garrisons' attorney, Ron Brewster, would have enlightened her in no time flat! Over and over he had stressed that they wanted someone who fully understood what she was getting into.

And she had spent months and months preparing herself *not* to feel the way she did right now.

So what had happened?

She brushed aside the disturbing voice as quickly as she did Neil's accusations. "Of course I did," she told him tautly. "I didn't let myself think of it as *my* baby— it was *their* baby. All I did was give Robbie a temporary home."

"Robbie? The baby was a boy?"

Her chin held high against his accusing voice, she nodded.

"How old, Jenna? How old is he?"

"He's nearly four years old," she said quietly. "He has a birthday in January."

Neil dropped into a chair. He sat there, his hands dropped on his knees, his forehead supported by his fingertips. When he finally looked across at her, his eyes had lost some of their fierce glitter, but his voice was bitter and flat.

"Damn it, Jenna, I can't believe it! A stranger! You had a stranger's baby!"

"They weren't strangers, Neil. Not from the minute I saw them, and especially not after I met them."

"And that's supposed to make a difference?" Anger hardened his features. "You got all cute and cozy with the husband and that makes it all right?"

Jenna could hardly believe his outburst. "I didn't sleep with him," she said sharply. "Artificial insemination is about as cold and sterile as you can get! You're an attorney—you should know how it works!"

"I know all I care to know, and believe me, you just took the words right out of my mouth. 'Cold and sterile' is exactly the way I see this whole thing! How much did they pay you?" he demanded.

"Very little!" she shot back hotly. "I was off work for less than six weeks and I accepted only what I lost out on salary. And the fee didn't even play a part in why I did it! Just the other night you were spouting off about wanting a home and a family, but *you're* the one who's cold and unfeeling! Is it so hard to understand that someone else has that very same need?"

His eyes remained locked with hers endlessly. Then finally he shoved an agitated hand through his hair. "All right, you've made your point. But we're getting married in less than six weeks, and besides, I can think of a dozen reasons right off the top of my head— moral, ethical *and* legal—why this shouldn't be a proving ground for childless couples."

"I'm not saying it's the answer for everyone." Her tone was quiet as her anger began to abate. "But it was right for them, and it was right for me, and I'm not sorry I did it." She hesitated. "Only I have to see Robbie again."

His eyes locked with hers, probing, questioning— and still angry.

"I'm not sure I can explain exactly why," she said with a feeling of helplessness. "I only know that it's something I have to do." She swallowed uneasily before forcing herself to go on. "And then—then you and I can go on with our lives together."

The harsh, grating breath he drew was the only sound in the room. "I think you're asking for trouble, Jenna. I'm not even sure I should let you do this—"

She shook her head quickly. "You can't stop me, Neil." Her voice was very quiet, yet there was an unmistakable ring of finality to it. "No one can." She paused. "Please, try to understand—"

"I don't understand," he cut in abruptly. "And even if I could, I think you picked one hell of a time to go running off! In case you've forgotten, we're getting married six weeks from Saturday!" He whirled around and headed for the front door. "If it's not too much trouble—" he threw the clipped words over his shoulder "—give me a call when you get back."

With that, he walked out on her for the second time that week. Silently Jenna made her way over to a chair and sank into the cushions. It was, she realized shakily, perhaps a good thing that she was leaving for a few days.

It would give her some time to think about Neil—something she realized she desperately needed to do.

CHAPTER THREE

THE DRIVE NORTH filled one of the longest days of Jenna's life. Anxious to arrive in Plains City, she'd felt the long hours stretch out endlessly, particularly the last half-hour after Waco. Her muscles were cramped and aching from the hours spent in the driver's seat, and her frame of mind nose-dived even farther when a fan belt broke just outside of Abilene and there was a two-hour wait trying to find a service station willing to repair it. And the matter wasn't improved any when her little Datsun became testier yet and she had a flat tire a mere half-hour after she'd finally gotten started again. Tired and frustrated, she finally arrived well after ten o'clock. She pulled into the first motel she saw and crawled into bed, exhausted.

She shielded her eyes against the bright glare of the sun when she stepped out of her motel room the next morning, looking up and down the main thoroughfare of the sleepy little town. There was a market, a hardware store, a feed supply store, a barber shop and a café.

It was in the direction of the café that Jenna guided her footsteps. She had awakened ravenous, since she'd been too tired the previous night even to bother searching for a place to eat. Stepping inside, she glanced around the matchbox-sized interior. There was room for perhaps half a dozen people at the small counter, and three well-worn booths lined the wall. The fragrant smells wafting from the kitchen sent hunger pangs growling anew in Jenna's stomach.

She sat down on one of the stools near the counter, waiting her turn while a threesome in one of the booths was being served. She looked up when the waitress, dressed in a crisp blue uniform and jaunty cap, approached her.

"Hi." Fresh-faced and open, the woman flashed a wide smile. "What can I get you?"

Jenna smiled back and eyed the hand-lettered menu before making a quick choice. "How about coffee and a cinnamon roll to start with?"

"Comin' right up."

Her eyes widened when the waitress placed a Texas-sized roll in front of her and a cup of fresh hot coffee. Pulling the warm, fragrant roll apart with her fingers, she savored the spicy taste of the cinnamon and gooey icing, resisting the impulse to lick her fingers.

"More coffee?" The waitress returned a few minutes later with the carafe in her hand. Jenna placed her hand over her cup and shook her head quickly. "How about another roll?"

"No, thanks." Jenna smiled and indicated her stomach. "It was delicious, but I couldn't take even one more bite."

"Not many people can handle more than one of Herb's cinnamon rolls." She grinned. "Fact is, he makes the best rolls in town."

Jenna nodded politely and commented, "It's so quiet here. It's hard to believe that Abilene is less than thirty miles away."

"It's not always like this," the waitress said with a wink. "After dark, things tend to liven up a bit. You know how some men are about dropping in for a few beers after work...." She shook her curly head and grinned. "They talk about women being no better than a bunch of cacklin' hens when they get together, but I'll never believe it."

The waitress took advantage of the lull in customers and returned the coffee carafe to the hot plate, then came back to Jenna. The look she gave her was amicable but inquisitive. "You stayin' at the motel across the street?"

Jenna nodded.

"Just passing through, I'll bet."

"Yes and no. Actually, I hope to be staying a few days." She hesitated, but couldn't help responding to the woman's friendliness. "I'm here to see the Garrisons—the Ward Garrisons. Do you know them?"

"Not personally." The woman shook her head, and a shadow passed swiftly over her face. "Don't see much of him anymore since... well, that's beside the point." She eyed Jenna curiously. "Are you a friend of the family?"

"A friend of the family?" For some reason the term sent an unexpected pain shooting through her heart. On blood ties alone, she was practically a *member* of the family. She resisted the impulse to laugh hysterically. Instead she gathered herself quickly under control and nodded. "Megan and I... were good friends some time ago. But I'm afraid I've lost the address after all these years." She tipped her head to the side and smiled encouragingly. "I don't suppose you happen to know where they live?"

The waitress shook her head apologetically. "Sorry—no. Wait a minute!" She snapped her fingers, already heading toward the kitchen. "I'll bet Herb knows. He's lived here forever.

"Take the first road to the left heading north out of town. Turn left again at the first intersection," she announced, bustling through the double doors a moment later. "It's the house at the end of the gravel road. Only one there, so you can't miss it."

"Thanks so much. I'll just be on my way, then." Jenna smiled gratefully and paid for her breakfast. Glancing back, she saw the waitress gazing after her with an odd look in her eyes. Jenna sent a little wave over her shoulder as she exited the tiny café.

She quickly walked across the street to where her car was parked in front of her motel room. She inserted the key in the lock, but suddenly she stopped, one hand poised on the dark blue roof as her mother's words from yesterday came back to her. How *would* Megan feel about her dropping in without any warning? It could be quite a shock, she suddenly realized. For a moment she hesitated, temptation almost overruling reason in this instance. Then, with a sigh, she turned and trudged the few steps to her room.

Inside, she sat down on the double bed and reached for the phone. The Garrisons' phone number popped into her head without conscious thought, and for a moment she sat stunned. Why was it that she remembered it after all this time? Was it because she hadn't *wanted* to forget? Her hand gripped the receiver as she recalled the last time she'd telephoned, to let them know her labor had started. Once again she could hear Megan's ecstatic voice coming over the wire.

"Oh, Jenna, I can't believe it! It's finally about to happen! A baby—our very own baby! We'll be there as soon as we can."

The memory was both poignant and sweet, and Jenna took a deep, shuddering breath to force back the odd sensation gripping her heart. She punched out the number with steady hands, aware of a faint flutter in her chest as she eased back on the bed and waited.

The phone rang once, twice and then again. Jenna felt her heart beating crazily.

"Hello?"

She couldn't prevent a note of breathless excitement from entering her voice. "Megan?" She sat forward on the edge of the bed, her body taut as a bowstring. "Is that you, Megan?"

There was a long silence, and then a female voice demanded, "Who is this?"

Recoiling from the sharp tone, she shifted uneasily as she realized it wasn't Megan who had answered. "I...my name is Jenna Bradford." She heard a soft gasp but paid no mind. Her tone was cautious but hopeful as she spoke to the woman on the other end of the line. "I've just driven all the way from Galveston and I was calling to see if I might be able to see—" *Robbie.* She stopped the word from slipping off her tongue just in time. "Megan," she finished hastily. A little puzzled by the awkward silence that followed, she bit her lip. "I'm sorry...I must have dialed the wrong number."

"No. No, this is the right number."

The admission came readily enough, but there was something in the tone...it was brusque, even a little hostile. Jenna's words were polite but guarded. "If I have the right number, then who are you?"

Again there was a long empty silence before the unknown woman spoke. "Eileen. Eileen Swenson." She seemed to hesitate. "I'm Ward's sister."

Ward's sister. No wonder the surprise at her name. "Then you know who I am," she said softly.

"Yes—yes, I do. And I think I know why you're here."

There was no denying the challenging note in Eileen Swenson's voice. If this was any indication of how Megan or Ward would feel... She could only pray it wasn't. She prickled a little but said politely, "If it's not too much trouble, could you put either Megan or Ward on the phone?"

There was a seemingly endless silence. "Megan's dead," the woman finally said quietly.

Dead...Megan was *dead*. Her mind reeled. It didn't seem possible. She'd never known her, not really. Was it possible to mourn someone's death without ever really knowing that person? But certainly Jenna knew all she needed to know. Megan was a warm, vital woman whose capacity for love went far beyond any ordinary measure, if indeed love could be measured. A dozen questions tumbled around in her brain. How had Megan died? And when? She couldn't suppress a burning feel of resentment against Ward for not letting her know, even while the rational part of her argued there was no need for her to know.

But suddenly she remembered Robbie. Megan was gone, but did that change anything? Her reason for being here? No.

"I'm sorry," Jenna said softly. "When...?"

Eileen Swenson had no trouble understanding. "About a year and a half ago."

She twirled the cord around her finger and thought a moment. "Mrs. Swenson, I'd still like to talk to Ward—"

"He isn't here."

Jenna took a deep breath. "Then could you give him a message for me?"

"I'm sorry. I—I don't know when I'll see him again."

The woman was beginning to sound a little agitated. "Look," Jenna said evenly, choosing her words carefully. "I'm really not here to cause trouble, but don't you think you should let Ward decide whether he wants to talk to me?"

"I'm not lying," the woman defended herself. "He isn't here and I couldn't say when he'll be back. I only stopped by this morning to check on the house while he's away."

"Where is he?"

"New Mexico. He's working on an irrigation project there."

New Mexico...Lord, and she'd come so far already. Her muscles tensed with an emotion she wasn't yet ready to name. "I see," she said slowly. "Is Robbie with him?"

"No. He's staying with me. But please don't ask to see him. I couldn't possibly agree without Ward's permission."

Jenna's body went limp with despair. "I understand." Her voice sounded as hollow as she felt inside. She wasn't such a fool that she didn't know that engineering projects sometimes lasted weeks, months even. But suddenly there was a glimmer of life inside her. Surely Ward wouldn't leave Robbie for weeks at a time. "Do you expect him back soon?" She made no attempt to disguise her hopefulness.

There was a heavy sigh on the other end of the line. "I'm really not sure. Early next week maybe, but as I said before, I'm not certain." It was obvious the admission was made with great reluctance. "I'll let Ward know you're here... if you decide to wait around that long. Where are you staying?"

"I'll be here," Jenna promised in a low voice. "I'm at the Sundowner Motel." She paused. "Mrs. Swenson...?"

"Yes?"

"I—thank you. Thank you for telling me."

The moment stretched out into a taut silence. When Eileen Swenson finally spoke, her voice sounded oddly strained. "Don't thank me yet. For all I know, you may have made the trip for nothing."

Jenna stared pensively out the window after hanging up the phone. The shimmering sunlight outside seemed a stark contrast to the dark emptiness of her mood. Apparently, all the odds were stacked against her. It had all started with her vague, restless feelings about Neil, and then he had warned her against coming. Then her car had broken down, and now—this. Megan was *dead,* and Jenna had been so certain she would let her see Robbie. It would be days before Ward returned, a hollow voice inside her protested. Better to go home now and forget she had ever come, forget she had even tried to see Robbie, forget he had ever been born.

But she couldn't. Dear Lord, she couldn't.

Refusing to give in to that tiny voice, Jenna got up, grabbed her purse and walked outside. Dispiritedly she walked the few blocks to the town's business district. There was more to the town than she had originally thought; she noticed at least three drugstores, a steak house and several more small cafés, one small but complete department store, one clothing shop, even a movie theater and a playhouse. All the amenities of a city, Jenna thought to herself halfheartedly, but without quite the variety to choose from.

Her steps eventually took her back to the motel, and Jenna found herself driving toward the Garrison place. The directions she'd been given earlier unconsciously guided her. Before she knew it, her car was parked in the gravel drive and her feet were carrying her toward the front door. Her footsteps echoed emptily as she mounted the steps, and for a fraction of a second, she stopped before lifting her hand to the brass knocker.

Silence greeted her.

After a long moment of almost fearful waiting, she turned and trudged slowly down the steps, her emotions so tangled that she felt unable to sort through them.

Taking a deep breath, Jenna forced her attention back to her surroundings. Beyond the cross-fenced boundaries of the small acreage the plains stretched for miles, rolling and dipping endlessly, glinting yellow in the bright September sunlight. In the distance she could see the sun-baked, gently rolling hills to the west. Settling herself under a towering cottonwood tree, she turned her eyes once again to the two-story farmhouse.

The yard was well kept, and the white clapboard exterior of the house looked newly painted. Although it was quiet outside, there was a warm, homey look to the house itself. A wide swing hung from the porch rafters near the front window. Jenna could almost visualize the inside, cheerful and cozy, a comfortable sofa laden with pillows in the living room, thick braided rugs covering the floor and knickknacks and treasures strewn throughout. The urge to scramble to the window and peer through the sheer curtains was so strong that she almost succumbed. Only the feeling that she would be spying, intruding where she had no business, prevented her from doing exactly that.

The thought sent a chill through her. Why had she come here? she agonized silently. Despite what Eileen Swenson had told her—that Megan was dead and Ward was gone—had she really believed it? Had she really expected the door to be thrown open and to be welcomed with open arms? She shivered. No. She could never expect that from Ward. She didn't know how she knew, but she did.

What if he said no? What would she do then? Could she deal with it, or would she handle it the way she had handled it all this time, sweeping her feelings under the rug once more? Denying the hopeless longing to see her child, to hold him, to *know* him? All these months— years!—she hadn't let herself think of him, but no matter how hard she tried, the memory was always there, lurking in some distant corner of her mind. Denied but never forgotten. For the first time, she realized how desperately afraid she was that Ward would refuse to let her see Robbie.

But her need outweighed her fear by far.

"Oh, Robbie," she murmured faintly, fervently. "I'm so close...." Slowly she closed her eyes, unable to stop a wave of despair from sweeping through her. She heard words spinning through her brain—words she couldn't speak. *So near and yet so far.*

Her entire body trembled as she stumbled to the car and started the engine. She drove back to the motel in the same trancelike state she had left it. Outside, the small town went about its business while Jenna shut herself away in her room. Neil...Megan...Robbie... Faces whirled through her imagination, the features obscure and blurred. The squall of a newborn infant resounded in her subconscious and she flinched.

Finally she stumbled over to the bed and lay down, her body curled in a tight ball. She knew she desperately needed an outlet for all the pent-up emotion inside her, but as always, the tears refused to come. All the pain was tightly locked up inside her, and her heart was an unbearable weight in her chest.

IT WAS NEARLY DARK when the wheels of the small Cessna touched down in a perfect landing on the small airstrip just outside Plains City. Skimming across the smooth surface, the plane gently glided to a stop in front of the metal barn that served as a hangar. Moments later, a lean figure emerged from the building and strode toward the house. Though the man was rapidly approaching forty, a rangy, muscled hardness to the six-foot-three-inch frame had not yet been softened by the years.

Though Ward Garrison was tired and weary to the bone, a kind of hurried impatience marked his long-legged stride as he took the porch steps two at a time, heading with intent toward the den.

The room was paneled in knotty pine, and sparsely but comfortably furnished. Bookshelves lined nearly every available wall space. The only decoration was a pair of old flintlock rifles mounted above the stone fireplace. Near the window stood a worn leather armchair that had seen many years of use. A massive desk dominated the room, and Ward directed his steps toward it.

The chair behind the desk creaked a protest as he sat down. He made no move to reach for the phone; instead his hazel eyes rested on the framed photograph that occupied a place of honor on the desktop. A shuttered look came over his face as he picked up the oak frame, studying the fragile features in the photo as if to memorize them. But there was little need. Even without the reminder of those laughing blue eyes and silky blond hair, the image was printed indelibly on his brain. She looked so happy and carefree.... And it seemed like a lifetime ago that *he* had felt that way.

"Megan," he said aloud. And then he wished he hadn't, as the familiar tightening began to build in his chest. He took a deep, shuddering breath, but long minutes passed before he set aside the photograph and leaned back in his chair.

"Oh, Meg," he murmured faintly. "Sometimes it's still so hard to believe you're gone...." She had been a part of fate, a moment in time...and she was no more.

His eyes flitted to a smaller picture, but one no less dear to his heart. He felt a surge of pride and possessiveness. His son. His own flesh and blood, the one bright spot left in his life. The son Megan wanted so badly but wasn't able to have. Despite the brief time allotted to them, no one could have been a better mother to Robbie than Megan. She *was* his mother, the only mother he had ever known.

Ward's eyes grew unusually soft as he reached out a finger and traced the outline of the miniature features so like his own. Robbie had his bold nose, the same square jawline. But his eyes...those vivid green eyes could belong to only one person.

The reminder was one he had learned to live with. Not that he was ungrateful...but there were times when he was strangely resentful of the woman who had given him his son, as well as of the fact that his own wife could never hope to conceive... while it had been so *simple* for her. And there were also times when Robbie would look up at him, his eyes unusually serious and urgent, yet so full of life and expression, and he felt a brief surge of anger jolt through his body, because he looked so *damned much* like her.

Ward reached for the phone and punched out a number. "Eileen?" He swiveled around in the chair to stare out the window. "It's me."

"Ward!" Mild surprise was registered in his sister's tone. "Are you home already?"

One side of his mouth quirked upward. "I pushed the crew as hard as I pushed myself so we could finish ahead of schedule."

"Well, thank heaven you don't do near as much traveling as you did five years ago." There was a brief pause. "It's hard on Robbie with you gone, as young as he is. He tries not to let it show, but I can tell."

"I know." There was a bitter edge to his smile. "You wouldn't believe how much I miss him. But with Tyler breaking his leg and laid up in the hospital, I had no choice but to fill in for him." He lifted a hand to smooth his rumpled dark hair. "Is Robbie still up?"

"No. I put him to bed right after dinner." Eileen's voice was full of apology.

Ward's smile was halfhearted at best, but he disguised his disappointment. "Well, don't bother waking him. I'll be over tomorrow to pick him up."

"Don't hurry on my account." Eileen laughed. "You know Robbie—always where the action is. And if there's nothing going on, he creates a little excitement of his own. But he keeps me busy and I love having him around. The house is so empty with Tim and Katie away at college." She stopped for a second. "But

I'm really glad you came back early. Frank's going to a cattle auction in Amarillo on Monday, so maybe I'll go along and do some shopping."

He nodded. "I'll see you tomorrow, then...."

"Ward, wait! There's something you should know—"

The sudden urgency in Eileen's voice stopped him from hanging up. Frowning, he spoke into the mouthpiece again. "Yes?"

"Ward..." Her voice dropped, and she seemed unsure of something. "I was at the house today to pick up the mail, and ... someone called."

Something in her tone brought his tired senses fully alert. He leaned forward in his chair and asked in a clipped voice, "Who?"

It was a full minute before Eileen spoke. He could scarcely make out her muted tones. "Jenna Bradford."

"Jenna Bradford!" Ward sat back disbelievingly, his fingers tensing around the phone. "What did she want?"

Eileen was silent, hesitating just a moment too long, but somehow he already knew. "Robbie."

His insides were suddenly tied in knots. Why now, after all this time...? "What else did she say?"

"Nothing really." Eileen sounded just as confused as he felt. "She just said she didn't want to cause any trouble—but wants to see Robbie. And she's staying until she talks to you about it."

"Staying? You mean she's *here?*" He felt as if he'd been struck.

"Yes. She's at the Sundowner Motel in Plains City." An empty silence hung in the air as their thoughts veered in the same direction. "Ward, do you think . . . ?'' Eileen swallowed, almost afraid to say the words aloud. ''Do you think she wants him back?''

''If that's the case, she won't be long in discovering she'll have one hell of a fight on her hands,'' he said grimly, ''because I'm not about to let *anyone* take my son away from me. And the sooner she finds that out, the better.'' On that unrelenting note, Ward slammed down the phone and walked out the door.

There was no point in putting it off—he intended to find out *exactly* why Jenna Bradford was visiting.

THE EVENING stretched out emptily after Jenna finally roused herself. She must have fallen asleep, she thought vaguely, switching on the bedside lamp. Sitting up, she glanced at her watch. It was just after nine. A dull ache throbbed in her temples, and she stumbled to the bathroom to splash some cold water on her face. As she dried her hands, she studied her reflection. She looked strained and rather drawn, her eyes the only splash of color in an otherwise pale face.

The lateness of the hour rather than hunger reminded her that she hadn't eaten since lunch. Rummaging through a small bag from a convenience store where she'd stopped on the long drive yesterday, she found a half-eaten package of tiny sugared donuts. She nibbled on one, but the sweet taste was unexpectedly cloying. The few bites she took sat like a heavy stone in her stomach, and she pushed aside the package distastefully. Suddenly she felt as if the walls were closing in on her, and she knew she couldn't remain in the stark motel room any longer. After running a brush through her long dark hair, she grabbed her purse and a light denim blazer and went outside, intent on getting a breath of fresh air.

Darkness had already settled over Plains City, but the parking area of the motel was lighted by the bright glare of the sign near the office. Jenna was in the process of closing the door behind her when she noticed a dark maroon Blazer pull to a halt in one of the stalls. As a man got out, something in his lean, muscular bearing caught her eye. He was tall and broad shouldered, and a faint breeze ruffled his thick dark hair as he dropped his keys into his pocket. The sharp blade of his nose bespoke arrogance, the thrust of his chin determination. She registered the deeply chiseled features with a prickly sense of unease as she watched him slam the car door shut with almost vicious intent. Hazy spears of light shone down from the streetlamp, falling full on his face for a moment, as he moved away from the car.

Jenna froze.

Dressed in a plaid shirt, jeans and boots, the man could have passed for just another cowboy, one of the many who seemed to populate the town. As if he were caught in the same current of awareness as she, the man slowly turned to face her. Jenna couldn't tear her eyes away from his as a flicker of recognition passed between them.

Ward Garrison didn't bother to smile; he didn't bother to tip his hand in greeting. He just stared at her for what she suspected was the longest moment in her life. Then he began to move toward her.

Jenna's breathing grew almost painfully shallow as those hazel eyes stared unwaveringly into hers. Her heart thumped as she watched his face grow colder with each step that brought him nearer.

She had the feeling that the battle for Robbie was over before it had even begun.

CHAPTER FOUR

THE PREMONITION held her pinioned where she stood for what seemed an eternity. She'd thought of little else but this meeting for the past few days, but now that the moment was upon her, she knew with an unswerving sense of certainty that it wasn't going to go at all as she'd planned. She'd intended to pave the way smoothly so that there were no surprises for any of them, to be calm and reasonable and persuasive, but above all—civilized. Becoming argumentative had been the last thing on her mind, but in the face of those cool and slightly hostile hazel eyes, she felt an unmistakable surge of anger.

She moistened suddenly dry lips. "You came here...to find me." Almost defiantly she waited for Ward to speak.

He inclined his head, his eyes never leaving hers. "Yes."

His even tone didn't fool her. She could feel his eyes on her, weighing her. Again she was aware of a forceful undercurrent rippling between the two of them, as if...as if they were both preparing to do battle.

As indeed they were. The thought was a jolting one, but she instinctively summoned all her pride. It took effort, but she met his gaze unflinchingly. "We need to talk." One hand still rested on the doorknob behind her, and she turned slightly to open it. "Shall we go inside?"

There was an uneasy silence as Ward breached the few steps between them. Again Jenna felt a debilitating sense of apprehension invade her body as he brushed by her and stepped into her motel room. For a moment, she was tempted to give in to it, to let herself face the truth and be done with it, to admit once and for all that the man at her side had no intention of letting her see her child. Not now—not ever. Not entirely to her surprise, Jenna found that her hands were shaking as she closed the door behind them. She quickly crossed to switch on the light above the long, maple-veneered dresser, then turned to face Ward.

He was still standing near the doorway. To Jenna, he appeared big and powerful and more than a little intimidating. It took no stretch of the imagination to realize that beneath the flannel shirt he wore there lurked a number of extremely well-developed muscles. Her stomach gave a peculiar lurch as her eyes rested briefly on the dark thatch of wiry hairs emerging from the opening of his shirt. He seemed to tower mere inches from the ceiling, and the unruly dark hair falling over his forehead, mussed from the wind, only emphasized the impression of strength and power. The faintly uncompromising look on his face as his gaze met hers did little to dispel the notion that she was coming up against a brick wall.

Jenna made a nervous gesture with one hand. "Please, have a seat." She indicated the chair nearest the doorway, then sat down in one of the two chairs flanking the tiny round table near the window. Once there, she laced her fingers tightly in her lap and dropped her eyes for an instant. Now that the moment was actually upon her, she wasn't sure what to say. A tremor ran through her body. Should they exchange a few civil words—though from the look on his face she doubted that was possible—or simply get down to business? God, how cold that sounded! What might have been a business transaction for some women had definitely *not* been one for Jenna, despite the contracts and legal mumbo jumbo between her and the Garrisons all those years ago. She had done it for Megan, and how she wished it were Megan she were facing right now!

Finally she cleared her throat and looked up at him. "I talked with your sister today. I—she told me you weren't expected back for some time."

He made an impatient gesture with one hand. "We finished ahead of schedule."

"I see," Jenna said carefully, her eyes meeting his for a fleeting second. "I—I was also at your house today. It seems a very nice place to—" her gaze slid nervously away from his for a moment "—to bring up a child."

"Is that why you're here? To see if Robbie is being provided a proper home? If that's all that concerns you, I'll set your mind at ease. My son is being raised in a normal, stable environment and there's no need to worry—"

His tone wasn't openly hostile, yet Jenna felt her temper rise at the faint bite in his tone. She hadn't even asked to see Robbie yet—as if it weren't already apparent what his answer would be! But she wasn't about to be pushed out of the arena when she'd done nothing wrong.

"I didn't come here because I was worried about Robbie!" she said sharply. "And I'd hardly call it a normal, stable environment when you decide to go riding off into the sunset and dump Robbie at your sister's! In fact, it makes me wonder just how often that happens!''

''I have to make a living and my job demands that I travel.'' The words were clipped, but inside Ward felt a wayward twinge of guilt. The extensive amount of travel was the only thing he disliked about his work, but both he and Megan had known what he was getting into. If anything, it had made the time they spent with each other all the more valuable. Nevertheless, that was the reason he'd decided to obtain a pilot's license and do his own flying. He preferred to schedule his own time rather than arrange it around commercial flights. He'd hated the hours spent hovering in and around airports. Over the years he'd moved up in the firm, and his trips away from home had decreased enormously since he was now a consulting engineer. Still, he couldn't help but remember how, in the first months following Megan's death, he'd thrown himself into project after project, welcoming any and every opportunity that took him away from his home and away from the painful reminders. No, he hadn't seen much of Robbie then, and he still regretted it to this day.

But he didn't need anyone, and especially Jenna Bradford, throwing it up in his face. Robbie was *his* son, and he wasn't about to stand on the sidelines and watch someone jeopardize that relationship—not when that person was the only one on earth who could come between them. And she was a threat. Of that he was convinced.

''I don't see the need to explain my actions to you,'' he said gruffly. ''Robbie is my son, not yours. I would think that you, more than anyone, would be aware of that.''

For an instant Jenna had regretted her carelessly flung words, knowing they weren't fair. But his, quiet though they were, stabbed at her like the point of a knife.

She could only stare at him. This, then, was what she was up against, the hidden fear she'd be afraid to give voice to lest it be true. Ward Garrison resented her presence, probably wished she had stayed in Galveston, forgotten by all concerned. After all, he and his wife had their lives, and she had hers. And the two had been intertwined for so brief a time. But she couldn't forget....

She forced herself to meet his eyes. ''All I want,'' she stated with quiet deliberateness, ''is to see Robbie. Is that so terrible?''

For just an instant Ward hesitated. Once... *once* he might have been able to appreciate her request, perhaps even honor it. But how could he now? He'd already lost Meg. That thought kindled a moment of pure panic. What would he do without Robbie?

He couldn't afford to let Jenna see his fear, he suddenly realized. He couldn't stand it if he lost his son.

He made a vague gesture with one hand. ''You shouldn't even be here,'' he said in a very low voice. ''Your part in Robbie's life is over and done with— finished. Can't you see that?''

Jenna drew a deep, uneven breath. ''I'm not saying I want to be a part of his life. I know that's not possible. All I want is to see him again. Just this once.''

Ward's mouth tightened. ''You're here. Don't you think that counts for something? How can I believe you'll stop at just once?''

She thought quickly. "All right." She bit her lip guiltily and looked away quickly. "I'll admit... I thought I'd stay a few days and—and I could see him while I was here."

"No."

The single word was like a cold blast of wind from the Arctic. Jenna felt a shroud of iciness steal around her heart. When she had come here she'd had so much hope... and he was shattering it as surely as if he'd taken her heart in his hands and crushed the life from it.

"Please..." She had to force the word past the unfamiliar dryness in her throat.

"Damn it, I said no! I can't take that chance!" He made a sudden movement, then abruptly checked himself.

Jenna caught the motion, watching as his hands balled into fists at his sides. Oddly, she wasn't intimidated by either his size or his actions. Still, she couldn't prevent her eyes from locking sharply on his face. Before she'd almost had to strain to hear his low, clipped responses. Now the sudden harshness in his voice startled her. His expression conformed with his voice, dark and brooding. But as she stared up at him for an intense moment, she became acutely aware of something else.

He looked—and sounded—almost bitter. And yet for a fraction of a second, she could have sworn she glimpsed something else in his eyes, and she wasn't sure she could put a name to it. Pain? Fear? No. Surely not fear. He had no reason to be afraid of her.

Little did she realize that was exactly how Ward was feeling. He was furious with himself for nearly letting his emotions get the best of him, but also angry with

Jenna for precipitating this ungodly situation. His thoughts in turmoil, he turned away. He'd had no choice when Meg was wrenched from his life, but now he did. He wouldn't stand by and let this woman snatch away the only thing he had left in this world. He loved Robbie so much. A life without him was something he couldn't even bear to think about.

So why was he feeling so all-fired guilty about protecting his own interests?

"Why?" he muttered. "Why did you come here? Damn it, *why?*"

It slowly dawned on Jenna that this wasn't any easier for him than it was for her. There was a muscle twitching in one lean cheek, and she watched him close his eyes as if in pain. For a moment a part of her wanted to reach out to him, to soothe away the hurt, whatever the cause.

But she knew instinctively that the gap between them was miles wide, particularly at this moment, and would not be so easily bridged.

She stared at the unyielding strength of his back, the muscular width of his shoulders, and wet her lips nervously. "Look, I know what you're thinking—"

"Do you?" Slowly he turned to face her. "I don't think so, or you wouldn't be here."

Jenna lifted her chin proudly. "I think I do," she refuted quietly. "It was never my intention to barge in and turn everything upside down. I know we all thought it best to each go our own ways after the birth, and I'm not aware of any reason we still can't do that. Seeing Robbie now isn't going to change a thing. And I've kept my promise to stay out of your lives—"

"Until now."

Ward's voice was low and controlled, yet he seemed to be looking right through her. Dear Lord, she could almost believe he hated her! Why—*why* did he think it was so wrong for her to want to see Robbie?

Denying the cold feeling of dread that was creeping through her body like a slow and deadly poison, she spread her hands beseechingly. "I-I'm getting married soon and . . . and I'll be having my own family eventually. I swear I'll never interfere again. . . ." She shook her head quickly, feeling she was making a terrible mess of this whole thing but not sure how to set it right. She drew a tremulous breath before going on. "Please. Surely you can understand that I *need* to see him—even if it's only a glimpse! As much as I need air to breathe. . . ."

The silent plea in her eyes cut into his soul. Those eyes so like his son's held no secrets, and he could see the fear, the longing, the desperation. And he could only thank heaven that Jenna didn't know he was just as scared as she.

"I'm not sure I can." He studied her. "Are you trying to say that after nearly four years you're finally having second thoughts? That you actually care about him?"

Jenna straightened with an indignant gasp. "Of course I care about him! I cared about all of you. And you can't accuse me of having done it for the money, because you know very well that had nothing to do with it!"

Damn! Why couldn't she just let go? She was leaving him with no other recourse. God, but he hated himself for what he was about to do! "Of course you do," he echoed firmly. "You cared so much you didn't even want to hold him when he was born!"

Jenna felt the world whirl giddily around her. Raw pain splintered through her, until she felt she would break apart from it. Dear God, why did he have to remind her? It wasn't because she *didn't* care that she hadn't wanted to hold him! It was because she *did*. And she hadn't realized just how much she'd grown to love that life that had bloomed inside her until she'd actually seen him. She'd been afraid that if she touched him, if she held him . . .

Seconds passed. Seconds that became long, intolerable minutes in which a mantle of gloom slowly descended over her. There was no movement in the small, stark room, no sound to break the deathly silence. How could she make Ward understand that it was love that held her back, love that brought her back now?

Her jaw wouldn't work properly. "For God's sake, there's not a child on earth who was more wanted than Robbie. And not just by you and Megan, but by me! He was yours. I knew that—I've always known that. But that doesn't mean I never cared about him. That I never stopped thinking of him. . . ."

Her voice trailed off. She couldn't go on anymore. Who was she trying to convince? Ward? Or herself? She did love her son, the son she had never really known, would *never* know. But it was less than a week ago that she had finally owned up to the truth—that no matter how she tried, she couldn't forget, couldn't erase the memory as easily as chalk on a blackboard. All these years it had always been there, like a pebble in her shoe. Dear heaven, what a comparison! For an instant, she almost hated herself. He was her son. Her child. Yet she wouldn't know him if she came face-to-face with him at this very moment!

"It won't do any good." Dimly she heard Ward's voice. "The answer is still no. I won't let you see Robbie."

Slowly Jenna raised her head to look at him. For a moment her mind was unwilling to believe her ears. But beside the cold finality of his words, she was stung to the core by the look of unyielding harshness in his face. His eyes were cold, totally devoid of any feeling. In that moment Jenna hated Ward Garrison, hated him fiercely, with every ounce of feeling she possessed. She wondered wildly if she could ever get through to him. If anyone could get through to him. He seemed so different from the man she remembered, the man who had been so protective and loving with his wife. She sensed a hardness, perhaps even a ruthlessness in him that she was sure hadn't been there before.

"Megan would have let me see him, and you know it," she told him in a low voice. Her hands curled into fists at her sides as the rush of emotion inside her began to swell. Both anger and resentment fueled her attack, forcing the words from her. "You're not the same man you were—not the loving, tender husband she thought the world of, the man I thought she was so lucky to have. What happened to him, Ward? Did he die along with his wife?"

For an instant Ward couldn't believe his ears. An agonizing pain ripped through him before he acknowledged that she was probably right. Megan would never have denied her. Couldn't he have let Jenna down easier? He wasn't sure. He couldn't afford to give her any encouragement. There was too much at stake.

His jaw hardened. He met her defiant gaze from across the room, inexplicably wanting to hurt her as much as he'd been hurt these past few years, even while

something inside stabbed at him and pricked his conscience.

"I won't deny it. Meg would have let you see him,"
he said flatly. "And since you know it, you might as
well know this, too. It won't do you any good to stick
around in hope that I might change my mind, because
I won't." His eyes drilled into hers. "Robbie is my son.
As far as I'm concerned, he no longer has a mother. He
lost the only mother he had when Meg died."

He turned and strode from the room. The door
slammed behind him with a resounding bang. His
footsteps pounded the pavement, not faltering until he
wrenched the car door shut beside him.

Once there he blew out a long, harsh sigh. It was
over. Done. No doubt Jenna Bradford thought he was
a bastard. A cold, selfish, unfeeling bastard who didn't
give a damn about anyone or anything but himself.
Well, perhaps it was best. He'd made sure she would
never again try to see Robbie. He'd succeeded in
crushing her hopes, smashing any dreams she might
have had of reuniting with Robbie. The look in her eyes
before he whirled from the room told him more clearly
than words that he'd succeeded.

But even then the tight knot of tension that sat like
a stone in his stomach didn't begin to ease. If anything, it curled even tighter, slowly moving upward,
until he felt as if he would choke on it. There was a
bitter taste in his mouth, a gnawing feeling that clawed
at his gut.

He knew this night would prey on his mind for a hell
of a long time. He stared into the stark blackness of the
night, suddenly seeing her face again, that look in her
eyes—haunted, full of anguish, dark with pain and
helpless frustration. Oh, yes, he knew that look. He'd

seen it often enough in the mirror. How many days had he awakened in the morning to that very same image? How often had he seen it eating into his soul?

With a muttered curse he slammed his hand against the steering wheel and shoved the keys in the ignition.

JENNA WASN'T AWARE how long she stared at the closed door. It could have been minutes, hours, or it could have been seconds. She began to shiver, whether from reaction or the coolness of the room she couldn't be sure. Wrapping her arms around her body, she got up and switched on the heat. But just as suddenly, she felt as if she were being smothered. The walls were closing in on her, and it was hot, oppressive.

Unable to stand the silence, she turned on the television. The newscaster's voice droned on in a dull monotone, but the sound was faintly reassuring. Somehow she didn't feel quite so alone. It wasn't until she had settled herself in the middle of the bed that reality began to set in.

She should have known Ward wouldn't let her see Robbie. She was an outsider, an intruder, interfering where she had no business. Now she remembered vividly the day she, Meg and Ward had signed the contracts in Ron Brewster's office.

"Please don't get me wrong," Ward had said, looking directly at her. "We realize how much you're going out on a limb for us. And I can't tell you how grateful we are to know that we're finally going to be blessed with our own child." He'd exchanged a tender look with Megan, who sat at his side, before turning back to her. "We're not dealing with money here. We're dealing with feelings. This is a very complicated situation and there's so much at stake. Though we've tried to think of all the problems that might occur, the one thing we don't want is for any of us—the baby included—to be hurt unnecessarily. That's why we both think it best if we stay out of one another's lives after the baby is born. No cards, no pictures, no phone calls. We hope you'll agree that this is the best way. The *only* way.''

Megan had looked a little contrite, rather uncomfortable, Jenna recalled. Though Ward's voice had been rather quiet, his look had been piercingly direct and there had been something totally unyielding in those hazel eyes. But it wasn't as if she minded—at the time.

No, she had wholeheartedly agreed with his stance. It was the only practical way to approach the experience. No messy, sloppy or sentimental feelings to clutter up the issue. Any maternal instincts she might have had had been swiftly suppressed. They simply didn't belong, she'd told herself. It didn't matter that she was doing it for love. She couldn't afford to love this child, because it really wasn't hers. Her whole being at the time was geared toward giving this couple what they wanted. A baby, *their* baby, and nothing else mattered, including her own feelings.

But that was before, and this was now, and how cold it all seemed at this moment.

It was all too much. Too much, and all at once. She leaned back against the pillows, suddenly unbelievably tired. She ignored the tight knot of pain that sat on her chest like a viper ready to strike and forced herself toward the bathroom to undress for bed. She really should call her mother, she thought as she slipped a thin cotton nightgown over her head, but she didn't have the energy. All she wanted to do was crawl between the sheets to nurse her wounds in private.

Tomorrow. There was always tomorrow, and then she would decide what to do. But for tonight, all she wanted was to sleep... and mercifully find forgetfulness.

DESPITE HER FATIGUE, Jenna's sleep was fitful and disjointed, broken by dreams of a harsh male voice that jabbed and accused. Dreams. More like nightmares, she thought as she swept aside the sheet and padded toward the bathroom early the next morning.

Even a hot shower didn't revive her. She felt as if she were eighty-eight instead of twenty-eight. A wry smile touched her mouth. "Good Lord," she told the face in the mirror, thinking back earnestly, "you haven't felt this bad since... since the first few months you were pregnant." She was one of those fortunate enough to be rarely sick, but she'd been sick often then; hardly a morning had passed during her first trimester that she hadn't been plagued by nausea. And tired—God, how tired she'd been, no matter how many hours of sleep she got.

The smile faded. The memory of last night came flooding back. What was she going to do about Robbie? Should she leave, or try to see him on the sly, perhaps? No, she couldn't. That idea was almost as unpalatable as leaving without seeing Robbie. It simply wasn't in her nature to go behind Ward's back, no matter what the cost. But was there any other way?

After dressing in jeans and a short-sleeved jersey pullover of jade green, she opened the drapes and stared out the window. The day was bright and sunny, and huge puffy clouds were being pushed by a steady wind overhead. An occasional car whizzed by, but Jenna's mind was elsewhere.

Exactly what kind of response had she expected from Ward Garrison, she demanded of herself impatiently. A little wariness, a bit of uncertainty, maybe—somehow they hadn't come as a surprise. Her mind delved further. Gratitude? Maybe. But certainly not what she'd gotten! If he had thought to deal her a low blow, he'd certainly succeeded. She shivered as she remembered his words. "Robbie lost the only mother he had when Meg died."

Still it was his right to say no, to deny her request. But did he have to be so cruel? So ruthless? Was that what grated her so? Partly, she acknowledged with a weary slump of her shoulders. But that wasn't all. It hurt to admit the truth, but she had to face it. When Ward had walked out the door last night, he'd taken a part of her with him, a part she could never hope to regain. But it wasn't fair, she cried silently. It simply wasn't fair that she had to leave before she'd even had the chance to say hello.

Jenna had always prided herself on being in control. It wasn't ego that told her she was a good nurse. Her composure was one of the things that made her so. But where Robbie was concerned, that was something over which she had no control, and she couldn't help the wave of helpless fury that surged through her. There *was* no choice to be made. Ward Garrison had seen to that, she thought bitterly. She would head back to Galveston this morning as soon as she was packed. There was no reason to stay. She wouldn't see Ward again. She simply couldn't stand to go through this yet another time.

A wave of despair swept through her, so intense it bordered on pain. The harsh knock at the door was almost welcome. Jenna opened the door wide without a thought as to who her early morning caller might be. She stood frozen as she saw who was on the other side.

For a moment she couldn't speak. Disbelievingly her eyes ran over the tall figure filling the doorway. Just as he had last night, he wore boots and a pair of jeans, but they were topped by a camel-colored sweater. He was hatless; his jet black hair tossed freely in the breeze. His lips were set in a straight line, though, and the curve of his jaw seemed just as unyielding as it had been last night.

A surge of resentment poured through her as he brushed by her and stepped into the room. The door closed with a silent click behind her. Her hands still curled around the knob, Jenna turned to face him.

"Come to kick me while I'm down?" Her chin lifted defiantly as his eyes swiftly toured the room. She had the feeling that nothing escaped his notice, not the rumpled unmade bed, or her robe and nightgown tossed carelessly over one of the chairs. She gave a silent thank-you to herself that she hadn't yet lifted her empty suitcase onto the bed to pack the few things she'd brought. She might regret it later, but she couldn't resist adding tightly, "I might be down, but I'm not out, and I'm not beaten. So if you came to gloat—"

"Do you still want to see Robbie?"

The clipped, quiet words almost slipped by her completely. Jenna stared at him, convinced she hadn't heard right. "Are you serious?" she finally breathed.

His head barely moved as he nodded. "But you have to understand—this is the only time I'll let you see him."

Jenna's eyes were fixed on his face. There was nothing soft in his expression; those hazel eyes were unerringly direct as he looked at her. "I—" Her voice cracked as she tried to cope with his sudden appearance. He'd changed his mind? It seemed too good to be true. "Yes, of course... of course I still do!" She sounded breathy and excited. Her hand came around to fiercely latch onto the other in front of her.

"He's still at my sister's. You can come with me to pick him up if you want."

Already he was brushing by her on his way out. Jenna's eyes were wide and disbelieving as he stepped out on the sidewalk and turned to face her. Under any other circumstances the curtly given invitation would have grated on her like a fingernail scraping a chalkboard. But right now the world could have come down around her ears and somehow she didn't think she'd have known. Her heart began to soar within her chest as she hurriedly slung her purse over her shoulder.

Robbie. At last she was going to see Robbie.

CHAPTER FIVE

UNFORTUNATELY the exhilaration skittering through Jenna's veins proved to be rather short-lived. She couldn't stop herself from studying the expression that met her glance for an instant over the roof of the Blazer. Ward looked every bit as unapproachable as he had last night. She felt her excitement dampened more than just a little.

Only one small thought kept her heart from plummeting straight to her feet. Ward had yielded enough to give his consent to let her see Robbie. She didn't know what was behind his change of heart, and since she suspected he was far too complicated a man for her to figure out, she didn't bother trying. She found herself wondering if she dared hope he would unbend even further and let her spend a little more time with Robbie.

Once Jenna had purchased some take-out coffee and they were on the main highway heading north out of town, she risked another glance at Ward. "Is it far?" she asked presently.

His response was more a growl than an answer. "What?"

Jenna wiped the palms of her hands on her slacks. What was it about him that set her so on edge? She'd never felt quite so ill at ease around anyone before—

and somehow she suspected it wasn't just because of all the friction between them now.

"Is it far to your sister's?" she repeated. "The drive—how long will it take?"

"About twenty minutes." The answer seemed to come grudgingly, as did his next words. "She and her husband have a four-hundred-acre ranch. They raise beef cattle—and a few horses, as well."

Jenna spoke without thinking. "I'll bet Robbie likes that. Most kids are fascinated with animals." An unconscious smile curved her lips as she let her mind wander, despite the disturbing presence at her side. At nearly four years old, a little boy's world probably consisted of sleep, eat and play, though not necessarily in that order. What were his favorite toys? Cars? Trains? Books? And what was he like? Quiet? Robust? Suddenly her mind was filled with questions. How old was he when he learned to crawl? To walk? When had he first laughed? And talked? What was his first word? Mundane matters, to be sure—but ones only a mother could express such a profound interest in.

Forgetting herself for a moment, she turned to Ward, curiosity overruling caution. Question after question formed on her lips. But the sight of his face, taut and grim, and his lean fingers clenching the steering wheel, stopped her short. Too late she realized her mistake. She shouldn't even be thinking of herself as Robbie's mother. Already her mind—or was it her heart?—had begun to trespass on forbidden territory.

Her fingers tensed in her lap. Lord, and she hadn't even seen him yet. She was going to have to do better than this, or she would only end up getting hurt.

Instead she asked quietly, "Does he stay there often? With your sister, I mean?"

Their eyes met as he flashed a quick, sidelong glance at her. There was a hint of annoyance in his eyes. "He only stays with Eileen if I'm going to be out of town." He sent another swift glance at her before stressing, "Which isn't all that often anymore since I'm a full partner now. Otherwise he goes to a sitter in town."

Jenna frowned. "Isn't your office in Abilene?" When he nodded and said that the sitter was in Plains City, she added, "You're a partner now? You weren't before, were you?"

"No. I was offered the partnership about a year ago."

So it was after Megan had died. She would have been proud of him, Jenna suspected. She almost voiced the thought aloud, but his tone was clipped and abrupt, and she was left with the feeling that he wanted nothing more than to be left alone.

That was something Jenna was only too willing to do. She turned her head to the side. Idly she saw that the terrain had changed slightly. They were leaving the flat plains behind and the road followed the dips and curves of gently sloping hills. Homes were few and far between. Cattle grazed in the distance and fields of wheat rippled in the wind.

Though she tried to content herself with the sweeping Texas landscape just outside the window, the strange sort of tension that had sprung up between them last night was in full force once again. Maybe it was because she didn't understand him. She couldn't even pretend to comprehend his hostility last night, or his abrupt about-face. But was it only that? No, there was something else.

More and more Jenna found her gaze touching on that strong, masculine profile presented to her. Ward's eyes were focused straight ahead. His nose jutted out forcefully and there was a faint bump on the bridge that made her wonder if he'd broken it once. The firm contours of his mouth pressed together in a straight line. Didn't he ever smile? She shifted uncomfortably on her seat. She didn't like looking at him, yet he drew her gaze like a magnet.

Her eyes slid downward. His hands were big and very strong-looking, the fingers long and lean, not in the least bit fleshy. One hand lay carelessly over the top of the steering wheel. The other was curled firmly below. She drew in a soft breath of surprise. How long had his sister said Megan had been dead? A year and a half. Her eyes lingered on the smooth band of gold that still encircled his wedding finger.

Her attention drifted back to his hands. Bristly black hairs covered the wide backs. The sleeves of his sweater were pushed up to his elbows, and Jenna's gaze followed the muscular definitions of his forearms. They, too were coated with a thick layer of dark hairs. Was he as hairy as that all over?

She caught her breath again, but this time it was for an entirely different reason. Warmth tainted her entire body, and she had the sinking feeling that a tell-tale trail of red was creeping into her cheeks—she, who hadn't blushed in years. *This drive is going to last a lifetime,* she thought to herself uneasily. She didn't like Ward Garrison and she definitely didn't like the strange way he made her feel.

"When are you getting married?"

The question, out of the blue as it was, gave Jenna a start. It was the first time Ward had spoken of his own accord. For a moment she was unable to speak. "In November," she finally responded. Neil... her marriage. They both seemed a lifetime away. "The first week. We—Neil and I have been engaged for six months now."

Ward took his eyes off the road long enough to study her for a moment. She was looking silently out the window. Meg had really liked Jenna, he remembered. She'd been impressed by that fleeting, almost shy smile and her quiet levelheadedness. She'd decided almost on sight that Jenna was the one.

"She's perfect!" Meg had told him enthusiastically. "Perfect! She even looks a little like you!"

He had agreed that she was the best choice, though not until after they'd interviewed her. Ron Brewster had really grilled her on her reasons for wanting to carry a baby for nine months and willingly then give it up. Her responses had been quiet, almost serene, but there was a world of emotion in those vivid green eyes. No one could doubt her sincerity after looking into those eyes.

But now Ward did doubt—for the first time. At this moment, he couldn't respond to her calm demeanor the same way he had when they'd first met. She was quiet, almost too quiet, as she gazed at the passing countryside. What was going on inside her head? Was she plotting? Scheming of ways to take away his son?

With a harsh sigh he leaned back against the seat. Damn it, he was letting his imagination run wild. Or was he? He didn't know. That was the whole problem. He just didn't know. Meg would have had his hide for being so suspicious; in those days he hadn't been. In fact, he hadn't been until now.

But Jenna *was* getting married, he reminded himself reluctantly. Although he tended to view her as a noose around his neck right now, after this one day she would be out of his life again. But for how long? He pushed away the nagging voice and instead found himself wondering about her future husband. Did it bother him that she was a woman who had voluntarily carried another man's child? Probably not, he decided, a wry twist to his mouth. Today's morals weren't exactly Victorian, and she was, after all, a very attractive woman.

The observation surprised him, as did the realization that he didn't even have to look at her to recall the slender curves of her body. She was so small boned for such a tall woman. The jeans she'd worn this morning had outlined her narrow waist and the flare of her hips. Once again he visualized the gentle thrust of her breasts against her top. Ward shook his head and his jaw tightened. Damn! He was suddenly almost painfully aware that this was the first time since Meg had died—since he'd known Meg, in fact—that he was actively taking note of a woman's appearance. An odd twinge shot through him and his mouth twisted.

Somehow it went against the grain to admit that the first woman he was even remotely conscious of was Jenna Bradford. He could understand the attraction if she reminded him of Meg, but they were nothing alike, not in personality and certainly not in looks. And she was the one woman on earth who stood to harm him the most.

The realization hardened his voice. "What does your intended think of your visit here? I assume he knows why you've come."

Jenna grabbed at the armrest as Ward made a swift turn off the highway onto a narrow side road. They bounced along for several seconds before she spoke.

She tilted her head to look at him. Her quiet voice seemed to hold a challenge. "I didn't need his permission."

"Then I suppose he's behind you all the way."

Jenna bristled at the insolent tone. She had the feeling he was goading her. "My fiancé," she ventured again in forceful but carefully measured words, "is well aware of my reasons for being here." Certainly it was the truth, yet she knew a niggling sense of guilt. Neil had probably known very well he couldn't stop her, but while he was aware of her reasons for coming here, he didn't understand them. He hadn't been at all as supportive as she'd hoped, but even while she told herself this, Jenna knew that even if his objections had been far more strenuous, it wouldn't have made one whit of difference.

But she couldn't be one hundred percent honest with Ward, considering this strange unnamed battle they were having. She didn't quite understand why, but they were adversaries, each on guard against the other. To admit that Neil didn't want her here would be akin to handing an arsenal of weapons to an army.

A dark shadow passed across Ward's face as Jenna fell silent. Meg would have laughed at him if he'd ever have said he had a tough-guy image, callous and hard-hearted, but he had the feeling Jenna Bradford thought of him that way. Last night he'd wanted her to think that. Hell, he'd acted like a mother hen rallying around her chicks, but with all the noise of a raging bull. But this morning . . . this morning was a different story.

He'd slept little the previous night. Her image had danced behind his eyelids all night long. He couldn't forget her expression when he'd left her. Even as he stared at the winding ribbon of road in front of him, the vision in his mind blurred and repeated itself. In her face he'd seen his son's tiny features staring back at him again, crushed and shattered, without a shred of hope to cling to.

He couldn't help but wonder—who was he hurting more? Jenna? Or Robbie?

No, he could have stuck to it if it hadn't been for that. He hadn't been able to live with his decision even one night—he couldn't say no! What if she were the one denying him the chance to see his own son? It was something he didn't want to think about, and for an instant, he hadn't been able to stop putting himself in her place.

Yet he despised himself for being so weak, and he hated the fact that she had put him in this position. It was one neither he nor Meg had given any thought to once Robbie was safely in their possession.

But he had no one to blame but himself, and like it or not, he would stick to his word and let her see Robbie.

The rest of the trip was made in silence, with Ward grimly giving his attention to the road ahead. Jenna stared pensively out the window, both afraid and excited. She was a bundle of nerves by the time the Blazer turned onto a narrow access road, and she began blotting her hands nervously against her thighs as she spied a house in the distance. Her heart was pounding so furiously she could feel the rapid rise and fall of her breasts against the soft jersey of her blouse.

She marveled that her legs even held her as they drew to a halt. Opening the car door, she had to force her attention to her surroundings. She was standing in front of a modest ranch-style house, nestled into a grove of trees. It was tranquil-looking despite the cluster of outbuildings and randomly parked pickup trucks several hundred yards away.

Ward gave her a cursory glance as he got out. "Eileen's probably inside," he said shortly. Just as he rounded the front fender, a flash of red and blue careered around the corner of the house.

"Daddy!"

In that instant, Jenna felt her heart stop beating.

It resumed with thick, uneven strokes as the small figure raced toward them as fast as his chubby, three-year-old legs would carry him. They came to an abrupt halt, and the boy, squealing with excitement, was snatched high into a pair of arms.

Transfixed, Jenna could only stare at him. So this was Robbie. This was her son. *Her son....*

"I missed you, Daddy. I missed you this much!" The little boy spread his arms as wide as they would go, then latched on to his father's neck once more. Tanned, chunky arms peeped out from a short-sleeved bright red polo shirt over which a pair of bib overalls was worn. On his feet were a pair of red canvas sneakers. "Did you bring me a present?" he asked eagerly.

"I missed you, too, champ." A warm kiss was pressed on one dirt-smudged cheek, and Ward drew away to gaze at his son. His lips curved upward as he winked. "And yes, I brought you a present."

So he can smile, after all. Despite the fact that Jenna's whole being was focused on her son, Ward's voice was so full of warmth, his eyes filled with such love and gentleness, that for an instant she was almost stunned. The harsh, unyielding man she had glimpsed last night might have been a stranger, a figment of her imagination.

But the shadow of the stranger was back when he turned to her—reluctantly, it seemed. She collected herself quickly as she saw Ward's smile fade.

"Robbie, there's someone I'd like you to meet." His arms tightened around the boy. "This is Jenna."

Eyes round with curiosity, the little boy wiggled in his father's arms to stare at her, but he didn't say a word.

That he didn't was beyond Jenna's comprehension. Again she felt the breath wrenched from her lungs as a rush of the sweetest, most delightful sense of pleasure shot through her. Robbie's mop of fine, almost black curls could have come from either her or Ward, but those vivid green eyes surrounded by bristly black lashes could belong only to her. *Her!*

In the space of a heartbeat, her joy was shattered as she realized how much of an outsider she really was. She was his mother, but she didn't belong in this tightly woven circle of love between father and son. Jenna was overcome by a rush of emotion so intense she almost cried out with it. Was it possible to feel both joy and pain at the same time? It was, indeed. The moment was both poignant and heartwarmingly precious.

"Hello, Robbie." Her greeting came out as a whisper, and she found herself unable to tear her eyes from that small cherubic face.

"Hi," he finally whispered back. Then he promptly turned and shyly buried his face in the strong column of Ward's neck.

Cast in the unlikely role of rescuer, Ward set the boy on his feet, then ruffled his thick dark hair. "Where's Aunt Eileen?"

His shyness forgotten, Robbie beamed up at him. "In the barn," he responded happily before dashing off.

Ward started off after him, then paused for a second and glanced back at her over his shoulder. Though her insides were still quivering at her first sight of Robbie, her legs felt as if they were leaden poles beneath her when she moved to where he was waiting for her.

The day was sunny and rather warm, lighted with brilliant patches of sunshine. Jenna shivered as they stepped into the barn. The temperature inside was noticeably cooler, so cool that she slipped into the denim blazer she'd removed against the warmth of the car's interior. The odor of fresh, sweet-smelling straw permeated her nostrils and mingled with the aroma of leather and horses. Beneath massive overhead beams, she kept apace with Ward's long-legged strides as he followed Robbie.

"Look, Daddy! Misty's gonna have a baby horse!" Jumping up and down, Robbie pointed toward a stall.

Jenna heard a feminine chuckle as they halted, and then a cheerful voice announced, "Looks like you're just in time, Ward. Misty Moon is about to drop a foal."

Jenna peeked around Ward's broad shoulder. The voice came from a woman with hair as dark as Ward's, worn in a crisp, no-nonsense hairdo that waved neatly back from a friendly, likable face. Eileen Swenson, she assumed. She guessed her to be in her early forties, perhaps slightly older than Ward.

Eileen was kneeling near the flanks of a horse. Jenna drew in a soft breath of surprise. There on a fresh bed of straw lay a beautiful chestnut mare, her golden brown coat glistening with sweat, velvety nostrils flared.

At the small sound, the woman looked up to where Jenna stood slightly behind Ward. Jenna saw the friendly expression vanish as Eileen's eyes darted from Jenna to where Robbie had come to thrust one dimpled hand into Ward's, then back again. Intercepting the look, Ward gestured between the two women and gave a curt introduction. "Eileen, this is Jenna Bradford. Jenna, my sister Eileen."

Aware of the closed expression on Eileen Swenson's face, Jenna murmured a polite greeting. Eileen nodded briefly. Then the mare's sides began to heave and she whinnied, a low sound that spoke of pain.

Moments later a much smaller version of the chestnut mare was awkwardly trying to stand. Inspecting the baby, Eileen announced it was a colt.

"What's a colt?" Robbie piped up.

Busy attending to the mare, Eileen looked up at him and smiled. "A boy. A girl is called a filly."

"Does he have any teeth?"

Eileen shook her head. "Not yet, but he will very soon. By the time he's six months old, he'll have almost as many as you."

Robbie moved a few steps closer. Eyes as wide as saucers were riveted on both mother and baby. "If he doesn't have any teeth," he persisted, "how will he eat?"

Eileen hesitated and looked at Ward, who took up where she left off. He glanced down at his small son. "Well, Robbie," he said, his voice very gentle, "his mother is going to take care of that for him for a while.''

Almost as if he knew he was the subject under discussion, the spindly-legged colt finally made it to his feet and unsteadily moved to nuzzle his mother's belly. The mare whickered softly and looked back at her offspring with velvet-soft eyes.

Somehow the gentleness in Ward's voice was Jenna's undoing. She had watched the foal's quick birth silently, but at the sight of mother and baby, her lungs constricted painfully. Suddenly feeling as though she were suffocating, she stumbled out of the stall and ran toward the wide double doors.

High in the sky, the sun shone down on her still figure as she stood motionless near a whitewashed fence. Several horses grazed peacefully in the paddock near the barn. Beyond, the wide sweep of prairie seemed endless. The land was a rich golden color, fields of wheat swaying in tempo with the gentle breeze.

Jenna saw none of this. Her lungs ached with the effort it took to breathe. Her head hurt. And her breasts; her nipples tingled and she crossed her arms across her chest as though to stop the milk that had never been allowed to flow.

She had declined the shot that would have dried her milk, she remembered vividly. Stubbornly, willfully refused it. She had elected instead to let nature take over the drying of her milk, stoically enduring the slow-going painful process as if...as if by doing so she could purge herself of the memory of the tiny being she had nourished and given life to for nine long months.

She grabbed the wooden railing tightly for support. Still, the memories lingered. And then, as now, the pain in her breasts was nothing compared to the pain in her heart.

Sensing she was being watched, Jenna drew a deep quivering breath and slowly turned. Robbie was standing several feet behind her, small hands clasped behind his back and one sneakered foot toeing the sun-baked dust.

The cobwebs of the past floated away like a dew-kissed mist before a softly sighing breeze. With a feeling strangely akin to relief, she noted he was alone.

"Hello again." She smiled reassuringly at him and inclined her head toward the barn. "Are Daddy and Aunt Eileen still inside?"

Wordlessly he nodded, his eyes huge in his small face.

She took a step forward, stopping when he retreated a step in response. "I'll bet you like the baby horse, don't you?" She deliberately didn't call it a foal, wanting him to feel they were on the same level.

Again he nodded.

"Do you know what Aunt Eileen is going to name him?" she asked coaxingly. Wanting desperately to hear his voice once more, she sighed when another nod was all she received. The green eyes studying her were thoroughly childlike in their curiosity—and their wariness.

She tried again. "You'll probably get to ride him when he's older. Won't that be fun?"

There was an answering sparkle in Robbie's eyes for a second. Seeing it, Jenna slowly moved toward him. She sank down on her knees before him and dug into her coat pocket, remembering the small packet of candy she'd purchased during the long trip from Galveston.

"Do you like jelly beans, Robbie?" She held out the cellophane package in her hand for his inspection. Her eyes ran over his babyish features as if to memorize them for all eternity. Being so close to him, she could see that his cheeks had the bloom and texture of a ripe, fuzzy peach. She longed to reach out and stroke the downy curve, knowing instinctively his skin would be as soft as it looked.

She smiled at him. "I like the red ones," she said. "I have since I was a little girl—not much older than you." She opened the package and poured a few of the candies onto her hand, then slipped the package back into her pocket. There was a look of longing in his eyes as she slipped one into her mouth. "Mmm, they're really good," she told him. "Are you sure you wouldn't like one?"

He hesitated for so long Jenna thought he would finally relent, but then he shook his head. Up until that moment, she'd always thought she had a way with children. She couldn't help but be disappointed that he wasn't responding as she'd hoped. She was just about to rise to her feet, when he smiled at her. It was a tiny, shy smile, but a smile nonetheless.

Jenna thought her heart would bubble over with joy. Suddenly she wanted to reach out and touch him, run her fingers through his silky dark curls and hold him to her breast, capturing the moment and holding it close to her heart forever. Trying not to move so quickly she would frighten him, she did indeed stretch out her arms to fold him close.

Her hands got no farther than his shoulders. At her first faint touch, his eyes widened and his lower lip began to quiver. Feeling as if she were a hot air balloon that had just been deflated by a mere pinprick, she felt her hands fall limply to her side. Slowly she rose to her feet as, with another fearful glance, Robbie turned on his heel and ran toward the house.

"Is everything all right?"

Ward's voice behind her startled her. She pivoted to face him, aware of a burning resentment building inside her. No, everything was not all right, she wanted to tell him bitterly. *Nothing* was right. Her eyes hardened for a fraction of a second as she let the bitterness take hold. This man ... *this man* was all that stood between her and Robbie. If it weren't for Ward Garrison, Robbie would be hers and hers alone.

She was immediately ashamed of the thought. It wasn't fair, any more than were her angrily flung words last night. She summoned a wan smile. "I'm fine," she murmured. She looked up at him, vaguely surprised to see a hint of compassion in those dark eyes.

Her reaction to the foal's arrival was silly, she decided. She had embraced the situation awkwardly. Birth, like death, was but one of life's everyday occurrences. One was a miracle and the other was something to be dealt with but not dwelt upon. She was, she realized, experiencing a kind of delayed reaction over her forfeiture of Robbie. Perhaps if she had forced herself to deal with the pain of her loss at the time of his birth, she wouldn't be feeling so desolate inside right now. And maybe she had expected too much of Robbie, of the moment. But now...before...what did it matter? The ache in her heart was there, and it was real.

Ward moved closer, studying her quietly. There was a shadow of pain in those luminous green eyes, and it took no stretch of the imagination to know that it had to do with Robbie. His unexpected sense of helplessness when she ran from the barn surprised him. He'd known instinctively that she'd been thinking of Robbie's birth. Especially in light of his feelings about her presence, the stab of pain he'd felt was unexpected, as well. But he couldn't help remembering the long and difficult labor she'd endured. Hours and hours of pain while he and Meg had sat waiting. Hoping. Anticipating. Talking in hushed, excited whispers about the baby they would soon hold in their arms.

It made him cringe to be suddenly reminded of what Jenna had gone through to give him his son and how he had repaid her. He had emerged from the barn in time to hear her say jelly beans were her favorite candy. Then when Robbie refused them, his throat had tightened oddly at the look of hurt that flashed across her face. Robbie loved jelly beans.

But the fact remained: Jenna's simple request to see his son wasn't simple at all. If he ever lost Robbie, he didn't think he could bear it.

"You'll have to forgive Robbie," he said finally. "He's a little leery of strangers."

For an instant Jenna's eyes collided sharply with his. But there was no hint of malice in either his tone or his expression, and strangely enough, she sensed his words were meant to be reassuring. She moved to step into the shade of a cottonwood tree, absently running a hand over the pale rough bark. "Don't apologize," she said in as light a tone as she could muster. She leaned against the tree before turning to face him again. "He's not too young to learn that he shouldn't take candy from someone he doesn't know." And she should have known better than to try to bribe him with it, she added silently.

He glanced over to where Robbie now played happily with a truck on the sidewalk in front of the house. Jenna's eyes followed, but when her eyes met his again she was stunned at what she saw. There was a flash of pride as he looked at Robbie, but the look changed completely as he turned back to her. Again she glimpsed the same elusive emotion she'd seen in his eyes last night. Fear? Something wasn't right. She almost sensed he was somehow afraid of her. *Of her?* No, that wasn't possible. He had nothing to fear from her; she could do him no harm. The ball was in his court, as it had been all along.

Both of them were lost in thought, and so neither of them heard Eileen come up silently behind them. Glancing uneasily between the two of them, she cleared her throat. "Will you two be staying for lunch?"

CHAPTER SIX

JENNA LOOKED AWAY quickly, leaving it totally up to Ward, as it should have been. She didn't want to influence him one way or the other. On one hand, she was admittedly reluctant to leave just yet, having only had a mere glimpse of Robbie. But she suspected the less time spent with both Ward and his sister the better.

Her thoughts proved to be right on target. Eileen insisted on preparing the light lunch of chicken soup and tuna sandwiches herself, and Jenna was left feeling awkward and out of place.

The jelly beans had left a sticky mess in the palm of her hand, and when she emerged from the bathroom and walked back to the living room, where she'd been ushered in to wait, the sound of voices carried through from the kitchen.

"You're making a big mistake, Ward." Eileen sounded tense, agitated. "Don't you realize the trouble you've invited?"

Jenna stiffened. There was no doubt in her mind what—and whom—Eileen was talking about. The deep sound of Ward's voice was muted, so she couldn't make out his reply.

She glanced around the room, trying to take her mind off the conversation in the kitchen. The overstuffed sofa and matching wing chairs looked inviting, but Jenna was too tense and restless to sit. She

stared at the array of photographs hanging on the pale
gold of the living room wall. There must have been at
least twenty. A boy, a girl—at various ages. Indoor
poses, outdoor poses. The same print of a waterfall in
three different sizes on the opposite wall. That was all
she really registered.

"I still can't believe you went ahead and did it. I
thought you weren't going to let her see him."

Eileen's voice again. If she was trying to stifle her
words, she wasn't doing a very good job of it. Or perhaps they were meant to be heard. In any case, the
conversation didn't make for the best atmosphere when
Eileen finally announced lunch.

They all seemed edgy and nervous as they gathered
around the butcher block table in the big, roomy
kitchen. All except Robbie and Frank Swenson. Wearing a battered Stetson and dusty boots, Frank arrived
at the table a few minutes late after washing up. Bar-
rel-chested and muscular, he had a thatch of graying
blond hair and bright blue eyes in a rugged, tanned and
weather-beaten face. Robbie chuckled delightedly when
he sat down and proceeded to tickle his ribs, and he
even succeeded in earning a reluctant smile from the
other three adults at the table.

As for Robbie, he could hardly sit still. Jenna could
see that he was a very active little boy who, in spite of
his reticence with her, was possessed of a sweet and
loving nature. He ended up spilling his milk, and the
few bites he took of his sandwich were punctuated with
an excited, "Can we go see the baby again before we
leave?" And then those big green eyes would turn
hopefully in the direction of his father.

Ward finally relented. "All right. One more time
before we head for home."

Frank went with them, leaving Jenna and Eileen alone. The silence that settled over the room was stark and uncomfortable. Jenna at last folded her napkin onto her luncheon plate, rose and carried her dishes to the cupboard beside the stainless steel sink. When she walked back to the table, Eileen cleared her throat and looked up at her.

"Robbie's quite a little boy, isn't he?"

Jenna gathered up the other cutlery and placed it on a plate. Surely this wasn't an overture of friendship, not after what she'd said to Ward. Eileen had been polite but no more during the meal. "Yes," Jenna agreed in a noncommittal tone, then looked directly at her. "But, then, you're in a much better position to know that, aren't you?"

The woman blanched and her tentative smile faded. At her stricken look, Jenna felt a stab of guilt. The episode with Ward last night, and even today's events, had left her defensive and prickly. "I'm sorry," she said quickly. "I shouldn't have said that."

"No." Eileen took a deep breath. "No, I probably deserved it." She paused, indicating that Jenna should take a seat. When she was sitting across from her, she studied the younger woman for a moment. "You heard, didn't you?"

Jenna hesitated. "It was hard not to."

"I'm sorry. I honestly didn't mean for that to happen."

Jenna silently eyed Eileen for a moment. What could she say? That it was all right? It didn't erase the feeling of hurt she'd felt. First Ward and then Eileen. But she looked so deeply contrite that it was hard to doubt her sincerity.

"Look, I'll be honest with you." Eileen leaned forward in her chair. "If it had been my decision to make, I'd have decided against letting you see Robbie. But since it wasn't, I think you should know that Ward's been through a lot since Meg died. Sometimes I think the only reason he's gotten through it at all is because he's had Robbie to think of and Robbie to hold on to." She shook her head. "I just don't want to see him hurt any more."

Jenna lifted her eyes. "And you think that's what I'll do?"

Eileen made a vague gesture with one hand. "You seem like a very nice person, but, yes, that's exactly what I'm afraid of."

"Please don't be." Jenna spoke softly, imploringly. Her dark hair swirled around her shoulders as she shook her head. "I don't want to hurt anyone. Not Ward and certainly not Robbie. All I wanted was to see him—" how she kept the quaver from her voice she was never quite certain "—and now that I have, I'll be going home."

JENNA REPEATED those words over and over in her mind late that day. Though it was early afternoon when Ward headed back to Plains City, the day's sunshine had given way to a dark covering of threatening purple storm clouds. They seemed to penetrate her soul as they hung over the earth. The meeting had been such a letdown, she acknowledged wearily. Robbie was shy and hesitant with her and refused to let her touch him, though Ward, surprisingly, encouraged him. Jenna was under no illusions about the softening of his manner. She had the feeling it was only because of the presence of his sister. What saddened her the most was that she felt Robbie would have come around—in time.

Yet time was the one thing she didn't have. The one thing she would *never* have with her son.

"Here we are." Ward pulled into the parking lot of the motel. He found an empty space next to her car, then switched off the engine. Turning slightly, his eyes drifted to his slumbering son, strapped between them in his car seat, then on to Jenna. "Will you be leaving right away?"

If I don't, will you run me out of town? The words were on the tip of Jenna's tongue. She had to fight to bite them back. She stared out the window, at the wind relentlessly pushing the clouds across the sky.

"Tomorrow, I think. It's a long drive." Her tone was almost curt as she tucked a long strand of hair behind her ear. "It's too late to leave today."

Ward nodded. "I suppose you have to be back at work Monday morning."

In spite of herself Jenna felt a skitter of excitement. He *had* yielded enough to let her see him this once.... She sensed he was as ill at ease as she was. And why the small talk unless... "No." She rubbed damp palms against her jeans. "I've taken a short leave of absence."

Out of the corner of her eye she saw him rub a hand against his jaw. "You were working for a doctor before, weren't you?"

She nodded. "He closed his practice and moved to Michigan. I've been working in the hospital emergency room for almost two years now." She held her breath and waited, waited for him to say he was willing to let her stay as long as she wanted.

She waited in vain. The small spiral of hope inside her died as quickly as it had risen when the words didn't come. One hand fumbled for the handle of the door before she turned in her seat, her throat constricting tightly.

Her eyes moved unerringly to the small boy at her side, adoring him, memorizing the tiny features to hold them close to her heart for all eternity. His lashes were dark and bristly, fanning out thickly on plump, pinkened cheeks. Her eyes soft with emotion, she ran the tip of her finger around his small bow-shaped mouth.

She drew a deep, quivering breath. She would never be able to hold him, or touch him, or do all the things a mother should do for her child. No longer caring that Ward was watching her, she slid her fingers through the silky dark curls on his smooth forehead and bent to kiss his cheek. "Goodbye, Robbie," she whispered softly. "I'll always love you." Her lashes fluttered shut as she kissed him again, her heart full of silent wishes and hopes... and a fleeting sense of despair.

A hot ache filled her throat and it took a moment to control it. When she finally lifted her head to look briefly into Ward's eyes, she had schooled her features into a mask of composure. What she had set out to do had been accomplished. She had wanted to see her son and she had. Now it was over, and she could ask no more of this man.

"Thank you," she said quietly. "Thank you for letting me see him."

Her legs were unsteady as she got out of the car and made her way into the motel. Inside the room she stretched out on the bed, but for the second night in a row, the tears refused to flow.

THE EMOTIONAL EVENTS of the previous day had drained her, but Jenna woke up in the morning feeling as if she'd slept little more than an hour or two. She dragged herself out of bed toward the window. Parting the thin material, she noticed that the leaden gray cloud cover still remained, dampening the morning sun's arrival.

Several large raindrops spattered the car windshield as she stepped outside a short time later and loaded her suitcase into the trunk. After dropping off her room key and settling the bill at the office, she crossed the street to the little café where she'd breakfasted on Friday.

Despite the fact that it was Sunday morning and church services were undoubtedly going on, every booth was filled. The same friendly waitress who had served her a few days ago bustled over when she slipped onto a stool at the front counter.

"So you're still with us." The woman gave a beaming smile. "How about another cinnamon roll today?"

Jenna shook her head. "No, thanks. Just coffee."

She lingered over several cups, trying to shake her listless mood. Finally she glanced at her watch. It was nearly eleven o'clock. If she didn't leave soon, it would be dark by the time she arrived home.

The waitress came back over, wiping the counter with a spotless white cloth. "Looks like we're in for a downpour, doesn't it?" She nodded toward the swirling turbulence of the ever-darkening clouds outside.

Forcing a smile, Jenna agreed. "If I were home, I'd say we were due for a hurricane."

"It's that time of year, all right." The woman eyed her curiously. "Where's home?"

"Galveston." She lifted the brown ceramic cup to her lips.

She didn't see the figure at the end of the counter move until he sat down in the stool next to her. Pretending not to notice his interested absorption, she stirred more sugar into her coffee.

"I couldn't help but overhear you say you're from Galveston." When he paused briefly, she could feel his gaze lightly resting on her profile. "I hope you don't mind my saying so, but I spent a good many years in Houston myself."

The voice was well modulated and pleasant, but the line was a come-on if ever she'd heard one, and a very bad one at that. She didn't mind small talk from the waitress, but she wasn't in the mood for unwanted attention from a male admirer. Her eyes flickered briefly in his direction. "Really," she commented in as polite a tone as she could muster.

From the corner of her eye she saw him nod. "I went to medical school in Houston," he added. Her mind deliberately ignoring him, she turned to deliver a suitably curtailing remark that she hoped would send him back to his seat at the end of the counter. When she did, her hand was seized in a brief, warm clasp. "Steve Reynolds here. And you are . . . ?"

His words finally penetrated, and the blistering comment on the end of her tongue never came. "Jenna Bradford," she said faintly. A frown etched itself between slender dark brows as she withdrew her hand. "Medical school? You're a doctor, then?"

Smiling, he nodded. Jenna finally took the time to examine him thoroughly. She guessed he was in his early forties, and with his long legs awkwardly tucked beneath the counter, he appeared thin and gangly. His hair was a sun-streaked shade of light brown, with a few threads of gray, as well, and he had the gentlest pair of brown eyes she had ever seen.

Her apprehension melted away beneath his warm smile. "A general practitioner?"

He nodded, cheerfully adding, "I've even been known to look at a few dogs and cats over the past ten years."

Jenna smiled. "What a coincidence, Dr. Reynolds. I happen to be an R.N."

"You are?" His eyes lighted up with surprise, and it wasn't long before the two were engrossed in conversation, comparing notes on their medical backgrounds. Dr. Reynolds, it seemed, had also served a brief stint as an E.R. physician years before.

"Can't say as I miss the hectic pace," he finished, several cups of coffee later. "I didn't mind all the stress back then, but it's a different story now." He laughed. "Don't think I could pry my wife and kids away from this town now if I tried." One shaggy eyebrow lifted as he studied her, a distinctly speculative look in his eyes. "I don't suppose you're ready to give up all the excitement of a big city hospital just yet. My nurse quit last week and I haven't found a replacement for her yet. I could use a good office nurse, if you're interested in a change of pace."

Jenna shook her head, declining with a smile.

Dr. Reynolds sighed and pushed his cup and saucer away. "I don't suppose you have any family in town who could entice you into staying."

"No. As a matter of fact, I was here for the weekend visiting—friends." How quickly she was falling into that lie. Friends. She and Ward were more like divine enemies. His hostility suddenly vaulted into her mind and she shifted, feeling rather uncomfortable. Plains City was a fairly small town. If the friendly atmosphere of this little café was anything to go by, it was the type of town where everyone knew everyone else.

Apparently Steve Reynolds's thoughts were following the same vein. "Oh?" He glanced over at her curiously.

Jenna nodded, feeling compelled to elaborate. "Uh, yes... Ward Garrison."

"Ward? He and his wife were two of my very first patients. I've known him for years." He looked at her intently for a moment, a flicker of concern in his eyes. "I've been telling him for months it was about time he pulled his head out of the sand and started looking ahead again. There's no sense living in the past."

Her heart began to thump unevenly. Megan. He was talking about Megan. Eileen, Ward and now Dr. Steve Reynolds... they had made no bones about telling her that Megan was dead, but she was beginning to wonder *how* she died. "Yes, I—I quite agree."

She held her breath and waited, hoping he would say more. But instead his features relaxed and a slow smile spread across his face. "Now that I've seen you," he added with a wink, "I can understand why a pretty lady like you would be enough to turn his head. If I weren't already very happily married, I might be giving him a little competition."

Competition? For a minute Jenna drew a complete blank. Then she realized what he was thinking. She and Ward? Good Lord, the idea was ridiculous. But all of a sudden she remembered the look of those strong, intensely masculine hands curled around the steering wheel and she couldn't prevent the rush of heat that coursed through her body. She started to tell Dr. Reynolds that he was totally mistaken, but he was eyeing her quizzically, a faintly puzzled look on his face.

"Now that I think about it," he said slowly, "you look rather familiar. Are you sure we've never met before?"

"No," she said quickly. "I'm sure we haven't. I've never been to Plains City before."

"Well." He studied her for a moment. "You sure you won't reconsider the job offer? My receptionist is already complaining I'm running her ragged. And after all—" a twinkle appeared in his eyes "—Plains City is a lot closer to Ward Garrison than Galveston."

Jenna smiled and opened her mouth to decline once more, but suddenly the impact of those words left her feeling giddy. "Plains City is a lot closer to Ward Garrison than Galveston." Not Ward, but Robbie. *Robbie.* Perhaps she could accept his offer, after all, even if it were only for a few days or a few weeks. As long as it took him to find someone permanent. There was really no reason for her to hurry back to Galveston. She'd taken care of all but the final wedding preparations, and there was nothing that needed her immediate attention. This job would give her the perfect excuse to remain here and see Robbie again. Why couldn't she stay?

The answer was like a tidal wave coming down around her, crushing her hopes with the same driving force. Ward. She flinched, remembering his adamant refusal. She had already pressed her luck with him once. Could she risk it again? Her shoulders slumped dejectedly. No. Ward would never let her.

She shook her head and forced a smile. "I'm sorry, but tempting as it sounds, the answer is still no."

Steve Reynolds looked disappointed, but they chatted for several more minutes before Jenna got up to leave. Her car was still in the motel parking lot, and she pulled up the collar of her Windbreaker against the steady pelt of the rain as she ran back across the street.

"Say, aren't you Jenna Bradford?"

She nearly ran headlong into the motel manager as he poked his head out the door. "Yes!" She had to shout to make herself heard above the driving force of the rain and the howl of the wind.

"Got a phone call for you!" he yelled back, motioning inside.

Puzzled as to who might be calling her here, she lifted a hand to her face to wipe away the rivers of moisture rolling down her cheeks and picked up the phone on the counter. "Hello?"

"Jenna, is that you?"

It was Ward. One hand tightly gripped the receiver while the other curled tightly at her side. He sounded rather strange. "Yes."

"Thank God you're still there! Can you come out here right away?"

She could think of only one reason for him to sound like this. "Ward, is Robbie—"

She got no further. "He's sick, Jenna! He was burning up this morning! Will you come out and look at him?"

"I'll be right out," she promised. Neither the impatience nor the urgency in Ward's voice was lost on her.

Childhood illnesses were many and varied, and Jenna knew she couldn't even hazard a guess as to what was wrong with him until she had seen him. Once there, she took the porch steps two at a time. Before she even had a chance to knock, the door was yanked open.

Ward looked so relieved to see her that if the circumstances had been otherwise, Jenna might have enjoyed a self-indulgent laugh. As it was, there was barely time to breathe before Ward grabbed her elbow and practically dragged her into the living room.

Clad in jeans and a Dallas Cowboys football jersey, Robbie was sitting on a braided rug in front of the fireplace, surrounded by a dozen Matchbox cars and trucks, playing quite contentedly.

She slid a sideways glance at the tall figure next to her. The hard, self-possessed man of yesterday was gone. Now his expression was harried. The blue denim shirt he wore looked as if it had been shoved hurriedly into his belt, but his hair... She tried very hard not to smile as she passed him. The thick, dark strands were standing in a dozen different directions, no doubt from his running his hands through them the way he was doing right now.

Stopping in front of Robbie, Jenna studied him for a moment. His cheeks appeared slightly rosier than they'd been yesterday, but he didn't look all that sick. When Ward finally dropped down in a gold upholstered chair next to her, she looked up. "What's wrong with him?" she asked softly.

Ward ran a hand over the bristly line of his jaw. "He's sick!"

Jenna's lips quirked a little. "Sick... how? Other than the fever, of course," she added on seeing his mouth open. "Not eating, or vomiting... what?"

"He's covered with spots!" Again he ran his hand through his hair. "I don't know. Maybe it's measles or something."

Spots? Jenna could see no such indication. It was clear Ward was in no condition to offer anything more substantial than what he already had, so she knelt down in front of Robbie, then curled her legs beneath her.

"Hi, Robbie," she said softly. "Remember me? My name's Jenna."

He avoided her eyes and wheeled a tiny truck in a slow circle, but he finally nodded. "Smart boy," she praised, hoping to gain his confidence and trust. "Do you know what a nurse is?"

He hesitated, then shook his head.

"That's okay," she said with a smile. "A nurse is someone who helps people who are sick. Did you know I'm a nurse?" There was a barely imperceptible shake of his dark head. Jenna glanced briefly at Ward, then back at Robbie. "Daddy says you're not feeling well, and I'd like to help you. Can you tell me where you hurt?"

"Don't hurt anywhere." His words were muttered into his shirt front, and Jenna had a hard time understanding him.

Ward leaned forward in the chair. "He said his head hurt this morning when he woke up," he told her in a low voice. "I gave him some Tylenol about an hour ago."

Jenna nodded. "It's probably taken effect by now." Moving slowly so she wouldn't startle him, she lifted the back of her hand to Robbie's cheeks, then lightly felt his bare arms. He was slightly warm to the touch, but certainly not "burning up" as Ward had said.

"Do you have a thermometer around?" she asked Ward. When he rose and went in the direction of the hall, she couldn't resist calling after him, "You might want to look for a comb, too.'' At the startled look he sent over his shoulder, she smiled and added softly, ''For yourself.''

His black brows drew together in a frown, and she half suspected he would bite her head off for even making the suggestion. But when he returned, handing her a fever thermometer, she noticed his hair was once again in order.

''Now,'' she said to Robbie, ''you just pretend this is a straw, and don't bite, so we can take your temperature.'' Surprisingly, he obediently clamped his lips around the thermometer and held it there.

Watching from the chair again, Ward commented, ''I wanted to take it earlier, but he'd just had something to drink.''

As Jenna suspected, Robbie had only a very low-grade fever. Replacing the thermometer in the case, she looked at him. ''Can you show me your spots, Robbie?''

Robbie frowned heavily, then looked at his father. When Ward nodded encouragingly, he lifted his shirt. Jenna leaned closer. There were probably a dozen tiny, reddened blisters on his rounded tummy and back.

''What's wrong with him? Was I right? Is it measles? Is it serious?''

Typical parental overreaction, Jenna thought with a silent smile. Ward seemed to have calmed down for a few minutes, but the anxious alarm was back in his voice.

''No, it's not serious,'' she said soothingly. She rose and sat on the couch across from him while Robbie went back to his toys. ''But you were close. It's not measles. It's chicken pox. His fever is very low and shouldn't last more than a day or two. It's hard to say how many more blisters he'll get, but they'll begin to dry up after a few days. The itching is probably what will give him the most discomfort, but baking soda baths will help."

"Chicken pox!" Ward looked half relieved, half aghast. "Damn! That's contagious, too!"

Jenna nodded. "One other thing. You'll have to keep him away from other kids. If you don't, every child in Plains City will end up with it."

"How long is it contagious?"

"Well . . . at the very least a week." She frowned thoughtfully. "Probably not more than two weeks."

Ward rose and began to pace around the room. To Jenna's mingled surprise and confusion, his expression again grew more harried by the second.

"Ward—" her tone was very gentle "—it's really not that bad. Except for the rash, I doubt you'll even know Robbie has it. There's no need to worry so about him—"

"I understand that." He drew a deep breath and stopped in front of the fireplace.

"Then what's the problem?" Puzzled, Jenna tilted her head to the side. Instead of looking relieved, as she had expected, he still looked as if the world were about to come to an end.

He made a helpless gesture with one hand. "You just said he shouldn't be around any other children."

"Yes, but . . ."

"His baby-sitter takes care of two other kids and has two of her own. She won't be able to watch him. I can't afford to take even one day off right now—let alone a week or two—because the firm is negotiating a deal to oversee a dam project in Oklahoma."

"I see," Jenna said slowly. Her fingers clenched the nubby fabric of the couch. One of the trials of single parenthood was child care, and finding someone to take care of a sick child could make things doubly difficult. She hesitated. "What about Eileen?"

Ward ran a hand through his hair, undoing all the neatness so recently restored. "She and Frank left for a cattle auction in Amarillo today. They won't be back until Wednesday." The response came absently. "Damn!" he muttered. "I've got meetings all day tomorrow and Tuesday and there's no way I can get out of them. What the hell am I going to do with Robbie?" He stared out the window, where the wind furiously lashed the tree branches and rain poured freely down the windowpanes.

Jenna's heart skipped a beat. The solution was obvious. Sitting in the very same room with him, in fact. Her mouth opened, then clamped shut in a tight line. She wasn't going to humble herself by offering to watch Robbie for him and having him fling it back at her. But if he chose to ask her, then that was another matter entirely.

"I see your point," she agreed blandly. "It might be wise if Robbie were at home, particularly the first week or so. Is there someone you could get to stay here with him during the day?"

"Not on such short notice." Jenna held her breath almost painfully. She saw his expression change, his eyes narrow thoughtfully as he turned to her. Jenna looked at the russet brick of the fireplace, the polished oak extending beyond the mantel, the smaller shelves beneath laden with pitchers and leafy green plants. Anything to keep from looking at Ward and conveying the silent plea she knew would be reflected there.

"I don't suppose—"

She could hear the hesitance in his voice before he broke off abruptly. She stilled the shaking of her hands by clamping them around her knees and then forced herself to meet his gaze. "Yes?" How she managed to quell the quaver in her voice, she was never sure.

"When did you say you had to be back in Galveston?"

Jenna could scarcely believe her ears. "There's no hurry. I can stay as long as I want." Or maybe a better choice of words would have been as long as she was needed, she added to herself.

Ward was silent for so long she began to give up hope. "I don't suppose," he said finally, "that you might be able to stay with Robbie." He considered for a moment, his expression guarded. "You'd be doing me a big favor and—it would give you the chance to get to know him a little better."

She wanted to jump for joy. She could almost see the wheels in motion in Ward's head, but she wasn't so naive as to believe Ward actually wanted her there. It was merely a matter of convenience to him.

But it didn't matter. Nothing mattered but the chance to be with Robbie. And if that meant putting up with his father, then so be it.

"I'd be glad to," she said softly. Suddenly she frowned, thinking out loud. "Except I've already checked out of my motel." She sighed. "I guess I'll have to go back and—"

"There's no need. You can stay here, if you like." The words were uttered with grudging reluctance. Nevertheless the offer came as a surprise. When her startled, uncertain gaze met his, he added, "There's plenty of room. And I wouldn't feel right if I put you to the extra expense of a motel just so you could watch Robbie for me."

The opportunity was heaven sent. By some miracle, she'd been granted more precious time with her son. She'd be a fool to say no. She *couldn't* say no.

And she didn't.

"Are you sure it won't be a problem?" she asked softly.

"No." He looked away from the gentle probe of her eyes. "No problem."

Outside it was still dark and dismal as they hurriedly collected her luggage from the trunk, but Jenna felt as if a ray of golden, glorious sunshine had burst inside her.

She only hoped that she and Ward didn't kill each other inside of a week.

CHAPTER SEVEN

JENNA FULLY EXPECTED Sunday to be the worst day for all of them. But as it was, once Ward seemed to have assured himself that chicken pox wasn't as deadly as the plague, he excused himself. "I'll be in the den, catching up on some work, if you need anything," he said, glancing at Robbie, then back at her. "Maybe you two should spend some time alone together so Robbie won't be surprised when he's left with you tomorrow."

The observation surprised her. She had the uncomfortable feeling she was walking on very thin ice when she was around Ward, and somehow she'd expected that he would spend the afternoon keeping an eagle eye trained on her while she acquainted herself with Robbie. As for tomorrow, Robbie would be forced to rely on her no matter what, but at his tender age, she agreed that the fewer surprises in store for him, the better.

She spent the next few hours playing with him, while he dragged out first one and then another of his toys from his room. While he rebelled slightly at having her touch him as she longed to do, more and more she found herself on the receiving end of his shy, sweet smile. By the evening she was certain that she would have very little problem with him the next day.

Ward, on the other hand, was another story. She was uncomfortably aware of him when they were in the same room. When he looked at her, it was hard to believe he was the same man whose eyes softened with warmth and love each time they rested upon his son. While his manner toward her wasn't precisely aloof, she did sense a definite coolness.

The bedroom he'd shown her to was light and airy. The white wicker accents, garden-fresh pastels and mellow pine furniture lent the room the charm of a country inn. Yet even when she was alone that night she couldn't escape his presence. Exactly what role, she pondered quietly as she slipped into the wide double bed, other than that of a live-in baby-sitter, was she to take? He had very effectively coped with dinner, a delicious casserole she couldn't have topped herself. After dinner, he had briefly discussed his son's routine with Jenna, then hustled Robbie into the bathtub. A short time later, the youngster was neatly tucked into his bed and sound asleep.

He was indeed a very capable man. The thought was strangely irksome, but suddenly remembering how tired he'd looked that evening, she realized for the first time that his role as a single parent couldn't be easy.

She finally decided sleepily to play it by ear. She could—if she wanted and if he would let her—make life a little easier for him. And after all, she had no doubt that if he had any objections, he wouldn't hesitate to tell her.

On that note, she rolled over and went to sleep.

SHE NEEDN'T HAVE WORRIED, however. Always an early riser, she awoke just past dawn and showered, then padded downstairs to start breakfast. She pulled out a frying pan, then cracked an egg into a bowl and began to whip it. Sensing she was being watched, she looked over her shoulder to find a pair of very bright, watchful green eyes peeping around a corner of the swinging door.

"Well, hello there! How are you feeling today?"

"Fine," he whispered shyly.

"No headache today?"

When he shook his head, she nodded. "Good." Crooking a finger at him, she grinned and beckoned him closer. "How would you like to help fix breakfast?"

A pajama-clad Robbie eagerly ran across the room, clambering onto the chair she pulled up to the cupboard for him. "Here you go." She neatly broke several more eggs into the bowl and handed him the whisk. "Think you can beat these while I set the table?" His smile revealed two rows of tiny, pearly-white baby teeth. It was coming her way more and more often, she thought with glowing satisfaction.

Between the two of them, they managed to have breakfast on the table a very short time later. Robbie grinned happily as she lifted him into his booster chair, and while she grinned back at him, Ward walked into the room.

Jenna felt as if someone had wrapped a huge rubber band around her chest. She stood stock-still, and for an instant she couldn't breathe. Compared to the ragtag figure she'd glimpsed yesterday, the man before her could have graced the pages of a fashion magazine. His dark hair waved crisply away from his tanned forehead, and the three-piece suit he wore was molded with ease to the lean lines of his body. Yet for all the imposing figure he presented, it was the air of raw virility surrounding him that caught her unawares.

A restless shiver snaked down her spine as she straightened. She was far too conscious of Ward as a man, far more conscious than she should have been ... and the thought was strangely unnerving.

"Good morning," she said.

He nodded curtly to her greeting and started across the room.

"Would you like some breakfast?"

"Daddy never eats breakfast," Robbie piped up.

Standing at the stove with a plate in her hand, Jenna glanced over in surprise. "You really should, you know," she admonished gently. "Breakfast is just as important for you as it is for Robbie."

There was a sheepish look on his face as he poured himself a cup of coffee. "I usually don't have time," he admitted, sitting down at the table, "what with dressing and feeding Robbie and getting him to the baby-sitter's on time."

"Sometimes Daddy doesn't hear his alarm." This latest offering from Robbie was made with his mouth full of scrambled eggs.

Jenna smiled at the embarrassed look that flitted across Ward's face. Walking over to the table, she set a plate heaped full of bacon, eggs and toast in front of him. "But you don't have to worry about that for the time being, do you?"

Strangely, the gesture seemed a kind of peace offering. She had reached out a hand, and though for a minute she thought he might slap it away, he didn't. Instead he reached for the fork she extended to him, and though he didn't smile when he took it, there was something in his eyes that hadn't been there before—at least when he looked at her.

It made her feel warm all over, both inside and out. She found her lips still curving upward when Ward finally left and she carried his empty plate to the sink.

She turned back to Robbie and loosened the strap on his booster chair. "Since you're such a fountain of information when it comes to Daddy," she said with a wink, "maybe you can tell me what to fix for dinner tonight."

His eyes sparkled up at her. "He likes berry muffins."

"Berry muffins!" Jenna laughed. "You mean blueberry muffins?"

Robbie nodded vigorously and scrambled down from his chair. With her hands on her hips, she grinned down at him. "Sometime this week we'll have blueberry muffins for breakfast, but I think we'd better come up with something else for dinner."

LATER THAT MORNING she made a much belated call to her mother.

"Mom? How are you?"

"Jenna! Thank heaven you finally called! I was beginning to worry about you!" Marie Bradford's voice was tinged with relief, but her next words were cautiously optimistic. "How are things going, Jenna?"

Twirling the telephone cord around her finger, Jenna sat down at the round maple table. Hazy streamers of sunlight poured through the window, and she turned so that the warmth caressed her shoulders and back. The rain-sodden landscape of yesterday was gone, leaving behind a world of glistening brightness. A gentle breeze ruffled the starched yellow tablecloth, and she smoothed it with her fingers before finally responding.

"Things couldn't be better." She smiled against the mouthpiece. It was good to hear her mother's voice. She had wanted to call sooner, but she'd been wrapped up in trying to inspire Robbie's trust so he wouldn't be frightened of being alone with her. When she had finally remembered, it had been rather late. Ward had already gone to bed and she didn't feel right about using the phone while he was asleep, even though she intended to charge the call to her home number in Galveston.

There was a smile in her mother's voice, as well. "I take it you've seen Robbie, then."

"Yes, oh, yes. He's beautiful, Mom. The sweetest little boy you could ever imagine." She laughed, a clear, tinkling sound that was as lighthearted and carefree as she felt inside. Sensing he was being talked about, Robbie looked up from the coloring book he was absorbed in across the table from her. "Even though he's covered with chicken pox this morning!" she added.

She went on to tell her mother of Ward's dilemma, including Megan's death, though she purposely eliminated the fact that it hadn't been an easy task to get her foot in the door in the first place.

"Jenna—" Marie's voice was a little dubious "—I'm glad that things have turned out as well as they have, but please remember that this is only temporary."

Her smile faded. Her mother was warning her not to get too involved. But Jenna knew the score. She always had. At least she wasn't foolish enough to disillusion herself that times such as these with her son could become a habit. And as long as she kept that firmly in mind...

"I know that Mom," she said lightly—perhaps a little too lightly.

"I hope so, Jenna. I hope so." Once again Marie sounded faintly worried, but she changed the subject. "Does Neil mind that you're staying a few more days?"

Neil. She felt an unwelcome pang of guilt. She had hardly given Neil a second thought since she'd arrived. And though Robbie was her first and foremost reason for being there, she'd told herself it would be a good time to hash out her feelings for Neil.

At her silence, Marie sighed. "He doesn't know yet, does he?"

An uneasy twinge shot through her. "No."

"Have you even talked to him since you left?"

Jenna bit her lip. "No, I haven't," she admitted in a small voice.

"Jenna, you know I'm the last person to lecture you. Heaven only knows I'm grateful you've been the kind of daughter who's never needed it," she interspersed gently, "but this is the second time you've come to me before going to Neil. And soon you're going to have to realize that some things are best told to your mother second and your husband *first.*"

It was on the tip of Jenna's tongue to blurt out that Neil wasn't her husband yet. But having already had a similar conversation only a few short days ago, she knew what her mother was trying to say. She smiled a little wistfully to herself. What wisdom was it her mother possessed that she knew when to prod and not pry?

"I know." Jenna sighed. The truth was, she wasn't looking forward to the conversation. She was afraid

Neil was going to be less than thrilled with her decision. "I'll call him today."

She chatted with her mother a few more minutes before hanging up, then dialed Neil's office. When his secretary perfunctorily announced he was out of the office, she left Ward's number and asked that he return the call.

Her smile was back in place, however, when she turned her attention to Robbie. This was her one chance in a lifetime, and now that he was beginning to warm toward her, she wasn't going to let *anything* stand in the way of this special time with her son.

Later she would wonder how a day that started out so right could possibly end up so wrong.

TO BEGIN WITH, Robbie woke up from his nap fretful and feverish, and all of Jenna's attempts to soothe him were met with his further withdrawal. The Tylenol she gave him reduced his fever, but he lay on the living room sofa, quiet and unmoving, with a picture book in his lap that was never opened. Jenna's heart ached for him as much as it did for herself. He didn't feel well; he wanted his father and he was stuck with a stranger, instead.

It was nearly six when she finally managed to coax a tenuous smile from him. During his nap, more blisters had appeared on his arms and chubby, reddened cheeks. As he took one look at himself in the bathroom mirror, his eyes widened to the size of saucers and the makings of a smile appeared.

Taking advantage of the moment, Jenna moved to sit beside him on the couch, telling him about her own bout with chicken pox when she was six years old. "And as my dad constantly used to tell me, covered with spots the way I was, I had a face only a mother could love!'' She pinched his cheek lightly. ''So what do you think, Robbie? Is this a face only a mother could love?''

At that precise moment Ward walked through the front door. Jenna's smile faded as she watched his expression tighten—as if a curtain were slowly being closed until not even a sliver of light remained between the folds.

She had said the wrong thing...at the wrong time...and perhaps worst of all, in front of the wrong person.

From that point on things went from bad to worse. Without a word, Ward walked straight to Robbie and began talking to him in a voice too low for her to hear. Jenna felt shut out, betrayed. The feeling persisted through dinner, when Robbie insisted that Ward, not Jenna, pour his milk and cut his meat, and continued when Ward finally carried him up to bed. That afternoon before his nap she'd persuaded him to press a damp and hasty kiss on her cheek; tonight all she got was a mumbled and disinterested good-night over his father's shoulder.

The strained silence hung in the air like an ominous rain cloud when Ward finally came down the stairs. The fragile peace that had existed that morning was gone, almost as if it had never been. Jenna tried to interest herself in a paperback she'd brought along for the trip, but she was so tense she actually jumped when the phone rang a few minutes later.

''It's for you,'' Ward announced curtly from the kitchen.

Startled, Jenna looked up. ''For me?''

He nodded and held out the receiver. When she got up and took it, he walked back into the living room. When he was gone, she spoke into the mouthpiece. "Hello?"

"Jenna. Sorry I couldn't get back to you sooner, but I just got back into the office. I've got the most fantastic news, sweetheart!"

Neil. She'd completely forgotten about him calling. Yet even knowing he probably wouldn't be pleased about what she was about to tell him, she knew a faint sense of relief at being allowed this small respite from Ward. The tense silence in the other room was about to strangle her.

She laughed a little shakily. "I've got some news for you, too, Neil."

"You go first, then."

She hesitated. "No, you first. Mine can wait."

Neil didn't waste a second. "Jenna, you're not going to believe this! Remember I told you I've been putting out a few feelers?" There was barely time to grasp what he meant, when he plunged on excitedly. "Bates-McKinnon Oil has offered me a job as a lobbyist. Can you believe it?"

Could she believe it? She was stunned. "Bates-McKinnon Oil?" She frowned. "But Neil . . ."

"I'll be making double my present salary, Jenna. Double! Do you know what that means for us? I'll have an expense account that's out of this world, and on top of it, they're throwing in a company car, a *luxury* company car. From now on, where we go and what we do, we do in style! And that's not all, babe!" He laughed exultantly. "That house we looked at last week? I called Mark and told him it just wouldn't do. We've got to have something bigger and better, especially with all the entertaining we'll be doing. In fact, that's where I was this afternoon. I found the perfect house, Jenna. It's beautiful—lots of high ceilings and glass. We can make it into a real showplace!''

Jenna's head was whirling. All this talk of showplaces, and entertaining. She liked the house they'd looked at. It was cozy and homey, much like Ward's house with its charming nooks and crannies. She took a deep breath. "Neil, I can't believe you'd actually take a job like that! After all you've done for Citizens for Texas... it's like going over to the enemy camp!'' The oil companies had been a particularly troublesome spot for Citizens for Texas, but when she mentioned the fact to Neil, he brushed it aside.

"I'd be a fool to turn down an opportunity like this, Jenna. Bates-McKinnon is one of the biggest independents in the state. This could open up a whole new career for me.''

She flinched at the cold disapproval in his tone. "Aren't you going to at least give it some thought?''

"I *have* thought about it, Jenna. I'm doing what I think is right—for both of us.''

"For both of us?'' Her voice rose shrilly. "Only last week you were telling me how much you wanted a family! I'm beginning to wonder if a family even fits in with your plans!''

"Of course it does,'' he said impatiently. "That doesn't change a thing.''

"I still think you should think about it, Neil. Have you already given them an answer?''

He was silent for a moment. His voice was rather sullen when he finally spoke. "No, but I'm going to have to very soon, or they'll start looking elsewhere.'' He paused. "I never expected this from you, Jenna.''

"What?" Her mouth tightened. "You never expected me to interfere?"

"Well, yes...now that you put it that way." He sounded defensive.

By now Jenna was furious. "Let me put it to you this way, Neil. Just in case you're interested, Robbie is sick and I can't say for sure when I'll be home." Hastily she slammed the receiver down.

Her anger dwindled as rapidly as it had erupted. Numbly she made her way back into the living room. Neil said things hadn't changed—but they had. She wondered if he was marrying her because he thought she would sit passively in the background, bear his children, do his bidding without a second thought. It was true that Neil didn't have much when he was growing up, but at least he'd always had his parents' love. Now she couldn't shake the feeling that he was trying to make up for his lack of material comforts, that he wanted too much, too soon.

He had said she would be the perfect wife, the perfect mother...and now he wanted a car, a house, a child, a family. Everything proper and in its place, she concluded miserably, everything contributing to the image of a young, successful attorney well on the way to the top of the corporate ladder.

Suddenly Neil seemed a stranger, someone she'd never really gotten to know at all. And on top of it, Neil hadn't even asked about Robbie. Somehow that hurt more than anything.

"Is something wrong?"

She jerked her head up. In her preoccupation with Neil, she'd nearly forgotten about Ward. He was peering over the top of the newspaper at her. "Everything," she wanted to shout. Instead she muttered, "No."

"I take it that was your fiancé who called." Raising a dark eyebrow, he added, "I also take it that all is not well in paradise."

Jenna glanced at him sharply. Something in his tone set her on edge. "What makes you say that?"

"You were shouting." He set aside the newspaper and looked at her. "I wasn't eavesdropping, but I got the impression it was something to do with his job." He paused. "What does he do?"

Jenna lifted a hand to massage her aching temples. "He's an attorney," she answered distractedly.

A dark shadow passed across Ward's face. He'd been waging a battle with himself all day, rallying first to one side and then the other. He hadn't been in the best of moods when he'd awakened that morning, but when he'd arrived downstairs to find Jenna and Robbie waiting breakfast for him, he'd found his tension easing.

Yesterday he had rationalized letting her stay with them to nurse Robbie through his chicken pox because he had hoped it would satisfy her and perhaps avoid trouble in the future. Yet his dark side had invaded once again when he'd arrived at his office. No matter what Jenna said, what if she decided this one time with Robbie wasn't enough? He wanted to believe and yet he couldn't. If he lost Robbie he'd never forgive himself. What if she made these visits a habit? What if she wanted to see him every year? What if—God forbid—she decided a yearly visit, a monthly visit, wasn't enough? What if she decided she wanted him as her own?

It was a gut-wrenching fear. Unfounded, perhaps. Unwarranted. Who could say? But the very fact that she had come in the first place counted for something. He'd told her he couldn't take any chances. And he couldn't.

Face the facts, mister, he told himself harshly. *You're working without a net. If you take a dive, you've got no one to blame but yourself.*

But there was one thing he could do, and that was to be prepared for the worst. Be one step ahead of Jenna. The law was on his side—he hoped. And it was then that he had decided to place a call to Ron Brewster.

Now he found himself driven by the demon that had plagued him since he'd learned Jenna wanted to see Robbie. He might as well have been punched in the stomach when he'd come home earlier. Her smile had faded the minute he'd walked in the door, and seeing those two dark heads spring apart at his entrance, he'd felt like an interloper in his own home . . . as if he'd ruined their fun. Hell!

"Knows his stuff, does he?" Ward asked, suddenly curious about Jenna's fiancé.

Though her mind was still in a muddle over Neil, there was something in Ward's tone that caught her attention. "He's been fairly successful," she answered guardedly. "He's been at it for about four years."

He stopped directly in front of her. "I see," he said coldly. He paused, then added very deliberately, "Did he tell you you don't have a prayer in the world if you plan to take my son away from me?"

The words hit her like a blast of frigid air. Jenna's mind reeled. She looked at him, stunned to see that the cold mask she was only too familiar with had once again fallen over his features. "How—how do you know that?" she gasped.

Hot anger swept over Ward. He was right—she *was* after Robbie—and this from her own mouth! He pounced like a vulture. "Because I checked with my lawyer this morning, that's why! You signed away every hope of that the day you handed him over! Your name isn't even listed on his birth certificate as his mother anymore! Robbie is mine and mine alone, legally and every other way that counts!"

His words sliced into Jenna's brain like a whip. She recoiled, pressing herself back into the chair. For a full minute she sat stunned, not wanting to believe that he'd actually gone so far as to contact... She wanted to run and hide, but she could retreat no farther.

God only knew what lay behind his reasoning, but there was no question in Jenna's mind that he fully believed she was capable of wanting to wrest Robbie away from the only home he had ever known without any qualms whatsoever.

The thought sickened her. She felt cold—cold inside and out—and empty. God, how empty! Ward thought she was insensitive, selfish. How could he, after what she had done for him—for both of them? Megan. If Megan hadn't died this wouldn't be happening! Jenna hugged herself as if for warmth, her thoughts a mad jumble inside her brain.

"You're wrong," she announced suddenly. The sound broke the tense, waiting silence. "Wrong about everything. The other night you accused me of not caring about Robbie, and now—now you're accusing me of trying to take him away." She looked at Ward then, all her anger and resentment bubbling to the surface like water gushing from a well. It seemed that she

was damned in his eyes, no matter what she did—or
didn't—do. "Make up your mind," she told him, her
voice shaking with emotion, "because it can't be both.
If you'd think for a minute, you'd realize I would never
try to take him away unless I *didn't* care about him—
and I do. I would never uproot him from his home and
his family because *I* know what it's like to wake up and
have everything and everyone you love just disappear
before your very eyes!" Her jaw jutted out stubbornly
as she sent him a fulminating glance. "I don't give a
damn about what your lawyer says. Robbie *is* a part of
me as much as he's a part of you. And that's something no legal document can ever take away from me.
And just for the record, Neil is an environmental
attorney who probably doesn't know much more than
I do about child custody!"

Ward blinked a little and ceased his restless pacing.
He stared at her before she ran across the room and out
the front door. The last words were fairly flung at him.
In fact, the entire speech was. Somehow he hadn't
expected such an outburst. Yet he knew he was making her miserable. Was it because she made him think
of Meg? Her memory had been with him all day long,
all day yesterday, just under the surface. After all the
long, lonely months, just when the ache inside had finally begun to ebb, Jenna had reappeared in his life,
and it was back again, as powerful and as painful as
ever. *Admit it, Ward,* he told himself grimly, *you
wanted to lash out at her and hurt her the way you've
been hurting.*

And apparently he'd succeeded.

In the moment before those defiant green eyes had
clashed with his, there was no denying what she was
feeling . . . the hurt and the vulnerability. He could rec-

ognize those feelings easily, being so familiar with them himself. She reminded him of a hunted animal, totally defenseless and at his mercy.

Taking a deep breath, he opened the front door and stepped onto the porch. The sun had set in an amber blaze of glory, with lingering wisps of pink-tinged clouds hovering just above the treetops. The autumn air was faintly cool as a gentle evening breeze whispered through the trees. From the corner of his eye, Ward could see Jenna sitting motionless on the wide wooden swing, her face drawn as she gazed at her hands, clasped tightly in her lap.

He swallowed. Damn! What the hell could he say? He felt guilty as hell and yet . . . Taking a step forward, he grasped the railing and stared straight ahead.

"I'm sorry."

Jenna's head shot up. His words were bitten off. That was supposed to be an apology? She stared at him, mouth tight. "Are you?" She couldn't contain the bitter edge that crept into her voice. "I wonder."

"Yes. Yes, damn it—I am!" Straightening his shoulders, he turned to face her. "I had no right to assume that he might have offered any kind of legal advice."

"Even if Neil specialized in family law, it's an issue that would never have come up—" her chin lifted proudly "—because I wouldn't have brought it up!"

She almost dared him to refute the statement. His eyes met hers, then slid away so quickly that she was left believing he was as angry with himself as he'd been with her earlier.

And much as she wanted to stay angry with him, she couldn't. Because suddenly she could define what she hadn't been able to until now, that elusive something she'd glimpsed in his eyes the night he'd come to her motel room and at the ranch when he'd held Robbie in his arms.

It was fear. The fear that she might somehow snatch his child from him. Compassion surged through her, but there was no denying the feeling that she'd been wronged.

The words came out almost unconsciously. "But if you had it to do over again, you would make the same choice, wouldn't you?" she asked in a very low voice. "You'd have checked with your lawyer to make certain that I . . . that Robbie could never be taken away from you." She glanced up at him, and she knew, even before she finished, that she was right.

Ward looked away from her steady gaze. When he finally gathered the courage to look back at her, he saw that her eyes were cloudy with pain. She looked so wounded that for an instant she reminded him of Robbie when he came running into the house after a bump or scrape. Only she wasn't crying. And she wasn't looking to him for comfort, as Robbie always did.

But that didn't stop him from reacting in much the same way. It had grown too dark for him to see the uncertainty that plagued her, yet he could sense it, knowing they had been at odds ever since her arrival. And it was his fault. He had to fight a crazy urge to take her in his arms, to stroke that silky, dark hair away from her forehead and soothe away her pain. The only thing that kept his hands at his sides was the certain knowledge that the only thing she wanted from him was his son.

He eased himself down into the swing, next to her, but not touching her. "Would you like to tell me why you were so upset about the phone call?"

Jenna hesitated. He caught the look and frowned. "You don't have to. I just thought it might help to talk about it."

"Maybe...maybe it would," she said slowly, and haltingly she began to tell him about Neil's job offer and her doubts about the move. Ward didn't offer any judgments, any solutions, and she expected none. It was, after all, something only she and Neil could work out. But oddly enough, it did feel better to talk about it.

"You said you knew how it felt," Ward said suddenly, "to have someone you loved taken away from you." He hesitated, then asked softly, "Your parents?"

Jenna nodded.

"Weren't you adopted?" He peered at her in the darkness, not sure where the memory had come from.

"Yes," she answered quietly. Then, in a low voice she began to tell him about the accident that had claimed both mother and father. Ward listened quietly, intently, while she spoke. She was lucky, she said, to have found two people to replace her natural parents, two people she loved with all her heart and who loved her the same way.

Lucky? he reflected with a touch of cynicism. She had been a child, innocent and alone, lost in a world without love...for over a year. She, too, had known grief and pain, loneliness and despair.

But what about him? Would he ever love again? He was unaware of the tightening of his hand around hers.

Jenna glanced down in surprise. Her fingers were twined tightly in his, resting against her thigh. The fingers of his other hand brushed gently across the inside of her wrist in a gentle caress. She didn't remember him reaching out to her...but he had. His skin was warm, his grip sure and strong. It was strange, she mused. Two days ago she wouldn't have thought it possible. She and Ward didn't trust each other—she didn't even think they liked each other. Yet the eyes looking down at her were warmed by compassion, by understanding.

She spoke softly. "You're thinking about Meg, aren't you?"

A flicker of pain flashed in his eyes. Slowly, almost reluctantly, he nodded.

His fingers tightened, then relaxed, but he didn't pull away. Reassured, Jenna looked at him. Moonlight spilled down from the sky, etching the strong, proud features in silver. "Ward, what happened to her? How...how did she—?"

She never got the chance to finish. Ward lurched to his feet so suddenly she felt her nails rip into his flesh as he pulled his hand away. He took a single step away from her, leaving her staring at his broad back.

"I think it's time you went inside," he said flatly. "It's getting cool out here."

Jenna swallowed and got up slowly. She moved so that she could see the rigid set of his jaw. He had removed his jacket after dinner and rolled up his shirt sleeves. His shoulders were stiff with tension as he grasped the railing, the muscles of his forearms knotted.

"Ward—" She reached out a tentative hand and moistened her lips. "Please, I'd like to kn—"

"Just leave it, Jenna. Please, just leave it."

There was such a world of agony in his low whisper that Jenna felt her heart contract. Deliberately she laid her hand on his bare arm. She felt his muscles tighten at her touch and her heart sped up fiercely in response, but she kept her hand there until she felt him relax.

She turned slightly so that she could see his face. With the moonlight and the small pool of light slanting through the window from the living room, it was nearly as bright as day. Each had caused the other too much pain and suffering already, she thought sadly. Some was unwitting, and some was not. But it couldn't go on. For either of them. "I think," she said softly, "you and I could both use a friend...a truce. Shall we call off the dogs—on both sides?"

His eyes searched hers for a long moment. What he found there must have satisfied him. A tiny smile hovered at his mouth as he asked gravely, "A new beginning?"

Her gaze never wavered from his. "Yes. A new beginning."

Something flickered in his eyes. "Jenna..." He paused. "I really am sor—"

She shook her head swiftly. "No more apologies, either. Agreed?"

Ward smiled then, and she felt as if something inside him, something that had lain dormant for a long, long time, had suddenly come alive. His lips quirked faintly. "Do I have a choice?"

A warm feeling flowed through her. "No." She tossed her hair back over her shoulder and laughed lightly. "As my dad always tells me, I am one very stubborn lady."

Ward smiled. His eyes roved over her face in the moonlight, touching on the faint mauve shadows beneath her eyes. "This very stubborn lady looks tired. Maybe it's time you turned in."

She started to shake her head in denial, then realized he was probably right. It had been a long day, and from the look of Ward, not an easy one for him, either. Even in the silvered light she could see the deepening grooves of fatigue etched around his mouth. Suddenly she ached with the need to lift her hand to his face, to smooth away his tiredness with the gentle touch of her fingers.

The urge left her feeling a little shy and awkward. Taking a deep breath, she turned away. "You're right. It's late." She took several steps toward the door, then paused and glanced back at him.

His eyes bored into hers for a moment. "Good night, Jenna," he said very softly. Then, before Jenna was even aware of it, he crossed to where she stood. He kissed her gently on the cheek and then brushed by her to go inside the house.

When he was gone, she found herself smiling. Her hand stole up to cradle the cheek he had kissed. For an instant, she was reminded of her fierce avowal never to wash her hands again after the first time she and Darren Phillips had ever held hands.

She was still smiling when she went to bed that night.

CHAPTER EIGHT

IF ONLY THE PROBLEM with Neil were as easy to solve as the antagonism with Ward, Jenna mused pensively four days later. He had called again on Wednesday night, and much the same angry scenario had been repeated. Jenna simply couldn't understand his dogged determination to take the job with Bates-McKinnon Oil, and Neil was just as determined that it was the right career move for him. Only this time it wasn't Jenna who hung up on Neil—it was the other way around.

Did most brides-to-be experience cold feet? She breathed an uneasy sigh and opened the refrigerator to pull out several chops. This impasse was more than cold feet, and it was time she admitted it. More and more she was beginning to wonder if marrying Neil was right for her. Every time she thought about it, she felt a tiny frisson of doubt and as a result she found herself burying the subject in a far corner of her mind. But the fact remained: she was going to have to make up her mind when she returned to Galveston.

That, too, was something she wasn't yet ready to face. After six days with Robbie, he was just really beginning to trust her, to show signs of genuine affection for her. His case of chicken pox was mild; the fever and headache had long since disappeared. She could tell that he was tiring of being cooped up inside, and tried to come up with as many different activities as she could for him. Unfortunately he came up with a few of his own—including trying to paint the pale blue of his bedroom walls with white shoe polish. Ward returned on more than one day to find her practically dropping on her feet.

But no matter how tired she was at the end of the day, how naughty or mischievous Robbie was, she loved every minute spent with him.

"Will you draw me a picture, Jenna?"

Waving a piece of paper at her, Robbie skipped over to the kitchen table clutching a handful of fat crayons. There was still time before lunch, so Jenna pulled up a chair and sat down.

"Sure," she said cheerfully, then cocked an eyebrow at him. "I'm not much of an artist, though, so don't expect too much." She picked up a crayon. "What do you want me to draw?"

"Soupman!" he replied promptly.

Jenna laughed. "Soupman! What—or who on earth is Soupman!"

His small brow pleated into a frown. "Don't you know who Soupman is? Daddy does!" he informed her staunchly.

"Well, Daddy will just have to enlighten me," Jenna said with a chuckle. "I can't draw Soupman if I don't know what he looks like, so what else would you like?"

Robbie's eyes lighted up and he began to bounce in his chair. "Matman! Or Wonder Worm!"

Jenna blinked. Soupman. Matman. Wonder Worm! His childish pattern of speech was adorable, and she'd had no trouble figuring out that the hem was coming out of his jeans the day he'd come to her complaining they were "broke," but this time she was at a complete loss.

She choked back a laugh. "Robbie, where have you seen these people?"

"They're not people. They're heroes—superheroes! And I see 'em on TV all the time!"

Jenna was finally able to grasp that he was talking about cartoon characters, and convinced him to let her draw something else. He settled for a man, a woman and a child. Jenna glanced doubtfully at the drawing—she wasn't exaggerating about her artistic ability—the characters were little more than stick people—but Robbie was thrilled.

"That's you and me and Daddy!" he exclaimed delightedly. "Can I draw one, too?" he asked eagerly.

"Of course." She ruffled his silky curls and helped him with his drawing. She smiled a little crookedly when Robbie insisted on clamping them both to the refrigerator with tiny banana-shaped magnets. To her nondiscriminating eye, it was hard for her to tell which was his and which was hers.

While Robbie napped that afternoon, Jenna, on a whim, turned on the television. A silly little grin curved her lips as she tuned in a cartoon channel, but at the end of an hour and a half she was completely baffled. There was no sign of Soupman, Matman or Wonder Worm. She frowned a little. Robbie had been so adamant....

Robbie had just awakened from his nap, when a knock sounded on the back door late that afternoon. Jenna heard a cheery, "Anybody home in there?"

Robbie ran across the floor to open the door. "Aunt Eileen!" he cried. Eileen Swenson bent to hug the small body, then smoothed the unruly curls from his forehead. "Good heavens!" She laughed, eyeing his blistered cheeks. "What happened to you?"

"Pox!" Robbie declared. He nearly poked his eye out in an attempt to point to his roughened cheeks.

Eileen laughed again and whirled him around. "Where's Daddy? I didn't see the Blazer outside."

Standing behind the doorway, Jenna knew Eileen wasn't aware of her presence. She stepped forward, saying lightly, "Hello, again. Ward's working late tonight. He won't be home until later this evening." She paused. "Did you just get back from your trip?"

Eileen nodded and set Robbie on his feet. Her face still registered stark surprise and Jenna could almost see the questions tumbling around in her head. "How did you know I was in Amarillo?" she finally asked, breaking the taut little silence.

A ghost of a smile curved Jenna's lips and she glanced at Robbie. Eileen looked just as uncomfortably uncertain as she, but they both knew what the real question was. "Why don't you sit down?" Jenna waved a hand toward the table.

Eileen was quiet while Jenna explained that her reason for being there was merely an issue of expedience—for Robbie's sake and Robbie's sake alone.

At length, Eileen's eyes lifted to Jenna's. "So you're staying here, then?"

Jenna nodded, sensing something in Eileen's tone. "You probably think it's not wise under the circumstances," she stated calmly.

The older woman frowned. "I'm surprised that Ward asked you," she finally admitted. "But I'm a mother myself... and now that I've had the chance to think about it, I can understand your need to see Robbie."

"I meant what I said last week," Jenna said quickly. "I don't want to hurt anyone—"

"I know that." Eileen reached out a hand to lightly squeeze Jenna's. "I guess we're not so different after all." She leaned back and shrugged. "And it's not as if there isn't room. This is a big house."

Jenna was touched at the gesture, and smiled gratefully, but suddenly her breath caught in her throat. It had never occurred to her until now how it might look to someone else. "I'm sleeping in the room next to Robbie's," she began quickly.

To her surprise, Eileen laughed. "Good Lord, don't look so guilty. Ward still hasn't gotten over Meg—" she frowned thoughtfully "—although maybe that's exactly what he needs...."

Her voice trailed off so that Jenna could barely hear. But the gist of her words wasn't lost on Jenna; now that she thought about it, she remembered Steve Reynolds's having said something to the same effect. And recalling Ward's pained reaction to the mention of Meg's name, it was very obvious that there was still a very deep attachment. She sighed. It was really rather sad....

But while Ward might be oblivious to any and all women, including her, Jenna was certainly not as unaware of him as she would have liked to be. Her palms grew damp as she remembered the sandpaper roughness of his cheek against hers, and she thought of how he had looked that very morning. As usual, he was still sleeping when she had awoken. The bedroom door was ajar and she'd caught a glimpse of him in bed as she'd tiptoed past his room. She'd tried to look away, and found herself staring, instead. The covers were pushed down to his waist—thank heaven he'd been no more exposed than that—revealing strong shoulder muscles that flexed when he turned on his side. His chest rose and fell evenly in sleep, and was liberally covered with dark, wiry-looking curls. She'd been rather dismayed by her reaction, and had been trying to vanquish the memory all day long. In the course of her job as a nurse she'd seen literally hundreds of men—both young and old—and many of them more good-looking than Ward. Yet she had never been quite so conscious of one man's body. But she'd never created a child with any other man, either, a niggling voice reminded her.

The sound of Eileen's voice dragged her mind away from that last disquieting thought. "How are all of you getting along?" she was asking.

"So far so good," Jenna quipped lightly, then crossed her fingers. There had been a few times she'd caught Ward looking at her with a wholly unfathomable expression in his eyes, and her heart would speed up for a second, but when she looked again, it was gone. Certainly their manner toward each other couldn't be called easy and carefree, but with each day that passed they seemed to grow more comfortable with each other. And at least they hadn't crossed swords again.

She glanced down at Robbie, playing on the floor between the two women with a box of bristle blocks. Eileen's eyes lighted up suddenly as she followed Jenna's gaze. "You know," she said, looking down at Robbie with a sparkle in her eyes, "I think this is a moment that should go down in history."

Robbie jumped up immediately. "Are you gonna take a picture at me, Aunt Eileen?"

"I certainly am going to take a picture 'at you,'" she said with a chuckle, echoing Robbie's words. She reached down from the bag she'd carried in and pulled out a .35 millimeter camera. While Robbie preened and hammed it up, Eileen must have taken a dozen pictures, including one when Robbie threw his arms around Jenna's neck and smacked her soundly on the cheek. Jenna looked at her in amazement when the camera clicked and whirred for the last time. "I thought you were going to take *a* picture!" She laughed a little. "He probably won't thank you for this when he's older—not with his face all covered in chicken pox!"

Eileen laughed. "All the more reason to take advantage. Believe me, this is par for the course. And I love taking pictures of Robbie. Tim and Katie always groan when they see the camera come out. 'Here we go again,' they always say. 'Our life in living color!'" She laughed once more and looked at her. "Haven't you seen the albums yet? I've been at it since I was fifteen years old, and Meg kept every picture I ever took of Robbie and Ward. There must be hundreds."

"No, I haven't." She paused. "Tim and Katie are your children?"

Eileen nodded. "Tim's twenty and Katie's eighteen. They're both students at San Angelo State," she said proudly. "Tim is studying drafting and Katie's enrolled in a preveterinary program. This is her first year."

Jenna noticed the wistful look in her eyes. "And Mom misses them both already," she teased gently.

"Well..." The other woman grinned rather sheepishly. "It's been less than a month since the semester started, but with Katie gone, too, breakfast for two after twenty years of eating with the kids can get a little lonely. Already I have the feeling I'm going to have a lot of time on my hands this year. That's why I don't mind having Robbie.'' Hearing his name, Robbie grinned up at his aunt. She winked back at him. ''He keeps me out of trouble.''

''Doesn't the ranch keep you busy?'' Jenna asked curiously. ''I mean, you were so good with the mare the other day.''

''I don't mind helping out with the horses, but when it comes to cattle—'' she rolled her eyes heavenward ''—that's Frank's department, and that's the way I intend to keep it.''

Jenna smiled. ''Sounds to me like you need a job, then.''

By the time Eileen left a short while later, Jenna was surprised but pleased at the outcome of the encounter, especially considering the shaky foundation that had resulted after their first meeting. She liked Eileen's warmth, openness and frankness, and she was glad that Eileen was a part of Robbie's life. Much as the thought pained her, Eileen was, after all, the closest thing to a mother the little boy had.

When Eileen was gone, Robbie pulled a chair up to the counter and clambered up beside her. She had learned very quickly that no activity was complete without his ''help,'' and he seemed to derive a great deal of satisfaction in the small tasks he was able to perform. Jenna smiled at him fondly when he asked if he could help with dinner. She handed him the silverware and watched, amused, as he carefully arranged it beside the two plates.

The afternoon wore into evening, and soon the clock on the mantel chimed eight-thirty. She had been reading aloud to Robbie from a book of bedtime stories, and when she felt his small body sagging limply against her, she glanced down at him. He drowsily smiled up at her, but his long-lashed eyes drooped heavily.

She leaned down to brush his hair off his forehead. "I think it's time you were in bed, young man." Upstairs she undressed him and put him in a pair of lightweight pajamas. Jenna smiled, thinking she could have dressed him in a hair shirt and he wouldn't have minded. But tired as Robbie was, Jenna had no more than slipped his small body between the sheets than his huge green eyes opened wide. "Daddy," he whispered plaintively. "I want my Daddy."

She lifted a hand to stroke his cheek. "Sweetheart, Daddy had to work late tonight. He still isn't home yet." His lower lip began to tremble, and she sighed. "How about if I have Daddy come in later and kiss you good-night—as soon as he gets home. Will that be okay?"

Robbie nodded, and apparently satisfied, he turned on his side, tucked a fist under his cheek and closed his eyes. Jenna stayed with him for a few more minutes, fingering his soft dark curls, brushing his dimpled arm, savoring the petal-soft feel of his skin and tucking the sensation away in a corner of her mind for the time when she would be with him no more.

Her heart was heavy when she finally drew the blanket under his chin and crept softly from the room. She had been with him for six days now. Six days. How many more would she have with him? Only a handful. Soon. Soon she would have to leave. She had carried him beneath her heart for nine months, nurtured him and given him life—she had secretly carried him *in* her heart all this time—and these few, precious days with him would have to last her a lifetime.

She had avoided the room next to hers up until now, but found her footsteps directed there beyond her will. She cautiously stepped inside, noting the pale yellow wallpaper and the serene pastoral scenes framed on the wall. Studiously avoiding the huge four-poster in the middle of the room, she walked quietly to the pine desk on the opposite wall. She scanned the shelves above the desktop. Then with a sigh she turned, and her eyes rested on the framed photograph staring back at her from the dresser.

Tentatively she reached out and picked it up. "Would you have approved of my being here, Meg?" she whispered. "Would you have minded my being a mother to Robbie?"

The laughing blue eyes that looked back at her were full of warmth and life, yet Jenna had never felt so cold inside.

She found what she was looking for downstairs in Ward's den. The picture albums Eileen had spoken of. She hesitated before reaching for one of the heavy leather-bound books, feeling as if she had just broken into a place that was forever barred from her.

Switching on a lamp, she sat down on the oval braided rug in front of the fireplace and tucked her legs beneath her. Eileen hadn't been exaggerating, she thought dumbly. There were hundreds of pictures. Literally. There was Ward as a fuzzy-cheeked boy, openly adoring an equally loving Megan, who wore a bouffant hairstyle that had gone out when bell-bottomed pants had come in. Jenna would have laughed if it hadn't been so damnably sad. Just yesterday she had noticed a few fine threads of gray in Ward's thick dark hair. Even when he was laughing and playing with Robbie, she occasionally glimpsed in his eyes a fleeting expression of sadness that made her ache inside.

Her throat tightened as she turned a page. There was Meg, flashing an engagement ring; later, her face was wreathed in a glowing smile beneath a lacy veil as she walked down the aisle in a flowing ivory wedding dress.... The years passed as the pages turned. Meg was still smiling, but those delicate Dresden features looked haunted.

Then Jenna stared. Her fingers traced the features of a tiny infant cradled lovingly in Megan's arms. Ward stood beside her, one arm curved protectively around his wife and newborn son, beaming down into her radiant face. And there was so much more: a bare-bottomed Robbie sprawled on a blanket in front of the fireplace; Robbie crawling across the room; then later, Robbie spreading his arms wide for balance as he tentatively raised a foot. Jenna made a faint sound as she imagined those first tottering steps forward.

A rush of joy swept through her, so intense she was totally unprepared for the shattering pain that followed. Yet it wasn't the first time she'd felt that way. It had happened before...the moment she had felt her baby's first faint quickening inside her womb and later, his more vigorous movements; at his birth when she had first glimpsed his soft down-covered head and wrinkled red body.

And as before, she knew she couldn't afford to love Robbie now... any more than she could then.

She hugged the book to her breasts and brought her knees to her chest. The haloed lamplight began to swim before her eyes as she blinked rapidly, her heart so full of emotion she thought she would burst.

That was how Ward found her. At first he thought she was asleep. She looked cold, huddled on the rug, her forehead resting on her upraised knees and her arms wrapped around her legs.

"Jenna?" He set aside his briefcase. Loosening his tie, he threw it aside and walked across the polished floor. Bending over her, he gently shook her shoulder. "Wake up, Jenna."

Slowly she raised her head and stared up at him. Ward went absolutely still. The torment in her eyes was almost unbearable, and touched a corresponding chord deep in his soul. He looked down and saw that she was clutching a picture album. Easing it from her white-knuckled grip, he held it before him and focused on the photograph of Meg bending over Robbie, the child's face smeared with ice cream and frosting from a huge layer cake. It had been taken on Robbie's first birthday. Ward's chest tightened. It hadn't been long after that...

Slowly he closed the album and replaced it on the shelf, wishing that both he and Jenna could close the door to the past as easily. Once he had told himself that time would heal all wounds, that time would ease the ache in his heart. But at that moment, he wondered if there would ever be peace for either of them.

"Jenna." His hand curled lightly around her shoulder. "You shouldn't be here. You should be in bed."

The gentleness both in his voice and in the touch of his hand was almost her undoing. She had to struggle to find her voice past the tightness in her throat. "Why... why are you always trying to pack me off to bed like—" she attempted a feeble, quivering smile "—just like a child?" She took a deep breath and tried to gather some control.

Ward smiled a little at her valiant attempt at normalcy. Then, driven by some emotion he didn't fully understand, he pulled her up to her feet and reached out to trace the soft curve of her cheek. "What's wrong?" he asked softly.

Jenna's insides were so knotted she could scarcely speak. She shook her head helplessly, unable to look at him. "I . . . are you angry?" was all she could say. The quiver in her voice was unmistakable.

Ward brushed a tendril of hair from her cheek. "Because you were looking through the albums?"

She nodded. "Eileen was here today and—she told me about them."

He hesitated. A week ago he would have been angry. A week ago he might have felt she was intruding, interfering where she had no business. Hell, who was he trying to fool? He *would* have. But this week had softened the blunt edges of his volatile emotions around Jenna. Seeing how warm and patient she was with Robbie—she could barely tear her eyes away from him when he was in the same room. Even if Ward had been angry, he couldn't have stayed that way after coming in and seeing Jenna so upset.

"No," he said finally.

"I didn't mean to pry."

His hands squeezed hers. "I know."

Spurred on by the warmth of his fingers, lightly grasping hers, she met his gaze shyly. "I—I feel as if I've missed so much," she said in a low voice. "I wanted for once not to be on the outside looking in...."

"And?" His voice was cautious. His shoulders tensed. Somehow he knew what was coming.

"And now I feel that way more than ever." There was such a wealth of sadness in her voice that Ward closed his eyes against it. When he opened them, she was gazing at him searchingly. He started to shake his head and speak, but she stopped him. "Please understand—" she lifted her shoulders helplessly "—I don't regret anything, even coming here. But there's so much I don't know." She paused. "Will you tell me, Ward? Will you tell me about Robbie?"

Ward let out a deep sigh, moved as much by the quiet plea in her voice as the look of blind trust in her expression. His voice rough with emotion, he asked, "What is it you want to know?"

Jenna made a vague gesture with one hand. For a moment she was afraid he might close her out as he had the time she'd asked about Meg's death. "Anything. Everything." The eyes she lifted to his were suddenly eager and shining once more, so much like Robbie's that he caught his breath. "Was he a good baby?"

Ward waited only a second before pulling her toward the small love seat across from his desk. It took a minute for him to gather his thoughts. "Did you know," he began with a thread of laughter in his voice, "that after all the horror stories I'd heard about a newborn's 2:00 A.M. feeding, that Robbie slept the whole night through his first night home?"

Jenna listened quietly, attentively, thriving on every word. She learned that Meg had stayed up with him at night nursing a croupy cough on several occasions, and that later, at the age of seven months, Robbie had crawled into the bottom shelf of the pantry and removed every single label from the canned goods stored there. Ward laughed a little as he recalled how many surprises they'd had at dinner after that.

By the time he finished, they had moved closer to each other, though neither one really seemed aware of it. A long arm curled lightly around her shoulders. It seemed the most natural thing in the world to nestle trustingly into the hollow below his arm, and that was exactly what Jenna did before glancing pensively up at him.

"It hasn't been easy for you, has it? Trying to raise Robbie on your own, without—" she almost stumbled over the word "—without a mother." She held her breath uncertainly, almost afraid he would lash out at her again. She had noticed how his voice became edged with pain at the merest mention of Meg.

He looked down at her with a frown. "We've managed." Then, surprisingly, one side of his mouth turned up in a wry smile. "Robbie and I ate a lot of burned oatmeal, peanut butter sandwiches and frozen casseroles from Eileen before I discovered what a cookbook was for."

"Ward..." Suddenly aware of just how close they were, she drew back slightly. "Now that Eileen is back, would you prefer that I... I mean, do you want me to—"

"Leave?"

The utter calm in his voice made her faintly uneasy. She nodded slowly.

"Is that what you want?" Ward asked quietly.

Jenna closed her eyes and half turned away from him. "Do you really have to ask?" she whispered.

The room was so silent Jenna could hear her heart pounding in her ears. She waited almost painfully for his reply. It was a long time in coming.

"If you left, I'd have to go back to eating burned oatmeal for breakfast. You've got me spoiled in less than a week, Jenna." His light tone disguised the sudden churning of his stomach. He was playing with fire, but as he caught a glimpse of the naked vulnerability in her eyes, he knew there wasn't a damn thing he could do about it.

Jenna gave a silent prayer of thanks that she was sitting, because she knew her knees would have gone weak with relief otherwise. The smile she offered was tremulous. Impulsively she laid a hand on his arm. "You've done a wonderful job with Robbie," she said shyly. Long dark lashes feathered down over her eyes and she hesitated. Her eyes darkened to the color of jade.

Ward caught the painfully acute look and frowned. "What? What is it?"

Her voice was a halting whisper. "I know that when I leave here, I won't be a part of Robbie's life anymore. But knowing that he'll be loved and taken care of here with you will make up for a lot." Her voice broke treacherously. "But Meg only had a year with him, and it seems so unfair..."

Yes, it was unfair. And it was also unfair that for a fraction of a second, as Ward stared at the tears that welled in her eyes and slid slowly down her cheeks, he wondered if it was a ploy. A ploy to gain his sympathy.

He dismissed the idea almost as soon as it entered his head. And suddenly he realized something else, realized it with a shattering certainty that nearly snapped the fragile network of emotions he had spent the past eighteen months learning to control.

Slowly he leaned forward and extended a fingertip to trace the watery trail of a glistening tear down her cheek. "For Meg?" he asked softly.

Her dark hair fell in a silken curtain around her face as she nodded, her head bent. She felt too full of emotion to speak. It was almost a shock to acknowledge that she was crying. Now, after all these years.... She had wanted to... wanted to so badly the day that Robbie was taken from her and she knew she would never again see her son. But she hadn't. She hadn't because she was afraid that once the tears began to flow, they would never stop.

But now the well inside her had finally been released. Jenna was helpless as the tears rolled freely down her cheeks—for Meg, for herself, for the son she would never see grow straight and tall.

With a muttered groan, Ward pulled her into his arms. His eyes were dark with remorse as he tucked her head beneath his chin, gazing off into the shadowed corners of the room. How blind he had been. How wrong he'd been to utterly mistrust this woman. But Meg had known. Meg had seen what he hadn't been able to. Until now, he hadn't realized just how caring a person Jenna was—how much giving there was inside her.

He was touched beyond words; the sobs she choked back tore into his heart like a knife, bringing back poignant memories of the many nights he had lain alone in his bed after Meg had died, the empty ache inside as deep and dark as a bottomless pool. For long moments the storm of emotion overtook them both.

It wasn't until Ward felt the moisture in his own eyes that he eased back from her. "Jenna." His voice was a hoarse whisper. "For God's sake, this isn't doing either of us any good." He gave a forced laugh, trying to lighten the intense situation. "If you don't stop crying, you'll drown us both."

Jenna blinked back a fresh supply of tears and wiped the moisture from her cheeks with the back of her hand. "This is crazy, isn't it?" she said shakily. "I can't remember the last time I shed a single tear." She looked up at him through misty eyes. "I'm sorry—"

Two fingers pressed gently against her mouth stifled the words. "No apologies, remember?" There was a faint twinkle in the dark brown eyes that moved over her tear-stained face. Then with a sigh, Ward slowly folded her still trembling body in his arms once more.

Incredibly tender fingers smoothed damp tendrils of hair away from her flushed cheeks, then slid through the long shimmering tresses to knead the tense muscles of her shoulders. Feeling exhausted, drained, Jenna wrapped her arms around his waist and sagged against his strength. Ward's touch was warm and caressing through the thin fabric of her blouse, a soothing balm to heal the raw edges of her emotions.

Somehow the effect carried through to both of them. His heartbeat was slow and strong beneath her ear. The pale blue shirt he wore was open at the throat, and beneath the skin, with its fine covering of silky dark hair, the pulse at the base of his neck echoed the gentle rhythm. Of their own volition, her fingers crept up to measure the slow, steady cadence, while the wiry hairs tickled her skin.

It was inevitable, perhaps, that she should be reminded... she and this man had created a child together, a sacred bond they would share through all eternity. And yet it was the first time they had touched, *really* touched.... It was incredible. It was beautiful.

It also made her achingly aware of Ward in a way that she couldn't quite control. Suddenly she was only too conscious of the intimacy of their bodies. Her breasts were crushed against the solid breadth of his chest. Somehow her legs had become entangled with

Ward's, and she was half sitting on his lap. She was helpless to prevent herself from wondering what it would have been like had Robbie been conceived in the normal way....

Ward felt the slight stiffening of her body. "It's all right, Jenna," he murmured against her forehead.

"No. No. I—I'm tired and—I'd like to go to bed." Even to her own ears, her voice sounded high-pitched and nervous.

She would have pushed away from his shoulders with her hands, but he prevented her intended motion by wrapping his arms around her more tightly. His brows drew together in a frown. "Are you all right?"

Jenna gazed into the deep brown of his eyes, unable to move, mesmerized by the tiny flecks of amber and gold she noticed, yet aware of a fleeting sense of alarm. Something of her distress must have shown in her face, for he brought a hand to her face. With the pad of his thumb, he brushed away the shimmering dampness on her cheekbones. "Jenna, what's wrong?"

His tone was so incredibly gentle. Yet she thought, irrationally, that his cold, angry words were almost easier to bear than his concern, his comfort, his closeness. She shook her head, unable to speak for the churning of her insides.

She would have pulled away then, if it hadn't been for the look in his eyes. He was staring at her intently, and for a heart-stopping moment, Jenna could see the same shattering awareness in him that had seized her only seconds before. His fingers slid down her cheek, over the curve of her jaw and down her throat. For a timeless moment his fingers rested on the frantic throb of her heart, his touch burning through the thin material to the bare skin beneath.

"Jenna..." There was such torment, such desperation in the sound of her name on his lips, that she wanted to cry out in sympathy for him. Again he touched her face, her eyelids, her cheeks, her mouth....

When he finally lifted his hand away, Jenna felt the desolation of her own loss. And then her senses were spinning, swimming, awash in a tingle of expectancy as he resettled his hands on her waist. His mouth was a mere breath away, and she knew with delicious certainty that he was going to kiss her.

And she knew she had never wanted anything so much in her life.

CHAPTER NINE

THE TIGHT ACHE of anticipation grew, until Jenna wanted to scream with frustration. She could sense Ward's uncertainty and see the conflicting emotions warring in his eyes. She wanted desperately to take his face in her hands and cover his lips with hers until nothing else mattered. But something held her back, kept her hands at his shoulders, curled tightly into his flesh.

Somehow this made the moment, when at last it finally came, all the more precious . . . all the more exciting.

A sigh of relief escaped her lips when Ward lowered his head, claiming her lips with such sweet tenderness that Jenna felt herself caught up in a whirlwind of emotion unlike anything she had ever experienced before. Her hands slid up to tangle in the thick darkness of his hair, urging from him what she herself craved with an intensity that left her breathless.

Ward's response was instantaneous. His mouth moved over hers almost fiercely, filled with such hunger that for a moment Jenna was totally overwhelmed. Yet her mouth opened beneath his, yielding to the gentle demand of his tongue. Searing pleasure licked along her veins and consumed all but the heady sensation of his lips against hers.

"Ward..." There was a note of wonderment in her voice. Her fingers glided down the fluid lines of his back, delighting in the feel of muscle and bone. She moved closer, molding her softly cushioned breasts against the hardened contours of his chest.

Suddenly Ward froze. He tore his mouth from hers. "Oh, God, Jenna, what are we doing?"

Stunned, Jenna looked up at him. The words were wrenched from deep inside him. There was a faint glitter in his eyes, a lingering ember of desire, but the look was compounded with remorse and anger.

She felt as if she'd been slapped in the face. Her breasts tingled from the rousing contact with his chest, and there was a yearning ache in the pit of her stomach. Her hands still rested on his shoulders, and she shook her head, as if in denial. She felt her eyes glaze over with the unexpected sting of tears, but then she stilled.

She fixed on a point just beyond his shoulder, where a pair of very accusing green eyes were leveled at Ward's back.

Ward caught the look and glanced back over his shoulder at the same time a disgruntled voice charged, "You didn't come up and kiss me good-night! Jenna said you would!"

Inexplicably Ward found himself torn between the trembling woman he held in his arms and the small pajama-clad figure in the doorway. Pressing her head down against his chest, he spoke over his shoulder. "Why don't you go back upstairs and wait for me, Robbie? I'll be up in a minute."

The little boy doggedly stayed where he was in the doorway.

Ward gave an exasperated sigh, and Jenna's throat constricted tightly. She realized her eyes must have been puffy and swollen from her tears, and her cheeks felt flushed, as well. She drew in a deep breath against his chest, feeling the steady thud of his heart beneath her ear. Ward didn't want Robbie to see her like this, to know that she'd been crying. It would hurt Robbie as much as it had hurt her. But she knew, just as certainly, that concern for her as much as for his son had prompted Ward's oddly protective gesture.

"Go ahead, Ward." Her voice was muffled against his shirt front. "I'll be okay."

"You're sure?"

She nodded. Ward drew back—reluctantly, it seemed. He looked at her for a very long time, his eyes deep and dark. He seemed on the verge of saying something. Then, without a word, he gently disentangled her from his arms and went to his son.

When Ward and Robbie had gone, Jenna drew another deep, steadying breath, straightened her clothes and, with careful, concise steps, made her way up the stairs to her room.

SHE WAS GONE by the time Robbie had been tucked into bed for the second time that night. Ward paused at the door to his den, not realizing how tense he was until the knotted muscles in his shoulders eased when he looked inside and saw that the lamp had been extinguished. He felt a niggling sense of shame at his relief that he didn't have to face her.

When he'd settled himself in the living room with a good stiff drink, he leaned his head against the back of the easy chair and tried to relax. Thoughts of Jenna invaded in spite of his attempts to resist. What the hell was he supposed to say to her, he wondered grimly. He had no explanation for his behavior—just as he had no explanation for her uninhibited response. And somehow he found her reaction just as unsettling as his own.

His hand tightened around the glass before he took a long draft. He would have liked to tell himself that the kiss had evolved out of a very natural desire to comfort, but he knew this wasn't true. He recalled her sweet fragrance, the velvet softness of her hair, the honeyed taste of her mouth. Damn! Who was he trying to fool? Gradually, during the past week, his feelings of resentment had faded, replaced instead by something far different.

He hadn't looked at another woman since Meg had died. And the thought of touching someone other than Meg had never even crossed his mind, even after she was gone. And now that he had, he couldn't help but feel guilty... as if he had somehow betrayed her. Betrayed her memory. But it was only a kiss, he argued with himself. Only a kiss....

Still, there was no denying that he was attracted to Jenna. Maybe it was because she was living here with him. Wasn't it to be expected with a woman in the house again? Or maybe it was simply because it *had* been so long since he'd acknowledged the physical ache inside him.

Or maybe it was because she was the mother of his son.

Ward squelched that thought as swiftly as he downed the rest of his drink. That was one subject that was best left alone—as Jenna herself was best left alone, he advised himself sternly. She was, after all, engaged to be married, and it was that realization that finally permeated his brain. Thank God things hadn't gone any farther! But from now on, he was going to have to keep his eyes, and especially his hands, to himself. Sitting up, he rubbed the back of his neck, suddenly reminded with startling clarity of what she'd said earlier about his always trying to hustle her off to bed like a child. He snorted derisively. Like a child?

There wasn't much chance of that, he thought grimly, picking himself up and heading for the stairs. Not much chance at all.

NINE O'CLOCK the next morning found Ward and Robbie putting the finishing touches on the last of the breakfast dishes. Robbie looked up as Ward lifted him down from the counter where the youngster had been sitting to watch him stack cups and plates.

"Where's Jenna?" the little boy asked.

From his worried tone and the way his fine dark brows puckered in a frown over his small nose, he reminded Ward of a small, wizened old man. He ruffled the dark curls and set him on his feet. "Still sleeping, I guess."

"Can we go see?"

A reluctant smile pulled at the corners of Ward's mouth at his eager tone. "No, we can't go see."

"Then can we wake her up?"

"Not yet." Especially if she hadn't slept any better than he had, he added silently. But Robbie's face crumpled, and Ward found himself yielding with a sigh and a grin. "I'll tell you what. If she isn't up by the time *Superfriends* is over, you can go up and wake her. Now is that a deal or what?"

"Deal!" Robbie slapped his tiny palm against his father's much larger one and giggled.

Ward's eyes softened as he bent over to pick up his son. "You like Jenna, don't you?"

Robbie's eyes brightened further. "She plays Leggos with me," he said with a vigorous nod. "Don't you like her, too, Daddy?"

"Yes," he said slowly, unaware until that moment how true it really was. "Yes, I like her, too."

"And she's pretty, too, isn't she?"

The sudden vision that appeared in his mind of flowing dark hair, creamy translucent skin and glowing eyes triggered a stab of awareness in his body.

"Isn't she, Daddy?" a little voice repeated insistently.

Ward was silent for a moment. "Yes," he agreed reluctantly. "She's pretty, Robbie. She's *very* pretty."

Robbie grinned delightedly and Ward couldn't help but grin back.

"Good morning."

The quiet voice from the doorway caused both males to look in that direction. "Looks like I interrupted a man to man talk," Jenna added with a shy smile.

Man to man? More like heart to heart, Ward thought, watching her advance a few steps into the room. She was wearing dark slacks that hugged the flare of her hips enticingly, not too tightly, and a simple scoop-neck pale yellow T-shirt that gently molded the curve of her breasts. Ward had to force himself to look away, remembering suddenly how his fingers had charted those slender curves.

Robbie was wiggling in his arms, anxious to be free, and Ward, feeling very ill at ease, let him down. He ran immediately to Jenna, who scooped him up in her arms.

Ward cleared his throat. "Would you like some breakfast?"

Pleasurably intent on the small snuggly body in her arms, Jenna laid her cheek against Robbie's. "No, thanks," she answered absently. "I think I'll just have coffee."

The sight of those two dark heads nestled together had a very strange effect on Ward. He felt something that was half pleasure, half pain, stir deep inside. In spite of himself, he smiled wryly. "I seem to remember someone telling me just a few days ago that breakfast was just as important for me as it is for Robbie. Don't you practice what you preach?"

There was something almost intimate in his tone, and Jenna glanced up in surprise. The mild amusement in Ward's eyes kindled a like response in hers, but not before she felt her heart flutter strangely in her chest. "Well, then . . . I'll have whatever you're having."

"We already ate," Robbie piped up, crawling onto her lap when she sat down at the table.

Jenna smiled at his cheery tone. Then her eyes slid to Ward. "Not burned oatmeal, I'll bet."

Their eyes met, and he smiled again. "No, not burned oatmeal," he returned softly. "I've progressed to bacon and eggs by now. Sound okay?"

She took a deep breath. "Sounds fine," she murmured.

While Ward busied himself at the stove, she watched him from the corner of her eye, and some of her tension dissolved. She had dreaded coming face-to-face with Ward that morning, and she'd given a silent prayer of thanks that Robbie was with him in the kitchen. She had scarcely slept the previous night, thinking of what had happened between her and Ward.

She'd found herself reliving the moment when his lips had first touched hers, wondering if he'd felt the same explosion inside as she. The next minute, she was telling herself it would be wise to simply forget it had ever happened—because surely it wouldn't happen again. But as he didn't seem to be dwelling on the incident...well, then, neither would she.

"You're up early today," she remarked as he set a steaming plate in front of her.

A grin tugged at his lips as he removed Robbie from her lap and settled him on his own so she could eat. "It was worth it not to have to take a cold shower this morning."

The fork she held in her hand stopped midway to her mouth. "Cold shower?" she stammered.

Ward smiled at her wide-eyed surprise, aware of what she was thinking. "This is an old house, Jenna. It could use a bigger water heater. You've beaten me to the shower every day this week, and I've had to pay the price."

Jenna was utterly warmed by the genuine amusement in his voice. "I'm sorry, I didn't know," she began. If only...if only she weren't so completely aware of him as a man, a very attractive man, she could be completely at ease with him.

"Daddy thinks you're pretty," Robbie interjected suddenly.

She held back a grin at the embarrassed look on Ward's face. "Does he now?" she asked. A pang of sheer pleasure swept through her.

"Uh-huh." He stopped playing with the buttons on Ward's denim shirt to look at her. "Do you think Daddy's pretty?"

Jenna looked startled. "Uh . . . well, Robbie . . . men aren't usually called pretty—"

"What are they called, then?"

"Well . . . handsome—"

"Do you think my daddy is handsome?"

Jenna felt herself go crimson. From the look on Ward's face, he was obviously deriving an enormous amount of pleasure over his son's bald-faced questions. "I suppose he is," she muttered gruffly.

"There are no secrets with a three-year-old in the house," Ward commented, chuckling.

Jenna let herself fall in with the light mood. It felt so right, so good, to be sitting there in that house, enjoying the bantering among the three of them.

She smiled good-naturedly as Robbie scampered off toward the living room. "Speaking of secrets . . ." She raised her eyebrows and looked at Ward. "Your son seems to think I was born in the Middle Ages because I don't know who Soupman, Matman and Wonder Worm are. Would you believe I watched cartoons all yesterday afternoon and the closest I could come up with were He-Man and the Masters of the Universe." She shook her head and laughed. "I'm not so old that I don't remember my childhood years, but whatever happened to Casper the Ghost and Mighty Mouse?"

She felt an eddy of pleasure whirl inside her as he laughed. "Casper the Ghost and Mighty Mouse are alive and well and featured in living color on Saturday morning TV," he intoned gravely. "As are *Super*man, *Bat*man and Wonder *Woman* . . . ." There was a decided twinkle in his eye as he added, "Otherwise known as Soupman, Matman and Wonder Worm to one Robert Edward Garrison."

There was a stunned silence. "You're kidding," Jenna said with a burst of laughter. "And I thought..." She tilted her head and looked at him. "Last night he asked me to frost his teeth. He was a little put out because I didn't understand him. What exactly—"

"*Floss* his teeth," Ward supplied with a chuckle. "How on earth have you two managed all week without an interpreter?"

She got up to carry her plate and cup to the sink. "I'm beginning to wonder," she said dryly over her shoulder.

Ward's eyes followed her as she moved back across the room, admiring the lithe grace of her movements. He enjoyed the low musical tone of her voice and the lilting sound of her laughter; he liked the way the smooth strands of her hair flowed over her slender shoulders....

He was still thinking about her when he walked upstairs half an hour later. The sounds of Robbie's delighted squeals drifted to his ears, and he glanced idly into the bathroom as he passed by. What he saw made him feel as if he'd been hit in the stomach with a cannonball.

A waterbug from the time he was born, Robbie loved his bath time and considered the extra baths to relieve his itching chicken pox a special treat. Jenna was kneeling by the side of the bathtub, and just as Ward looked sideways, Robbie sprawled headlong into the soapy water, drenching Jenna from the waist up in the process.

"All right, young man, you've had enough," she announced, laughing and wiping the moisture from her cheeks. "One more dive like that and there won't be a single drop of water left in the tub. It'll all be on me!"

It was already, Ward thought, totally nonplussed. Her T-shirt was plastered to her body with a thoroughness that left absolutely nothing to the imagination. Her breasts lifted beneath the clinging material as she reached for Robbie's small squirming body. Ward stood rooted to the floor, unable to tear his eyes from the gentle, swaying movement those soft curves made as she briskly rubbed his son's body dry.

When she was finished, she wrapped the towel around Robbie, trailing her fingers lightly across his bare shoulders. It was then that she became aware of Ward watching her from the doorway. "He's so soft," she murmured, casting a slightly embarrassed look at him from the corner of her eye. "Touching a baby's skin is like... touching a feather."

His eyes moved slowly upward to linger on a faint bloom in her cheeks. And *hers* had the same dewy softness and texture as a rose petal, he thought to himself. His fingers tingled as he vividly remembered the feel of her beneath his hands, the taste of her on his mouth. An odd twinge shot through him, a twinge not unfamiliar to him, but dimly recalled nonetheless. It took a moment before he recognized it for what it was. Desire. Desire so strong he almost shuddered from the force that cut through his body. Compulsively his eyes slid downward once more.

God, how long had it been? he wondered achingly. How long had it been since he'd made love?... Too long. Not long enough. He knew some people, particularly other men, might say he was crazy, but there had been no one since Meg. The idea of making love—even going through the motions with his body and not his heart—sharing himself in that way with anyone but Meg, left a vile taste in his mouth. It was something he hadn't even thought about.

Until now.

He tore his eyes away from her breasts, aware of his breath coming jerkily "You'd better go change," he muttered. "I'll get Robbie dressed."

His tone wasn't really rough, but there was an edge to it that caught Jenna by surprise. When she glanced up at him, his terse nod indicated her clothing. Aware of its sodden state, she started to comment laughingly about Robbie's "bath" manners. But when she looked down she noticed her shirt clinging wetly to her body as if it were a second skin. The skimpy little bra she wore did nothing to disguise the pucker of her nipples through the thin material.

She hugged her breasts defensively and gave a forced laugh. "Yes, I suppose I should."

Ward stepped aside so she could pass, dragging his eyes from her figure as she went toward her room. It was, he thought, groaning inwardly as he pulled a polo shirt over Robbie's head, going to be a very long weekend.

THERE WAS A VERY definite change in their relationship after the incident the previous night, and Jenna wasn't sure who was more keenly aware of it, she or Ward. That night, and the following morning, as well, they had shared something—a kinship, a feeling of togetherness. For that brief time, Robbie wasn't *his* son, or *her* son, but *their* son. Regardless of how much either one of them wanted to skirt the issue of his birth, there was no denying it.

And somehow that acknowledgment set the pattern for the days that followed. The time spent with Robbie was precious. Jenna knew with a poignant sweetness in her heart that these gilded days of sunshine would have to last her a lifetime. But just as precious were the moments when her eyes met Ward's in a glimmer of shared amusement over something funny Robbie said or did; the feeling of utter peace that swept over her as they tucked Robbie, who now insisted that Jenna assist with his nightly routine, into his bed; the warmth that flooded her as she watched Ward and Robbie tussle on the floor after dinner. Nor would she forget the day Ward, realizing she'd only brought a limited amount of clothing with her, handed her a neatly folded pile of laundry, several items of which were lacily embroidered bras and panties.

If only he hadn't kissed her. What had seemed so right at the time later took on monstrous proportions in Jenna's mind. Regardless of her trouble spots with Neil, she was engaged to him, only a single step away from a lifelong promise to love, honor and cherish. And yet the minute Ward touched her, Neil momentarily ceased to exist. She almost wished she could forget... almost, but not quite.

Along with their newfound closeness grew another element, an element that stemmed solely from that not-so-innocent kiss, an element that magnified tenfold when they were alone. By the simple act of walking into a room, Ward precipitated a reaction in her that she was totally unable to control and—which was even more frightening—wasn't sure she wanted to. She couldn't deny the sheer pleasure she derived from observing the rugged male beauty of his face and body. Yet her heart raced dangerously, vying fiercely with her thundering pulse. There was no way she could attribute the reaction to the unease she'd experienced when she'd first arrived in Plains City. After their first tense days together, he seemed to have accepted her presence in his house with an alacrity that continued to surprise her.

Still, it was almost a relief when Monday came and she was left alone with Robbie. She needed some time to sort through her cluttered thoughts. She was at a total loss to explain this very strange attraction to Ward, especially when she was so closely tied to Neil. If only she knew more about Ward . . . and Megan, as well.

The perfect opportunity arose that very afternoon when Jenna answered the knock on the back screen door. Eileen stood there, dressed in a neatly tailored cinnamon-colored blazer and slacks that added deep tones of russet to her dark hair. Despite the crispness of her attire, her shoulder bag was pulled haphazardly over one shoulder and she looked ready to keel over with the slightest breath.

Jenna opened the door wider. "You look," she said with a smile, "like a woman who has just blown her last dollar on an all-day shopping spree." She glanced at Eileen's station wagon, sitting in the driveway. "Don't I get to see any of the loot?"

Eileen walked in and promptly collapsed on the nearest kitchen chair. Hearing voices in the kitchen, Robbie ran in from the dining room, where he'd been playing, gave his aunt a hug and kiss and promptly dashed out again.

"I wish," Eileen said glumly after he'd gone, "that I *had* been shopping. At least I'd have something to show for my effort besides two aching feet."

Jenna pondered the weary set of her shoulders. "Would you like some tea? I was just about to make some." Eileen nodded gratefully. After setting the tea kettle on the stove, Jenna looked over her shoulder. "If you haven't been shopping," she ventured curiously, "what have you been doing?"

"Job hunting," came the grim response.

Jenna pulled down two cups from the cupboard. "Job hunting?" she echoed. "With no luck, I take it?"

"Exactly."

Their conversation of last week came back to Jenna in a flash and she gasped. "Surely not because of what I said—"

Eileen waved a placating hand. "Oh, don't feel bad. It's not your fault. It's just that I hadn't considered how difficult finding a job in a town of less than two thousand people might be. By noon I'd hit every business in Plains City and Silver Falls—" Jenna knew that the Swenson ranch was midway between Plains City and Silver Falls "—so this afternoon I decided it wouldn't hurt to try Abilene, instead...." Her voice trailed off, and Jenna didn't need to ask to know how she had fared.

"Have you worked before?" She placed a cup and saucer before Ward's sister.

"Actually, I've never been trained in anything." She looked rather sheepish. She shook her head and gave a rueful smile. "I guess if anything ever happened to Frank I'd be a classic model for a displaced homemaker. I haven't had a job since before Frank and I were married, and that was clerking in the drugstore on Main Street."

Jenna reached out to cover her hand. "It's nothing to be embarrassed about," she said gently. "My mother would have been in exactly the same position." She paused. "What does Frank think of the idea?"

"Of my getting a job?"

Jenna nodded.

"Oh, he's all for it." A smile flitted across her tired face. "And so are the kids. They called this weekend." She laughed a little. "Of course it might be a different story if I told them lack of training was the problem and that I was gearing up to enroll in college along with them."

"They shouldn't knock it," Jenna observed with a wry smile. "It's been known to happen." She patted Eileen's hand comfortingly. "I wouldn't be so discouraged so soon, though. What kind of job did you say you were looking for?"

"I've done a little typing and bookkeeping for the ranch. I thought I'd try to find something in that area."

Jenna's eyes narrowed thoughtfully. At the look, Eileen prompted with a laugh, "What? Go ahead and spit it out. I'm open to any and all suggestions."

"I was just thinking of all those photographs at your house—the ones on the living room wall. You took those, didn't you?"

Eileen looked puzzled. "Yes, but . . ."

"I didn't give it a second thought at the time. I just assumed they were taken by a professional."

"A professional!" Eileen gasped, then laughed. "I've taken some classes in technique and developing and have a darkroom at the house. And I have some good equipment. But photography has always been just a hobby. Good heavens, a professional—"

"No, really!" Jenna interrupted, beginning to gather enthusiasm herself. "You're good, really good—at least *I* think you are. And as long as you're looking for a job, why not make it something you like?''

For the first time there was a genuine spark of life in Eileen's eyes. She looked at her in amazement. ''You really think I should?''

Jenna spread her hands. ''That's entirely up to you, but as long as you don't actually need the money, you're not really out anything by looking. And if nothing turns up, you can always try something else.''

''Jenna—'' she reached across the table and hugged the younger woman ''—you are a lifesaver.''

Jenna was touched by the spontaneous gesture. She smiled back at Ward's sister, and it was then that Eileen's gaze dropped to where Jenna's hands were curled around her teacup.

''I didn't know you were engaged.''

Jenna flushed, a little puzzled at the odd look in Eileen's eyes as they lingered on the engagement ring.

''When's the big day?''

''The first Saturday next month,'' Jenna murmured, suddenly very uncomfortable.

''Next month! My goodness, that's so soon!'' Eileen sounded shocked. Their eyes met for the briefest of moments, and Eileen looked away, visibly embarrassed. ''It's just that . . . when I think of the last few weeks before Frank and I were married . . .''

Jenna had no trouble deciphering Eileen's thoughts, or picturing a younger Eileen, glowing and radiant, in a trailing white wedding gown with a lacy veil. She would have been wildly ecstatic . . . and not hundreds of miles away from her fiancé.

Suddenly the tiny gold band with its sparkling chip of diamond seemed to weigh heavily on her finger. If

Neil were to walk through the door at this very moment, how would she feel?

She didn't know, and the realization was more than a little disturbing.

Oddly, the thought of her own marriage only brought her around to the subject of Ward and Meg. She took a deep breath and eyed Eileen assessingly. "Eileen, would you mind telling me about Ward—and Megan?"

For just a moment Eileen was startled. Jenna could see it in her eyes. "It's funny you should put it like that," she said slowly. "After all this time, I still find it hard to think of one without the other. Meg and Ward. Ward and Meg."

Jenna hesitated. "I feel awkward about asking you, but Ward—"

"I know." Eileen nodded understandingly. "He doesn't talk about Meg to anyone, not even me. He'll mention her name in passing once in a while, but that's as far as it goes." Her eyes darkened. "Except for once," she added softly, so softly Jenna could hardly hear.

"Are you sure you don't mind telling me?" she asked tentatively.

"No. Not at all." Eileen shook her head firmly. "I think I actually wanted to dislike you, but I couldn't—I mean I can't." She waved a hand in the air and laughed a little shakily. "It's crazy, but how many times have we met . . . three? I guess what I'm trying to say is, I feel as if you're family."

"It's not crazy at all," Jenna said quietly, oddly touched by her honesty. "Because I feel the same way."

Those were the only words necessary as they smiled at each other. Then Eileen's tone became brisk again. "Well. What is it you want to know?"

"Anything. Everything." Jenna's head began to whirl. "You said it was hard to think of one without the other." Her shoulders lifted. "Why?" she asked simply.

Eileen gazed through the window, where a restless breeze tossed the branches of the trees. Watching a faraway look come into Eileen's eyes, Jenna could almost feel her sifting back through her mind.

"Our family lived in town then," she finally began. "I was nine and Ward was six when Meg's family moved next door early one fall. From that day on, Ward carried Meg's books to school for as long as I can remember. They were inseparable. Where one was, the other wasn't far behind." Her smile grew wistful. "My parents used to tease each other and say those two were exactly like Mary and her little lamb—and they were."

"So they were childhood sweethearts," Jenna murmured.

Eileen nodded. "I think I could count on the fingers of one hand the number of girls Ward dated during high school and college and still have a few fingers left over. It was the same way for Meg. We all knew they would get married eventually, and they did, right after Ward graduated from college. They had the kind of relationship that was almost too good to be true. They were the couple with everything—a fantastic marriage, a nice home, stable career...." Her voice grew very soft. "And in fact it *was* too good to be true. There was only one thing missing. And other than each other, the one thing they wanted most was the one thing they couldn't have."

Jenna knew Eileen was talking about a child.

Eileen touched her arm gently. "You'll never know how much happiness you brought to Meg—to both of them."

Jenna's throat constricted tightly. Oh, she knew. But it wasn't without a loss of her own. Through a haze of pain she heard Eileen's voice.

"Robbie has been Ward's only salvation," she said quietly. "The day of Meg's funeral, Ward told me he felt as if he'd lost a part of himself forever, a part he knew he would never regain."

"How long had they been married when...?"

"Fifteen years," Eileen said quickly.

Jenna wet her lips. "Eileen..." She had wondered so often, and she knew, now more than ever, that she couldn't ask Ward. Her voice was a tiny thread of sound. "Exactly what happened?... I mean, *how* did Meg die?"

The silence stretched out endlessly. Jenna held her breath and waited... waited in vain.

Eileen shook her head sadly. "I'm sorry, Jenna," she said quietly, "but if you asked Ward and he didn't tell you... well, maybe it would be better if it came from him." She paused briefly, then gazed across at her. "Is there anything else you'd like to know?"

Jenna shook her head quickly. In some ways the day had brought the answers she sought. But in other ways... She had wanted to know about Ward, and now she did.

She no longer wondered why he still wore his wedding ring, though somehow she had known all along. Ward was still very much in love with his dead wife.

She sighed, her mood a soulful contrast to the bright and cloudless day outside. She didn't even wonder why the knowledge hurt so much.

She only knew that it did.

CHAPTER TEN

THE MOON CAST a pearly glow against the enveloping darkness when Jenna slipped outside several nights later after a brief phone call to her mother. Lacy patterns of ebony and silver disappeared and reemerged as a smoky cloud wandered across the crescent that lighted the night-dark sky.

She lifted her face to the soothing caress of the breeze before crossing silently to the swing. The days had been filled with warm, brilliant sunshine. But the crisp, chill October nights foretold the waning of summer and nature's silent entrance into autumn.

And with each evening that passed, she was reminded that soon she would have to leave; Robbie was almost well. *Soon....*

"Beautiful night, isn't it?"

She turned her head to find Ward's form outlined in the doorway. Nodding silently, she watched as he came toward her and extended a mug identical to the one he had. She congratulated herself when her heartbeat fluttered only slightly before settling down to a normal rhythm as he sat down beside her.

She smiled as her hands closed around the warm cup and the tang of sweet-smelling chocolate drifted to her nostrils. "Is this a hint, Ward?" she murmured teasingly. "You're trying to bundle me off to bed again so you can work late?" Just this week Ward had told her about the roadblocks his firm had been running into with the project in Oklahoma. Consequently, it had been after midnight when he'd finally emerged from the den and gone past her room last night.

"Not at all." There was a thread of amusement in his voice. "Though I did hear you tossing and turning all last night."

Jenna looked away. She and Neil were still going around in circles, and her thoughts regarding him were a muddle of confusion, at best. Yes, there were reasons for her fitful sleep, the least of which was her budding awareness of her growing feelings for the man sitting beside her. She sipped her chocolate. "If you heard me, you must have been awake, too."

Ward stifled the urge to groan. If only she knew.... "Score one for the lady in blue," he said with a chuckle. His eyes swept over her, resting for a moment on the gentle thrust of her breasts beneath the thin sweater she wore. A now familiar ache swept through him, and unable to resist, he reached out to gently touch the downy curve of her cheek.

"You must be getting stir-crazy by now," he commented softly. "Plains City must be quite a change from life in the big city."

Ward's tone implied that she must be bored stiff, but that wasn't the case at all. Her cheek tingled pleasantly as she glanced at him in surprise. "A change, yes—but definitely a change for the better," she said firmly. "It's peaceful and quiet, and I can't honestly say I miss the hubbub of the city at all. I'm not the kind of person who has to be constantly on the move to be happy."

Somehow he had known that even without her saying so. "But surely you must miss your fiancé."

Jenna's fingers stilled around the smooth surface of the cup. He knew. She didn't know how, but somehow *he knew*. She gazed off into the distance. Just beyond the slatted boundaries of the property, wheat fields undulated gently beneath the starry sky.

"Did Robbie settle down all right after I left you two alone?" she asked, changing the subject. She knew Ward was aware of her ploy, and deliberately looked away from his strong features.

He was quiet for a long time. "Yes," he said finally. A wry smile suddenly curved his lips. "I suppose by the time I finally get used to being greeted in the evening with, 'Daddy, I itch!' Robbie will be over his chicken pox."

Jenna smiled wanly. "Probably," she agreed, though her heart wasn't in it. She was still disturbed by Ward's mention of Neil. She sensed he was trying to get at something—but what?

"He loves you, you know."

The oddly gentle tone, as much as the words and the freely given admission, stirred something deep inside Jenna. Coming from him, did he know how much that meant to her? She felt Ward reach for her hand and clasp her fingers lightly in his. "The feeling is mutual."

And how do you feel about me? Through the silvery darkness, Ward studied her delicate features. Her head was bent and her lips were clamped together. She was gazing downward, her feathery lashes veiling her eyes, the one thing he wanted most to see. The question echoed in his mind. If he were to ask and she were to look at him, he would know what was in her heart.

There had been something between them almost from the beginning, and he knew he wasn't the only one to feel it. Yet these past days he'd fought a constant battle with himself. Though he had wanted to, there was no way he could ignore the fact that she was a very attractive, desirable woman. Robbie's frequent baking-soda baths had seen to that. His mouth turned up fleetingly. The last time he had resigned himself to cold showers in the morning, found the toothpaste tube squeezed from the middle instead of the end, or folded women's underclothes while doing the laundry was when Meg was alive.

The reminders of Meg were many, the actual similarities between the two women few. He liked having a woman in the house again, and it had nothing to do with being relieved of some of the household burdens. But not just any woman, he corrected staunchly. Jenna. He liked her warmth, her sweetness, her quiet, loving nature. It was, perhaps, a very good thing that Jenna was involved with another man.

He expelled a harsh breath. No, it was Meg who complicated his attraction for Jenna. Meg who made him feel as if he were torn in two and unsure of himself for the first time in years. His eyes were drawn to Jenna, the slight vulnerability in her parted lips, the warmth of her hand lying trustingly in his, the dark uncertainty in the eyes that finally lifted to his face.

And he knew that he was growing weary of the battle.

He passed a hand over his face to clear away the fog, and felt her hand tense slightly in his.

"Robbie—" Jenna wet her lips tentatively "—Robbie doesn't remember Meg, does he?"

It was a moment before he shook his head. "No. No, he doesn't." He paused. "You've seen how Eileen is with her camera...I've tried to keep her memory alive to him that way...." His voice drifted off. It was oddly gentle, yet there was something in it she couldn't define.

She hoped it wasn't meant to be a warning. "Ward," she began hesitantly, "did you and Meg ever intend to tell Robbie about me?"

The air had been alive with the sounds of the night. A gentle breeze sighed through the trees; an owl hooted in the distance. The stillness seemed to drag on forever. Jenna could feel her blood thrumming in her ears.

With a sigh of dismay she blinked back her disappointment. She pulled her feet beneath the swing and began to rise.

"Don't go...." He spoke so low that if the wind hadn't momentarily abated, she might never have heard.

Her mouth dry with expectation, Jenna sat back down. The ensuing silence was so awkward that she almost fled once more; only the light, reassuring squeeze of Ward's fingers against her own stopped her.

Ward hesitated. No matter what he said, it would hurt her. He knew this and hated his inability to prevent it.

"I don't want to hurt you, Jenna. You know that, don't you?"

Her throat constricted at the intensity of his voice. His concern moved her beyond words, but it didn't erase the need in her heart, the questions in her mind. Her thoughts about Meg were a tormenting mixture of gratitude and pain. Megan had taken another woman's child—no matter that it was also her husband's—taken that child and raised him as her own, *loved* him as her own. Why—why did the idea hurt so? Because she had always thought of Robbie as *her* son. She'd never said the words aloud, but she'd felt them in her heart . . . so many times. And now more than ever.

But Megan was gone—and Robbie did have a mother. And Jenna didn't want to be relegated to a nameless, faceless person.

Slowly she raised her eyes to his. "I need to know, Ward. I *have* to know."

Moonlight silvered her features, accenting her vulnerability. He ached with the need to fold her into his arms and ease her uncertainties. But he knew he didn't dare.

"Meg wanted to tell him about you when he was old enough to understand . . ." he said slowly.

Jenna tensed at his hesitation, sensing what was coming. She forced the words from her lips. "And what about you?"

He let out a harsh breath and looked away. His voice sounded strained. "I thought it was best to let him think Meg was his natural mother." He shook his head. "We thought we had plenty of time to decide . . . nothing was ever really clear-cut. . . ."

He was trying to soften the blow. She understood that and could even appreciate it in an anguished kind of way, but it didn't stop her from resisting his attempt to slip an arm around her shoulders and draw her to him. Gently but firmly she withdrew, gathering her tumultuous emotions like a cloak around her shoulders, as if to shield herself from the pain of her world splintering around her. If he touched her . . . if he touched her she would shatter into a million pieces.

She drew a steadying breath. "I think I'll say goodnight now," she said carefully.

Upstairs in her room she prepared for bed mechanically, but the minute she slipped between the cool sheets, her numbness began to wear off. She stared at the shadows dancing on the ceiling. These past few days she had felt, little by little, that she wasn't on the outside looking in, that she was a part of her son's life.

But what did it mean, she cried out silently. What was the use? She had come here, filled with an all-consuming need to know who he was, where he was, what he was. But what would he know about her? Nothing. Ward would never tell him about her—never. She felt helpless, betrayed, shut out, almost as if she had never existed.

She turned over and clutched her pillow to her chest. Much as she would have liked to, she couldn't be angry with Ward. He didn't deserve to be hurt anymore. Even now she ached to go to him, to seek solace in his arms and forget the storm in her heart. And she knew that it could happen.

Despite the kiss they had shared, she'd been telling herself for days that Ward wasn't interested in her as a woman. But wasn't there something—a flicker, a spark—whenever their eyes met? Always...always one of them would quickly look away. Whatever the feeling was, it was happening to both of them.

But the realization only complicated an already complex situation. If she weren't pledged to Neil...and if only he weren't still in love with Meg....

JENNA AWOKE to the sound of a childish giggle. Prying open an eyelid, she looked straight into a pair of impish green eyes. She felt the dark mood of the night before disappear the way a dewy morning mist might evaporate under the bright rays of the sun.

"Hi, sport." Delighted, she propped an elbow on the pillow to confront her visitor. Robbie still wore a pair of light blue pajamas but looked amazingly wide-awake.

Smothering a yawn with the back of her hand, she sat up and glanced at the bedside clock. "Six-thirty!" she groaned. She was sorely tempted to bury her head beneath the pillow and sleep an hour longer, but another shy giggle from Robbie stopped her.

Instead she reached out and lifted him to the side of her bed. "You little rascal!" she said with a chuckle. He squealed happily when she began tickling him on his tummy and sides. Jenna laughed aloud herself, feeling gloriously alive and lighthearted.

"Can we make berry muffins this morning?" he asked eagerly after their horseplay, throwing chubby arms around her neck.

Jenna laughed and hugged him tightly, breathing in deeply of his delicious baby smell. "You've already learned I can't say no to you, haven't you?"

The fragrant aroma coming from the kitchen lured Ward downstairs an hour later. Jenna wasn't aware that he had entered the room until she heard Robbie's squeal of greeting and a deep, "Good morning," behind her. She turned, an oversized hot mitt still on one hand.

"How are you this morning?" He lifted his cup to his lips and gave her a faintly questioning look over the rim.

Jenna managed a tentative smile. "Fine," she murmured, turning around once more. He looked almost unbearably attractive, but there were faint lines etched in the tanned skin around his eyes. She felt her heart go out to him.

"What's for breakfast this morning?"

"Berry muffins!" Robbie's voice sang out before she had a chance to respond. Jenna grinned as she piled half a dozen warm muffins onto a plate.

"My favorite," Ward remarked beside her. His look was full of wry amusement as it traveled from his son to Jenna. "Do I need to ask how you knew?"

The three of them sat at the table and the muffins disappeared at an amazing pace, though Robbie didn't eat more than a few bites of his. She was just about to comment on this, when Ward carried his plate over to the sink. He turned back with a smile.

"Which of you do I thank for breakfast?"

"I helped!" Robbie shouted, beaming.

Ward laughed. "I'll just bet you did." He lifted Robbie from his chair and pressed a kiss onto his forehead. "Now Jenna!" Robbie demanded. "She helped, too!" He squirmed in his father's strong arms to point at Jenna.

Jenna felt her cheeks flush as she discerned his meaning. She watched Ward lower Robbie to the floor, then move to where she sat.

"With pleasure," he conceded softly. Her eyes widened as he bent over her and she saw that he actually meant to kiss her. Fingers knitted tightly in her lap, she turned her face slightly and raised her cheek, expecting a chaste, perfunctory kiss.

What she got was something else entirely. A finger beneath her chin tipped her face to his, and her heart began to pound furiously as his gaze dropped to her mouth. His touch was warm and sure as his knuckles brushed the curve of her jaw. He was so close their noses almost touched, and for a moment she sat breathlessly awaiting his next move. Her lashes fluttered shut when at last it came and his mouth brushed gently across hers. The smell of his after-shave whirled around her as his lips returned, pressing the kiss firmer, deeper. Every cell in her body reacted to his nearness in a totally intoxicating way that was both confusing and alarming. She was helpless to stop the melting sigh that escaped her lips when she reached up to tangle her hands in his thick hair.

The sound of two small hands clapping delightedly finally broke them apart. Shocked at the urge to let herself be swept away by her feelings—and in front of a three-year-old child, no less!—her mortified gaze sought Ward's. He grinned a little sheepishly as he slipped into his coat, ruffled Robbie's hair and then walked out the back door, leaving her staring after him.

Her legs felt like two heated wax candles beneath her. She was thankful she was sitting. Because if she hadn't been, she was very much afraid she'd have fallen into an ignominious heap on the floor.

SHORTLY AFTER Ward left Eileen dropped in. She had been a frequent visitor during the week, and Jenna found she liked her more and more with each day that passed. Eileen was throwing herself wholeheartedly into launching what she laughingly called her "career," and that morning she brought along a portfolio of photographs she had taken to see what Jenna thought of them.

The house was very quiet after she left, and after a quick call to check in with her mother, Jenna walked into the living room to find Robbie curled up in a chair with a book. Despite his early morning enthusiasm, it became increasingly obvious as the day wore on that Robbie wasn't feeling well. His eyes lacked their usual luster; he picked at his lunch and crawled listlessly into her lap early in the afternoon. By the time he awoke several hours later, she could feel the heat emanating from his small body.

He turned lethargically in her arms, snuggling his face against her breast. His dark hair clung damply to his forehead. His chicken pox were gone except for a few scaly blisters on his arms and legs. She studied him when he opened his eyes to stare up at her. Though his complexion was clear and unblemished once more, his cheeks were flushed with fever.

"You don't feel good, do you, sweetheart?" she asked gently.

Robbie shook his head. His lashes fluttered closed once more, fanning out darkly against his pale skin. Jenna eased him gently onto the sofa and retrieved the thermometer from the medicine cabinet in the bathroom. Minutes later, her suspicions were confirmed as she pulled the thermometer from his mouth. His temperature was 104 degrees.

"Robbie—" her fingers smoothed the matted hair from his forehead "—can you tell me where it hurts?"

Mutely he opened his mouth and pointed inside. Jenna could see from the brief glimpse she was afforded that the tissue at the back of his throat was fiery red.

Jenna went immediately to the phone, thumbing through the small directory nearby until she found the number for Dr. Steve Reynolds's office. A moment later she hung up, uttering a silent prayer of thanks when the receptionist informed her she could bring Robbie in right away. She wasted no time in bundling Robbie's limp body into her car and driving hurriedly into town.

There were several patients ahead of them, but it wasn't long before the receptionist called Robbie's name and they were led into one of the examination rooms.

Steve Reynolds's brows lifted in surprised recognition when he opened the door and entered the small room. "Well, hello again!" He glanced from Jenna to the small boy nestled in her arms. "Isn't that Ward's boy?" When Jenna nodded and stood up, his sharp eyes went over Robbie. "Not hard to figure out which one of you is the patient," he murmured. "Just getting over chicken pox, is he?"

Jenna nodded. "His throat is red as a firecracker, though it doesn't look like his tonsils are affected."

Dr. Reynolds held out his arms to Robbie. "How about if we take a look, young man?"

Despite the doctor's warm, kindly manner, Robbie refused to leave her arms, so Jenna sat on the small rectangular table with him while Dr. Reynolds checked his throat, glands and ears.

Finally he straightened up. "I think we'd better do a throat culture to check for a strep infection."

Jenna sighed. "That's what I was afraid of. It's not unusual with chicken pox, is it?"

"No, it's not," he confirmed. After swabbing Robbie's throat, he sat down at the small desk in the corner, then handed her a prescription. "We won't have the results of the culture for a few days, but I think we should start him on antibiotics right away." He handed her a prescription, then gave her an inquisitive smile. "Didn't you tell me you were heading back to Galveston?"

"Yes . . . well . . ." Jenna could feel herself flushing.

Steve Reynolds laughed. "No need to explain," he said, waving a hand. "As I said before, I think it's the best thing for Ward—"

"I'm afraid you've misunderstood," Jenna broke in hurriedly. "It was really Robbie's chicken pox that kept me here. I've been taking care of him, you see. Actually, I knew Megan *and* Ward...." Suddenly an idea began to blossom in her mind. She had wondered so often about Megan's death. Ward wouldn't tell her about how she'd died, and neither would Eileen.

But Dr. Reynolds had said that Meg and Ward were two of his first patients. Glancing down, Jenna noticed that Robbie had fallen asleep. The moment couldn't have been more opportune. She felt a little guilty at her deceit, but other than asking point-blank... She took a deep breath and plunged ahead. "It was so unexpected when Meg died. We were all so shocked...." She let her voice trail off, hoping he would pick up the conversation and tie up the loose threads.

His face was suddenly grim. "It was certainly the last thing in the world I ever expected. I diagnosed her infertility in the first place, you know." Jenna nodded, and her arms tightened around Robbie. She hadn't known that, but she let him go on. He shook his head. "Who can say why it happened? It was God's will. I tried to tell Ward that. There was no reason for him to feel responsible—there was no way anyone could have known it would happen—but I often wondered if my talk did any good. I think he still blames himself."

He shrugged dismissively and stood up. "We'll call if the results of the culture are positive. You'll be at Ward's?" When Jenna nodded, he shook his head and winked at her. "I still haven't found an office nurse. Let me know if you change your mind."

Jenna stopped at the pharmacy to have Robbie's prescription filled, but her thoughts were a mad jumble on the short ride home. She didn't really know any more about Meg's death than she had before, except that Ward blamed himself for some reason. What could possibly have happened that everyone was so reluctant to speak of it? She bit her lip thoughtfully, ruling out natural causes. Meg hadn't been that old, and as far as Jenna knew, she'd been healthy except for her infertility. And besides, Ward would never have held himself responsible for that. An accident, perhaps?

She sighed and reached out a hand to touch a lock of Robbie's dark hair. Her confusion was like a maze with only one way out: Ward. And yet, he had already been through so much she couldn't find it in her heart to ask him again.

His Blazer was already parked in the driveway when she arrived back at his place. She checked her watch briefly. Almost five-thirty. As she unbuckled Robbie from his seat belt, she noted that he seemed a little cooler. Thank heaven, she thought, cradling his limp body over her shoulder. He roused slightly when she lifted him, and she stroked the back of his head as she climbed the steps.

"Ward?" She looked around and stepped into the living room. Robbie smiled drowsily up at her when she put him on the sofa. "I'll be right back, sweetheart," she told him. "I'm just going to find Daddy and tell him we're back."

Ward wasn't in either the den or the kitchen. Maybe he was outside, she thought with a frown. She was standing near the stairway, so she decided to run up and drop her purse in her room.

That was the last place she expected to find him. "There you are!" she murmured with a soft laugh. "Were you looking for me—" She stopped short at the expression of stark relief in his eyes when he turned and saw her. He was standing just inside the doorway. The look on his face puzzled her for a moment—but only for a moment.

His eyes flitted quickly from the empty suitcase that sat near the closet door to where she stood in the hallway, and comprehension washed over her in an icy wave. For an instant she refused to believe... refused to believe that *he* could believe...

"Have you been home long?" she asked in a low voice.

"No." He shook his head and dropped his eyes before the silent accusation in hers. "I just got here."

"I see." Her voice shook with the effort it took to control her anger. "And I suppose the first thing you noticed was that my car was gone."

Ward closed his eyes and swallowed. He didn't bother to answer. She already knew.

"And when you came inside to an empty house, with both Robbie and me gone, you just *assumed* that I... that I..." Bitterness choked her. She couldn't say the words—she couldn't even *think* them. How *could* he? "I'm surprised you trusted me enough to stay with him all this time!" she flung at him. Anger and hurt combined to wrench the words from her. "Is that why Eileen has been dropping in so often all this week?" she lashed out furiously. "Checking up on me to see that I haven't run off with *your* son?"

"Jenna..."

She ignored the hand stretched toward her, the silent pleas in his eyes, the despair in his voice. His features were twisted into a dark mask of pain. He made no effort to conceal the agony that lay just beneath the surface. But there was no way Jenna could respond to it then.

"In case you're interested, I took Robbie in to Dr. Reynolds's office this afternoon," she informed him icily. "He may have strep throat." She spun around on her heel.

Ward was beside her in an instant. "Is he all right?"

"He will be," she said flatly, moving past him toward the stairs. "He'll be on antibiotics for a few days, but he'll be fine."

Dinner that night was a grim, silent affair. Robbie ate no more than she and Ward. The pall that hung over the table was like a heavy mist that entrapped the earthly world beneath. Exactly as she was trapped, caught between father and son.

She glanced at where Ward held a pajama-clad Robbie in the living room, rocking him to sleep. Robbie looked up at his father with quiet adoration. Though all she could see of Ward was the back of his head, the loving way he touched the child's cheek and his dark curls was more eloquent than words in describing his feelings for his son.

Her anger melted beneath a rush of sensations so strong they made her feel giddy. There was no denying the charged awareness that sizzled whenever she and Ward were alone together. She could see that now more than ever. He made her feel . . . strange. But it was an exciting feeling, a feeling she had never experienced with Neil. Neil, whom she was supposed to love, but who existed in a dark, shadowy corner of her mind. Not like the flesh and blood man before her.

She wiped her hands on a dish towel. Her eyes lingered on Ward, trying to understand the conflict in her heart, the tumult in her mind. What was wrong with her, she wondered silently. Ward was just a man, a man like any other man. But he wasn't, a voice insisted. He was the father of her child, the child she had nourished within her, given life to. The child she loved now more than ever, who was as much a part of Ward as he was of her. The child they had created together.

The sterile atmosphere in which this small child had been conceived was of little or no consequence. The bond between her and Ward was as constant and unchangeable as the tide that washed upon the shore.

But they were paradoxically tied by the one thing that stood between them.

The thought brought a wealth of sadness in its wake. She couldn't have said how long she stood there, staring at Ward and Robbie, before Ward carried his son upstairs. The next thing she was aware of was a gentle touch on her shoulder. With a gasp she looked up to find Ward standing in front of her.

"Who called?" At her blank look, he frowned. "The phone rang while I was putting Robbie to bed. Didn't you hear it?"

"No. I—I'm sorry. I didn't." Nervously she got a grip on herself and squared her shoulders.

"It doesn't matter," Ward said softly. "Whoever it was will call back."

For a long moment their eyes clung. Hers were dark with uncertainty as she remembered her bitter words to him not so long ago. His weren't quite so easy to read, but she could see a muscle working in his jaw.

"Did I tell you I have to go to Tulsa the week after next?"

Jenna shook her head. As casually as she could, she dropped her gaze and moved past him.

"I was just thinking—" there was a trace of hesitancy in his voice "—maybe before I leave we could go somewhere, just the three of us. Maybe a picnic the Saturday before, if the weather stays warm. There's a place just north of Abilene..."

"Just the three of us"? What about the two of them—he and Robbie? Jenna was standing near the dining room table, and her hands gripped the back of one of the chairs so tightly her knuckles showed white. She hated the bitterness that crept into her soul, but she couldn't help it. Only a few short hours ago he had thought she'd kidnapped his son! Was this his way of making amends?

"You will stay, won't you? At least until I get back from Tulsa?"

Despite what had just happened, how could she refuse? Silently she nodded.

"Do you think Robbie will be up to a picnic?"

"I don't see why not, since it's over a week away." Her voice sounded hollow. "His chicken pox are nearly gone, and his throat should be better by then."

"Shall we make it a date, then?"

His tone was light. She didn't have to look around to know that he had moved nearer. She swallowed. "If you like." He was standing next to her, so close she could feel his breath stirring her hair. Simply to have something to do with her hands, she reached for the small paper bag on the dining room table. "What's this?"

"Something for you." There was a slight pause. "I stopped at the candy store on the way home."

Her hand stopped in midair. "For me?"

Ward nodded, his eyes on hers. "Open it."

Hesitantly she reached for the sack. Inside were jelly beans—dozens and dozens of shiny red jelly beans. How had he known— Of course. That day at the ranch. She hadn't thought he'd been listening then. The gesture was silly, sentimental...and so sweet. Jelly beans. Blueberry muffins. She felt as if a giant hand were squeezing her heart when she realized that he had done this and then come home to an empty house and believed that...

"You'll have to share them with Robbie, I'm afraid. The red ones are his favorite, too."

For a moment she couldn't speak. Her throat tightened as she shook her head, unable to look at him. "You said he'd come around," she whispered.

"And he did, didn't he?" Ward's touch, like his voice, was very gentle as he tucked her hair behind her ear so he could see her face. "You know what they say—like father, like son. In this case, it's like son, like father."

Jenna closed her eyes and turned away. What was he trying to say? She was almost afraid to think about it. Her body trembled. Last night—and now. All the signs were there. She should go home, home before this charade went any further. If she stayed, there would only be more heartache. It was inevitable. She was blind if she couldn't see what was coming.

"Jenna..." Strong arms came around her and drew her up against him. Ward could feel the tenseness radiating from her body. He lifted a hand to stroke her hair, over and over again. When he finally felt her relax against him, he closed his eyes and rested his chin against her hair. "I'm sorry, Jenna. God, I'm sorry!"

She stiffened against him, but he held her firm. At his words, all the hurt she'd felt earlier came rushing back. "I thought you trusted me," she whispered brokenly. "How could you think I could actually do that to you . . . to Robbie . . . ?"

He drew her yielding body up closer to his and spoke above her head. "What can I say, Jenna? Somehow I always seem to be apologizing to you. Hurting you is the last thing I want, yet it seems to be what I do best." His voice held such anger, such self-contempt, that she gazed up and saw a face that mirrored her own anguish. "When I arrived home and you weren't here, I panicked. I thought..." He expelled a harsh breath and shook his head. "God knows what I thought." His eyes looked deeply into hers. "If there's any way I can make it up to you . . ."

Her eyes misted over with tears. "Hold me, Ward," she pleaded with an ache that penetrated clear to his soul. "Please, just hold me."

He did. There was no force on earth that could have stopped him. He gathered her fiercely against him and held her close to his heart as if he would never let her go. But in spite of his attempt to communicate his regret, her eyes were still dark with pain when he finally tipped her face to his.

Her lashes were long and spiky, wet with tears, before her gaze fell and her eyes were hidden from him again. The curve of her cheek was damp, as well, gleaming in the muted lamplight. But the sight of her soft lips, trembling ever so slightly, tore right into his heart. He caught his breath as his gaze dropped to her mouth.

And he could think of only one way to stop the quivering.

CHAPTER ELEVEN

HIS LIPS WERE WARM, undemanding, and brought such a storm of tenderness rising within Jenna that she almost cried out. With a helpless moan, she twined her arms around his neck and let her body melt into his.

Ward felt something snap inside him the minute she molded herself to him. The cushioned softness of her breasts crushed against his chest was driving him wild, and he yearned to mold her gentle curves to the shape of his hand. He longed to touch every square inch of her delicate skin. With a muffled groan his hands stole down her back, tracing the curves and hollows of her spine. She fitted him perfectly. He knew he should stop, knew he should put her from him that instant and forget he had ever held her in his arms. But she was too soft, too pliant in his arms, and he was like a man starved for the taste of her.

"God, you're sweet," he murmured huskily against her mouth. He gathered her closer still. "So sweet..."

A soft sigh emerged from her throat at the feel of tautly muscled thighs against hers. A welter of excitement skidded through her body as the kiss deepened to a heady intimacy. His tongue gently traced the shape of her lips before sliding within. Jenna could feel his heart pounding wildly in a feverish tempo that matched her own.

Her eyes flicked open to stare directly into Ward's. His were smoky with desire and spoke of hunger long denied; his wordless message sent the blood rushing hotly through her veins.

He kissed her again, his body silently communicating his longing. She was almost painfully conscious of the firm swell of arousal pressing into the hollow of her stomach.

His fingers tangled in her hair and he drew back slightly to gaze down at her. The muted lamplight behind him softened the harsh planes and angles of his face, but Jenna was aware that his warm chocolate eyes were smoldering with passion. "I want you," he whispered intensely. "I want you so much."

His hands tightened on her waist, as if he were waiting... as indeed he was. He was giving her the chance to pull away. Now, while there was still time. There was an agony of emotion tossing in her breast as she silently held his gaze, and desire—God, yes, desire!—pounded along her veins in a torrent so strong she felt consumed by it.

"Ward..." She murmured his name in a soft sound of protest. She knew, in some distant corner of her mind, that there were many reasons this shouldn't be happening... and all were forgotten in the storm that followed. Every muscle in Ward's face was taut. He looked as if he'd been carved in stone, and she could sense the control he was exerting over himself. But his eyes... one glimpse of the tightly leashed passion in those smoky brown depths was all she needed. She couldn't fight it any longer. She wanted him, she realized breathlessly, wanted him with an all-consuming passion that left no room for denial. She lifted her hands and drew his face to hers to ease the yearning ache in his eyes. This was the moment she had waited for, wanted without even knowing it, and nothing else mattered.

When next she spoke his name it was a whisper in the dark, a promise in the night. How they came to be in his bedroom, standing next to the huge four-poster, Jenna could never have said. The moon was rising to the east, spilling silvered pools of light through the windows. Ward's face was highlighted as she reached for her, undid the buttons of her blouse and slid the material from her shoulders. Her flimsy lace bra followed, and soon she was naked.

Entranced, she watched as Ward threw his own shirt aside and reached for his belt buckle. When at last he stood as naked as she was, he looked bigger, more powerful than ever before. His sinewy chest was matted with curly dark hair that arrowed downward; his legs were long, supple and strong. Moonbeams gilded his flesh, and she was unable to take her eyes from his stark masculine beauty.

An evening breeze rippled through the sheer lace curtains. She shivered, but it had nothing at all to do with the cool caress of the wind.

"Cold?" Ward's voice was tender. He reached for her, and Jenna met him willingly, eagerly.

"Not anymore," she murmured. With trembling fingers she reached up and smoothed the sensuous curve of his lower lip, loving the feel of his beard-roughened skin beneath her sensitive fingertips.

Ward groaned softly and slid his fingers into her hair, lifting her face to his. Her hair was smooth and silky against the bare satin of her shoulders. In one smooth fluid motion he lifted her and laid her on the bed, smiling tenderly as he joined her.

The smile faded as his gaze roved over her slender body, bathed in moonlight. Never had he seen anything so incredibly beautiful. His throat ached at the sight of her firm ripe breasts with their dusky crowns. He reached out a trembling finger to touch the swelling flesh he worshipped with his eyes.

Jenna thought she would die from sheer pleasure at the feel of his hands on her breasts. A tight ache began to build inside her, swirling and gathering force as he pulled her to him so that their bodies were touching from head to toe and his hands searched out and learned the secrets of her body. His mouth took hers with a searing hunger that amazed as well as pleasured her in a way she had never even dreamed of. She clung to him, exploring, hazily aware that soon there would be no turning back for either of them.

And Ward knew it, too. Desire licked through his veins like a raging inferno. He knew he couldn't hold back much longer. It had been too long, far too long since he'd made love to Meg... *Meg*...

Suddenly he froze.

The seconds ticked by while Ward fought a silent inner battle. But the more he admitted how much he ached to share himself with Jenna, the more his guilt magnified in his mind.

"I can't do this," he muttered hoarsely. His face was buried against the smooth column of her neck. "I can't..."

Jenna glanced at his face... and bit back a cry of pain, a cry of frustration, at the turmoil she saw in his eyes. His body was still hard and warm where it covered hers, but Jenna suddenly felt as if she were bathed in a sheet of ice. And she knew...

She wanted to rage at how unfair it was, but all the pain was tightly capped inside her. She struggled to be free of him, and though he rolled aside, he refused to let her leave the bed. His arm shot out across her waist to hold her pinned to the mattress.

"Let me go, Ward," she cried desperately. "Please..." She glanced down at where his bronzed forearm rested across her stomach, but all she could see was her own nudity, stark and glaring. The earlier pleasure she had experienced might never have been. Now she felt ashamed and exposed.

Ward saw the look and gently pulled the sheet up over both of them. He no longer touched her, but his arm still banded her body. "Please, Jenna. Let me explain."

Jenna looked everywhere but at him. The ceiling, the walls, the bureau. Her eyes suddenly riveted on the photograph there, and the room seemed to close in on her. Her breath came jerkily. She was in Megan's house, Megan's bedroom, making love with Megan's husband. *Megan, Megan, Megan.* Her thoughts were wild, disjointed, the name a silent scream that echoed in her mind. And to think she had actually felt guilty about being able to be with Megan's husband and son! She felt hysteria rising up inside her.

Strong hands shook her. "Jenna, for God's sake, don't look like that! It's not the end of the world—for either of us!"

Wasn't it? His world had ended when Meg died. She struggled to choke back the words, realizing she hadn't succeeded when Ward stared down at her, a muscle tightening his jaw.

"You're wrong," he said slowly, taking a deep breath. He reached over and flipped on a lamp. "At one time I did feel I'd lost everything when Meg died...." He hesitated. "But now, more than ever, I know I haven't." He sat up and ran a hand through his hair. "We need to talk, Jenna," he said quietly. "Clear the air."

Jenna shook her head. She slumped back against the pillows, suddenly drained. "There's no need," she said in a small voice.

Ward made an impatient gesture with one hand. "There's every need. Look, I don't want you thinking it's you—"

"Don't you think I know that?" The words were torn from her. She felt as if her heart were breaking in two. "There's been no one since Meg, has there?"

There was a seemingly endless silence. "No," he said quietly.

Her fingers curled tightly around the sheet. "And there's no one *but* Meg—not for you." She swallowed, wondering how she could speak at all for the pain and misery churning away inside her. "Don't you see, Ward? It wasn't me you wanted to make love to—" her voice broke treacherously "—but Meg...*Meg*."

"I wish it were as simple as that," Ward said heavily. He stared across the room. He wanted to say—so many things. But how could he explain what he didn't fully understand himself? "The thought of making love with my head and not my heart leaves me cold. If it's no more than physical release, it's not love, it's an act. A biological function. In a word—lust," he said flatly. The expression in his eyes softened as he looked at her, hating himself for the naked vulnerability in her eyes and knowing he had put it there.

"You're the first woman I've touched since Meg died," he said quietly. "The first woman I've *wanted* to touch." He drew a deep, unsteady breath, feeling as if he were baring his soul to her. "I do want you, Jenna," he said fervently. "I want you so much it scares me. The way you make me feel scares me—" his voice faltered uncharacteristically "—because I never thought I'd feel this way again. And—I'm still trying to get used to it." His eyes were cloudy with pain. "But somehow the fact that it *is* you only complicates things even more."

The emotion in his voice shook her. A part of her rejoiced when he said he wanted her, but the agony in her heart still festered.

"I'll never forget the day at Eileen's when you first saw Robbie again," Ward continued. "And the night you said you didn't give a damn about what my lawyer said—that Robbie was a part of you just as much as he's a part of me. That statement haunted me for days afterward, because I've always thought of him as mine—and Meg's."

Jenna nearly cried out. Why was he doing this? Couldn't he see how much this was hurting her? Every word he spoke was like salt on an open wound. She turned on her side to hide the torment she knew was reflected on her face, silently praying that he would stop.

But he didn't.

He hesitated, wishing he could see her face. Then he touched the curve of one bare shoulder gently, closing his eyes when she flinched.

"Do you remember that day in Houston when you were pregnant? The day Meg insisted I feel Robbie move inside you?"

Jenna nodded, a barely imperceptible movement of her head on the pillow. How could she forget, she cried silently. He had placed his hand on her abdomen and then snatched it away abruptly. It was as though an invisible glass wall had dropped between them. She had felt his withdrawal then as acutely as she had felt it only moments ago.

"That haunted me for days afterward, as well," she heard him say in a voice she didn't recognize. "It was a shock to see you and know that a part of me was curled up inside you. Then, when I felt Robbie move...you were carrying my baby inside you and I felt—I felt it should have been Meg, not you." His voice dropped to a pained whisper. "I was tied to a woman I barely knew in a way I had never been tied to my wife. I wasn't prepared for it, and crazy as it sounds, I felt as if I'd been unfaithful to Meg. I resented you for it. For a while I think I almost hated you, even while I knew I had every reason in the world to be grateful."

Somehow that hurt more than anything. She'd suspected his feelings toward her were far from friendly, but she'd never suspected... "Ward, don't...don't say any more." She threw off the sheet and reached blindly for her clothes. Her hands shook, but somehow she managed to dress.

But when she would have risen from the bed, she felt Ward's arms go around her from behind. "Jenna, please...please." His voice was a throbbing whisper. "I—I have to say this, not only for you but for me. Please listen and try to understand."

On the verge of struggling, she felt herself go slack.

Ward released her, resisting the urge to take her in his arms. He swallowed with difficulty. "When you came back, it was all there again...the hurt, the resentment. Because of you, I found myself thinking of Meg, bombarded with a million memories just when all the hurt inside had finally began to go away. But these past few weeks, all that's changed. She's been on my mind less and less and—and that's good." His hand touched her arm gently. "Instead I've found myself thinking of you."

"Good! How can that be good? You feel guilty, Ward. Guilty!" The words were a cry of anguish she could no longer hold inside. "Because of me! How do you think that makes me feel?"

"I *know* how that makes you feel," he said fervently, and this time he did take her into his arms. His heart turned over as, with a muffled cry, she nestled her face against his shoulder. "And it doesn't make me feel any better to know how much I've hurt you—yet another time." There was a ragged edge to his voice as he slid his fingers through her hair. "I may feel guilty, but it doesn't change how much I want you. And I want you so much it hurts inside."

The rhythmic sound of his heart beating beneath her ear was faintly soothing, somehow giving her a measure of courage. "I'm sorry," she whispered. The hair on his chest prickled her cheek. Her mouth barely moved as she spoke. Then, without her being aware of it, she pressed her lips against the skin stretched tautly over his collarbone.

Ward's fingers stilled in her hair. "Sorry that it happened?"

There was something in his voice that drew her eyes to his. Lines of strain were etched around his nose and mouth, and Jenna couldn't help but feel responsible.

Miserably she nodded.

"Oh, Jenna," he groaned softly. His fingertips stroked gently over her cheekbones, and then he took her face between his hands and looked deeply into shimmering green eyes. "Don't be sorry, because I'm not." At her faintly puzzled look, he went on. "It shouldn't have ended the way it did, but I'm not sorry it happened."

Stunned, she looked at him. "I don't understand. You're tied to the past—"

His hands dropped away from her. "And you're tied to another man." His quiet tone was like a bomb dropping in the stillness of the night, and his eyes, which had darkened momentarily, were suddenly harsh and accusing. "Does that explain what happened here tonight? Does it change anything? No!" He answered the questions with an anger that stunned her. "You don't love him and you know it! If you did, you'd never have let me lay a hand on you—"

"Don't! Don't say anymore!" It was a plea for mercy. Didn't he see what he was doing? Neil... oh, God, was this why she and Neil had never made love? He had pressed her occasionally, but she had always put him off, preferring to wait until they were married, saying she wanted the time to be right, for it to be perfect. What a change that was. How had things turned around so quickly between them?

It *would* have been perfect with Ward. She knew it as surely as night followed day.

The thought was like a knife to her heart. She drew a deep, shuddering breath, devastatingly aware of the warmth radiating from Ward's body. She wished he would move. As if he sensed her thoughts, she saw him from the corner of her eye get up and shrug into a robe.

But it didn't make any difference. She still couldn't think with him so close.

The mattress sagged as he sat down next to her. Sitting on the very edge of the bed, her toes curled and bare feet poised on the floor, she looked like a frightened rabbit ready to flee. She had precipitated this entire ungodly situation by coming here. It had been a mistake, a mistake from start to finish. And wasn't this where it ended?

"I can't stay here any longer, Ward," she decided. Her voice was high and tight. "Robbie—Robbie's chicken pox aren't contagious anymore. You could take him back to his baby-sitter's. I should leave—"

"So you can forget about tonight?"

She swallowed. His voice was sharp and she knew an unwarranted twinge of guilt. There was no need to answer. He already knew.

Ward's eyes narrowed on her ashen face. "I can't forget and neither can you. And I don't want to."

No. She couldn't accept that. They were both tied to the past—he to Meg and she to Robbie—and neither was willing to let go just yet.

"Ward, please—" She could feel what little control she had mustered slipping away from her. "How can you say that when just seconds ago you admitted to feeling guilty about Meg?"

"I can say that because I feel it here." She watched as he touched his hand to his heart. His voice had dropped almost to a whisper. His eyes never left her face. "All I need is a little more time, Jenna. Time to adjust."

"Why? So you can ease your conscience about Meg?" If she did as he asked, what then? She would be leaving soon, anyway. Picturing Ward with Meg, let alone another woman, hurt too much to even think about. Her response was wild and a little panicky. It was her only weapon against the sensual magic of his voice. "Then you'll be totally free again, Ward. A bachelor once more. Free to go where you want, when you want, with whomever you want." The spiteful words had no sooner left her mouth than she wished she could recall them. They simply weren't fair to him. And they weren't worthy of her, either.

A taut silence reigned for a moment. "I didn't have that kind of life before Meg and I were ever married," he said curtly. "I don't want it now." He paused and his voice softened. "Don't leave yet, Jenna. Stay... a little longer. At least until I get back from Tulsa."

Time. He was talking about time, and that was the one thing she'd been trying so hard not to think about—the fact that her time with her son was rapidly drawing to a close. Didn't he know she was living on borrowed time already?

It was a stark reality she couldn't hide from any longer. Still, the thought triggered a burning ache in her breast.

Without being aware of it, she had moved to the doorway. She stood wavering on the threshold, as if that single step into the hallway would take her out of his life.

It was a step she found herself unable to take.

Ward came up behind her and drew her back into a secure embrace, cocooning her with his strength and his warmth. "I don't want you to go yet," he murmured into the dark cloud of her hair. "Please stay, Jenna. Robbie needs you...." He could feel her indecision in the tautness of her body. Did she realize what he was asking? His arms tightened around her; his lips pressed gently against the soft skin of her temple. "*I* need you," he whispered.

Jenna sighed at the ache in his voice. Her hands lifted to tear his arms from where they were nestled around her waist; instead her fingers closed around his muscular forearms, loving the feel of the crisp dark hair beneath her skin, gently gauging the shape and feel of him. He was tense as a thin metal wire, she realized suddenly, and felt her resolve crumble.

Little by little his warmth seeped into her. There was no easy way out, no matter what she did. Would another few days really make any difference? Her mind seized on the thought. A few more days, a few more memories to hoard in her heart for the empty days she knew stretched ahead of her.

And Ward . . . he'd said the thought of making love with his head and not his heart left him cold. Her breath caught in her throat. She would be leaving— *leaving*—and neither one of them could afford to become involved with the other.

But weren't they already involved? Wasn't tonight proof of that?

It was a question she refused to answer. They were both so vulnerable, each in his or her own way. Her shoulders sagged wearily as she gently disengaged herself from his encircling embrace.

"I don't want either one of us hurt anymore," she whispered haltingly. "I think—I still think it would be best if we both put tonight out of our minds and—and go back to the way things were before."

"You'll stay, then?" His eyes, dark and intent, were riveted on her face. Yet there was nothing in his expression to indicate what he was thinking.

She nodded slowly. "I'll stay."

THE DAYS THAT FOLLOWED were like a roller coaster ride for Jenna, full of highs and lows. Each day that Robbie crawled into her arms, his small body warm and sweet smelling, and she rocked him to sleep, she felt her heart swell with happiness. Sometimes she caught Ward looking at her with a strange light in his eyes, and she sensed some tension in him, but on the whole, he seemed more relaxed than she had ever seen him, and for that she was glad. And though he scarcely touched her, except in the most casual of ways, she was as quiveringly aware of him as she had been that night they had lain together with nothing between them. There was an undeniable warmth in his eyes when they rested on her, a warmth that disturbed her even while it excited and frightened her. Could she hold on until Ward left for Tulsa? She hoped so, because if she didn't leave soon, she was afraid she might do something foolish, something very foolish, indeed.

She tried to counter her riotous emotions by telling herself she would have a lifetime with Neil. But the truth was, she didn't *want* to leave. She wanted to pretend this was a part of her life that could last forever. Yet she was invariably reminded that never again would she hold her sleeping son. Never again would her eyes meet Ward's across the table in silent amusement over something Robbie said or did. *Never.* She would have to bear that terrible finality for the rest of her life.

Jenna was glad for Eileen's company during that time. She dropped in nearly every day, even if it was for a few minutes. It was nice to feel that Ward's sister liked and respected her for herself, and she and Eileen had become fast friends, even though Jenna didn't feel quite comfortable in discussing her feelings about Ward. And much as she hated to admit it, those feelings blossomed with each day that passed. Frank and Eileen had stayed for a few impromptu dinners, and it was obvious that the two shared a very special relationship, a relationship much like her own parents'. They were friends as well as lovers, and she felt a stab of envy. More and more Jenna was beginning to feel that she and Neil could never share that special kind of closeness.

On Thursday, since Robbie was feeling better, Eileen asked Jenna and him to accompany her while she drove into Plains City to run some errands for Frank. Jenna was thankful for the opportunity to stop at a ladies' wear store and add a little to the weekend wardrobe she had brought with her. After coming out of a feed supply store, Eileen suggested they stop in somewhere for lunch. Robbie insisted on sitting next to Jenna in the booth, and Eileen pretended righteous indignation at his decision.

"You're a fickle little man," she accused laughingly, "deserting me like that at the first pretty face that comes along."

Robbie giggled when she reached across the table and tweaked his button nose, but when his squeals turned into shrieks of delight both women looked around in embarrassment and tried to shush him.

"That'll teach me to keep my sexist remarks to myself," Eileen said with a laugh after promising Robbie a chocolate milk shake. She winked at him and added, "You just cost me another dollar, young man."

Jenna eyed her over the menu. "That reminds me. How did the job interview go yesterday?"

Eileen grimaced. Her interview had been with a firm that specialized in school and sports pictures. "What interview?" she said dismally, unable to hide her disappointment. "After I got there, I was politely informed that someone had already been hired for the job and they'd neglected to get in touch with me." She frowned into her coffee cup. "I've been thinking about checking with a few photo processing labs in Abilene."

"That's not really what you want, though, is it?"

"Not really," Eileen said with a shrug. "But it's a start."

"Have you ever thought of opening your own studio? Children's pictures, family portraits, that kind of thing?"

Eileen nodded. "I might yet," she admitted. "And I wouldn't mind that, but actually I'd like a little variety." She smiled rather wanly and picked up her napkin when the waitress delivered their sandwiches. "Pretty picky for a lady who doesn't even have a job yet, huh?"

"You've only been looking for a few weeks," Jenna pointed out.

"In other words, don't give up yet."

"Exactly." She smiled a little at Eileen's glum expression. "I'm sure it's only a matter of time."

"Actually, I like doing candid shots. Catching people by surprise, that sort of thing." She grinned a little sheepishly. "Tim and Katie always hated that, but I loved it."

"Too bad this isn't New York or Los Angeles." Jenna reached over and poured a generous amount of catsup near Robbie's French fries. "You could work for one of those scandal sheets."

Robbie's eyelids were drooping heavily by the time they finished lunch and walked out to Eileen's station wagon. As Jenna fastened the seat belts around herself and Robbie, her engagement ring caught the sunlight.

Her eyes rested on it briefly. She had adored the ring when she and Neil had picked it out, but the jewel's flash in the midday sun suddenly seemed cold and artificial. She couldn't help but recall the conversation she and Eileen had had the previous week when she'd learned of Jenna's marriage, now a mere three weeks away. Jenna hadn't been the blushing bride-to-be Eileen seemed to expect then any more than she was now. And perhaps it was time she stopped lying to herself.

In three weeks' time she wasn't sure she would be a bride at all.

CHAPTER TWELVE

THE SATURDAY MORNING before Ward was to leave for
Tulsa, Jenna found him in the kitchen, standing over
the stove.

"Chicken? For breakfast?" She peered at the contents of the frying pan and raised her eyebrows. "You
and my dad would make a fine pair," she commented
tongue in cheek. "He likes catsup with his pancakes."

"And I like catsup with grilled cheese sandwiches."
He grinned over his shoulder at her, then glanced over
her approvingly. "But this isn't for breakfast. It's for
lunch." And he nodded at the table, where a large picnic hamper sat.

"Lunch?" she echoed blankly.

"You forgot, didn't you?"

"Forgot?" She searched her mind frantically, then
laughed a little sheepishly. "I guess I did."

Ward began to transfer golden brown chicken legs
and breasts from the pan to a platter. "We," he as-
serted, "are going on a picnic. Unless the idea of a day
out doesn't appeal to you?" He studied her questioningly.

The oddly tender light in his eyes incited a kind of
restlessness deep in her body, but instead of ignoring
the insidious warmth inside her, she found herself responding to it. "I can't think of anything I'd like bet-

ter,'' she answered softly. ''I'm sure it will be a day to remember.''

That brief exchange seemed to set the mood for the day.

It was late in the morning by the time they loaded the Blazer with the hamper, cooler and blankets and settled Robbie in the car seat between them. The weather was bright and sunny, with just enough of a crisp October bite in the air for Jenna to decide to throw in light jackets for all of them at the last minute.

As they sped along in the Blazer, all the tension and dark thoughts of the past weeks seemed to drift away. She gazed appreciatively at the pastoral landscape just outside the window. A coat of burnished gold covered the hills, and herds of cattle grazed peacefully beneath the noonday sun. Jenna knew the picnic was only a temporary reprieve from the dismal days that would follow when she left next week, but with her son beside her—and yes, Ward, as well—*especially* with Ward—she was determined to enjoy the day to the fullest.

There were several other cars in the small parking area Ward pulled in to, but the park was quiet and so peaceful that she felt a measure of tranquillity steal into her soul. Ward had no sooner set Robbie on his feet than a pair of squirrels emerged from behind the trunk of a huge oak tree. Robbie was after them like a flash of lightning. His chubby legs pumped furiously in an effort to catch them, and Jenna laughed at his forlorn expression when the squirrels quickly scurried up the tree and scampered across an outstretched branch to stare down at him, their bushy tails madly whipping the air.

They ate their lunch on an outspread blanket beneath a towering cottonwood tree. Replete from the salad, chicken and crusty bread Ward had packed, Jenna leaned back on her elbows and watched as an eagle looped gracefully through the vivid blue sky until it seemed no more than a lone speck in the distant ceiling overhead.

"Ducks, Daddy! Look!" Robbie called in high-pitched excitement. He pointed and began to run as fast as his legs could carry him.

Both Jenna and Ward followed. There was a small pond at the bottom of a gently sloping hill, its glass-like surface glinting silver in the sunlight. Trees and wildflowers lined its edges, and Ward caught up with Robbie just as he was about to plunge headlong into the water after the ducks, who were halfway across the pond by now.

"Oh, no, you don't, young man," he emphasized firmly. Swinging Robbie high in his arms, Ward leveled a stern look at his small son. "You can watch from here as long as Daddy or Jenna is with you, but you are not to go into the water."

"It's a good thing you remembered to bring along an extra set of clothes," she murmured. There was a flicker of concern in her eyes, however. Children as young as Robbie knew no fear, and she shivered a little as she looked at the deceptively smooth surface of the pond. It was impossible to tell how deep it was, but then, it wouldn't have to be deep at all for a child as small as Robbie to invite trouble.

Ward cocked an eyebrow at her. "That was one of the very first rules I learned as a single parent. Never go anywhere without at least one change of clothing."

He sounded so nonchalant, almost blasé, that Jenna found herself looking for the now familiar darkening of his expression, or perhaps a flicker of pain in his eyes. Granted, no mention of Meg had been made, but she still half expected it. Instead she found herself on the other end of a gaze so warm and affectionate she felt as if a hundred tiny fireworks had just exploded in her veins.

She hurriedly dropped her eyes. "I wonder if there's anything left over from lunch we could feed the ducks," she muttered. "I think I'll see."

When she returned, Robbie was standing by the water's edge, though Ward had crouched to curve a protective arm around him. Ward looked up when a crackle of twigs announced her presence.

"Find anything?"

She held out a small sack. "Just some bread crusts and the popcorn we were saving for later."

"Popcorn?" He raised both eyebrows.

Jenna laughed. "If ducks are at all like sea gulls, they'll eat anything."

She smiled to herself over his skeptical look and moved closer, watching as he gave a few of the crusts to Robbie. There were six ducks in all, and they were apparently used to being fed. The water rippled as they swam toward Robbie, who laughed delightedly when they began to gobble up the pieces he eagerly threw out one by one.

Ward wandered a few yards away and, apparently on a whim, threw out some of the popcorn from the bag he still held. One duck swam toward him, wasting no time in swallowing all the kernels.

He rolled his eyes heavenward as Jenna flashed a triumphant grin. "There's no accounting for taste," he said with a shake of his head.

"That's exactly what I thought this morning when you told me you liked catsup with grilled cheese sandwiches," she retorted promptly. She nodded toward the duck that had separated itself from the others, its tail feathers wagging prettily as it seemed to wait for another treat. "I'll bet that's a female."

Ward grinned over at her. "I guess I'm the kind of person that dogs and children adore."

"And ducks," Jenna added dryly. Her eyes dropped meaningfully to the first duck, who had been joined by the rest of the flock, apparently deserting Robbie's bread crusts for Ward's popcorn.

Ward's eyes twinkled. "Maybe it's my cologne." Robbie scowled indignantly when his newfound friends scuttled away, but promptly joined his father and dug a small hand into the bag to come up with a fistful of popcorn.

When the ducks' appetites were more than satisfied, Jenna took Robbie over to a small play area near the spot where they had picnicked. His back propped against a rough tree trunk, Ward watched while Jenna pushed Robbie on the swings and merry-go-round. The sound of their mingled laughter drifted to his ears as the pair came sailing down the slide together, Robbie perched on her outstretched legs.

Not for the first time, he was struck by how warm, how patient, how loving she was with Robbie. Yet this time was different. He felt he was seeing her—and his world, as well—in a different light, unclouded by the doubt and uncertainty that had colored his perception for so long. She was an immensely sensitive woman whose capacity for love made her vulnerable—as he had learned for himself.

Leaving her son wasn't going to be easy for her. He felt a stab of pain in knowing the anguish it would cause her. Nor did he want her to leave. She had stayed because he had asked. Because he needed her. And he did, God knows he did. She had brought so much into his life, made him feel as if he were slowly gaining back a part of himself he had lost.

He remembered how he'd felt the night Robbie was sick with strep throat, the night he'd come home and they were gone. He'd been afraid, yes—but underpinning that fear was something else, something that had nothing to do with Robbie. Jenna had brought light where before there had only been darkness, and he didn't want to think about how empty his life would be when she left. His hand clenched as he thought of her fiancé. She didn't love him. She didn't. Otherwise she couldn't have stayed in Plains City so long.

His eyes softened as they rested on her. The sun caught the reddish highlights in her hair as she flipped it back over her shoulder with a careless hand. He remembered its silky texture when he had run his hands through it, and the warmth of her skin beneath his fingertips, and the taste of her mouth under his. A shudder of longing wracked his body, but he knew that desire was only part of what he felt for her.

"Is that your little boy over there?"

The voice startled him from his thoughts. Ward looked up to find a woman standing before him. A little girl of perhaps five held her hand. He recalled having seen them in the playground with Jenna and Robbie.

"Yes, he's mine," he said with a nod. There was a flash of pride in his eyes as they rested on his son.

The woman laughed. "It wasn't hard to figure out who he belonged to." Her gaze sharpened for a moment on his face. Then she nodded toward the playground. "Although I think he favors his mother a little more."

Ward smiled. "I think you're right. He definitely has her eyes."

It wasn't until the woman had wandered off again that he realized what he had said, and more, comprehended the scope of his thoughts. For the first time, he had let himself think of Jenna as Robbie's mother, and it hadn't hurt at all. In fact, quite the opposite. He felt something soar free and easy within him.

"His mother," he said aloud, as if testing the words. "Robbie's mother." He felt his lips curve upward. "My son's mother—*our* son." He hoped no one was listening to his muttering—they'd think he was crazy.

As it happened, Jenna dropped down on the blanket just seconds later, winded from running with Robbie as he chased the bright yellow ball he'd brought along. "What's so funny?"

"Wouldn't you like to know." Ward's eyes, warm and intense, lingered on her face before he impulsively bent over to brush his mouth lightly across hers. The kiss was brief and sweet, tender with just a hint of passion. Her heart fluttered like the wings of a butterfly, and she thought she almost felt it skip a beat.

A warm flush tinted her cheeks as Ward chuckled. His eyes dropped meaningfully to where her breasts heaved beneath the thin cotton fabric of her pale blue shirt. "Because of me, or our son?"

Our son. This time her heart did skip a beat; she was sure of it. "Robbie, of course," she murmured breathlessly. "Just remember, your turn's next."

"Of course," he echoed somberly, an almost wicked glint in his eyes. Then he laughed. "I'm used to the way he wears me out. That's why I'm letting him run you ragged for a change."

"That's big of you," she grumbled good-naturedly. Sitting cross-legged on the blanket, she propped her shoulder against the tree trunk. Suddenly very glad they had come, she breathed in deeply of the crisp, clean air, drinking in the sights and sounds around her. She chuckled as Robbie ran in raucous circles around the blanket. "Where does he get all his energy? Although I guess that's a silly question when he's been cooped up inside for so long with chicken pox and strep throat."

Aware of the two pairs of adult eyes that followed his every move, Robbie's antics grew more winsome by the moment. "And what would he do without his adoring public?" Ward murmured, grinning. He glanced at Jenna, who responded with a brilliant smile then again turned her rapt attention to Robbie, who was now intent on somersaulting across the emerald field of grass. Ward's heart swelled at her tender expression and the look of sheer pleasure on her face, but there was a poignant longing in her eyes, as well, that tore into his soul.

They had come such a long way in the past three weeks, he thought to himself, suddenly overwhelmed by the feeling of closeness, the feeling of togetherness, the undeniable knowledge that the three of them were so right together. He reached out a hand and laced his fingers through hers, breathing a sigh when she didn't draw back as he half expected her to. Instead she smiled a little shyly, he thought, as he rested their clasped hands upon his denim-covered thigh.

Tiring at last, Robbie finally came over and sat between them, and it wasn't long before he was sound asleep, his head pillowed on Jenna's lap. From the direction of the pond she could hear frogs croaking throatily and the steady drone of crickets nearby. Slanting afternoon sunlight enhanced the faint yellowing of the trees and proclaimed the coming of autumn. The pond reflected the golden color of the surrounding landscape.

She lifted her head, letting the utter peace and tranquillity of the setting fill her senses and her being. But it wasn't so much the place as the company that filled her with contentment. *Company?* She smiled to herself. It was perhaps an odd word to apply to her son and her son's father. A rush of pleasure swept through her. She could hardly believe that Ward had actually called Robbie *their* son. The comment inexplicably filled her with happiness, and she wanted to pinch herself to see if she was dreaming.

But the warmth of Ward's hand tightly enfolding her own was real, as was the pressure of Robbie's head on her legs. Jenna slipped her fingers through his tousled dark curls, marveling as she had so often at how long and dark his eyelashes were against his flushed cheeks. A feeling of love, sweet and pure, bubbled up inside her.

Aware of Ward's eyes on her, she finally looked up. "It's beautiful here," she murmured. "Did you come here often with Meg?" Too late she realized what she had said. Her breath suddenly stopped for fear of shattering the mantle of contentment and companionship that had settled over them.

Ward was silent for so long that she began to think this was exactly what had happened. But then he turned his head slowly to look at her. "It's funny you should say that," he remarked, "because this is the first time I've come here since she died."

Jenna was almost afraid to look at him. But there was no animosity in his expression, nor were his eyes shadowed with pain, as she had expected.

His hand tightened almost imperceptibly around hers. "Jenna—" he spoke in a very low voice "—would you mind if we talked about her for a while?"

Her. There could be no doubt who he meant. For a wild, panicky moment, she almost refused. She had wanted to know for so long, but understanding the heartache it would cause him, how could she make him discuss Meg? Then she remembered Eileen's having said that Ward never talked about Meg to anyone, not even her.

"Why, Ward?" she asked, unable to prevent either the words or the faint catch in her voice. "Why now?"

Squirrels chattered in the branches high above. A breeze whispered through the trees. "You were right, Jenna," he said softly. "I've been tied to the past. But now . . . maybe it's time to close the door. . . ."

"It may not work, Ward. Believe me, I know." She swallowed the ache in her throat. For three and a half years she had tried to banish the memory of her son. And she had never succeeded. But now . . . now she didn't *want* to. "Memories are precious," she said unsteadily. "Don't let them go. Don't let anyone take them away from you, not when they're all you have."

He was quiet for a time. "Perhaps that was a poor choice of words. What I'm trying to say is that I think it's time I stopped dwelling in the past. It's time I went on with my life." He paused. "It's what Meg would have wanted," he finished softly. His fingertips grazed her chin, and he looked deeply into her eyes. "I want to tell you, Jenna. Please."

Something in his quiet entreaty made her hurt inside, even while she fought an inner battle. Suddenly she didn't want to hear how much Ward loved Meg, how he would love her forever despite his avowal to go on with his life. Her lungs burned with the effort it took to control her own selfish longings, but she sensed that his need to purge himself was as strong as her instinct to protect her own emotions.

Her fingers tightened around his as she silently gave him her answer.

The quiet was marred only by the sound of his voice as he talked. And talked. Once he started, he couldn't seem to stop. And Jenna thought despairingly that she'd been right, after all. Ward was purging himself. Much of what he said she had already learned from Eileen. That he and Meg had grown up together, had been childhood sweethearts.

But wisely she said nothing. She only listened, or tried to, with her head and not her heart.

She almost lost control when he spoke of the day she died.

"It was such a shock." He shook his head as if he still couldn't believe it. "I thought she was a little pale, but I never dreamed... Then when I came home—" His words trailed off, and it was a very long time before he could speak again. When he did, his voice was low and tense, seemingly ready to crack. "I knew right away something was wrong. Robbie was wet, crying hysterically.... Meg was lying on the floor, unconscious. I felt..." His eyes closed and his tone was almost violent. "God, I've never felt so helpless in my life! I called an ambulance, but somehow even then I knew... By morning—" he paused, faltering "—by morning she was gone."

The silence that followed seemed like the deadly calm before the storm. Before Jenna could say a word, Ward's eyes opened, two pools of darkness. "She was pregnant, Jenna. Pregnant!" He had almost spit the word. "Ironic, isn't it," he said, his mouth twisting bitterly, "that the very thing she wanted for so long should end up killing her. We'd been told by countless doctors that she could never even hope to conceive. And she didn't even know."

Jenna's mind whirled. *Pregnant! But how...?* Comprehension suddenly dawned. *A tubal pregnancy... She hemorrhaged....* Jenna was almost afraid to speak because of the bitterness etched across Ward's features. "You didn't know, either, did you?" she whispered. "Until...later."

Ward nodded.

Unthinkingly she wrapped her other hand around his. Tubal pregnancies are dangerous and difficult to diagnose. She recalled a few cases. The problem is that unless they are diagnosed very early, the enlarging egg can rupture the fallopian tube and the patient will likely hemorrhage. And that was apparently what had happened to Meg.

In the same instant, another realization swept through her. "You blamed yourself, didn't you? You felt responsible because she was pregnant."

His mouth was a grim slash on his face. "I *was* responsible. She hadn't been feeling well. She was pale and she'd been having some abdominal pain. I tried to get her to go see a doctor, but she thought it was just a flu bug." He inhaled deeply. "I guess I didn't try hard enough."

Jenna shook her head, her eyes beseeching. "You couldn't have known. No one could have. You can't continue to take the blame for something you had no control over."

After a long time he said quietly, "I suppose you're right." He leaned his head back wearily against the tree trunk, and Jenna's heart went out to him. She would have given anything to be able to take his pain as her own, to erase all the heartache and months of unhappiness. She felt helpless, as helpless as Ward must have felt when he'd lost Megan.

But all she could do was murmur tremulously. "I wish there were something I could say...."

Ward's face suddenly softened. "You don't have to say anything. Just the fact that you're here with me is enough." He turned his head to look at her and groaned at the glistening emerald of her eyes. "Oh, God, Jenna, I've done it again. You said this would be a day to remember, but I don't want it to be because I've made you cry again." He lifted a hand to brush the dampness from her cheeks, but at the delicacy of her skin beneath his knuckles, he felt something give way deep inside him. Slipping his hand beneath the silken fall of her hair, he tugged her gently forward.

Their lips met with the lightness of a feather, the caress so gentle and sweet that Jenna felt another tear slip from beneath her closed eyelashes. Yet the tear she shed wasn't only for Ward, but for herself—part for the anguish he had suffered and part for the gift he had just given her without even being aware of it. Her heart threatened to burst with tenderness for this man as she realized how special the day really was. Ward had trusted her, trusted her with a part of him that he had shared with no one, not even his sister. With a sigh, she looped her arms around his neck and gave herself over to the moment.

"Are you guys gonna get married?"

They drew apart as if they'd been burned, both glancing down at the same time. Jenna looked embarrassed, while Ward's eyes lighted with amusement, and Robbie looked utterly delighted as he stared up at the two adults.

"That was a very short nap, young man." Ward reached for his son just as Robbie bounded up. He ruffled the little boy's hair, then stood up. Robbie's gleeful laughter filled the air as he was tossed skyward several times and caught in Ward's strong hands. Holding the youngster securely in one arm, he turned to look down at Jenna.

With the blazing sun at his back, his dark hair appealingly tousled by the wind and a smile softening his craggy features, he made a very captivating picture. Jenna felt her heart surge with a heady, powerful emotion as her eyes traveled from father to son.

She had loved Robbie even before she had met him, loved him without knowing him. And now that she did, she loved him for the sweet, bubbly child that he was. She loved him because he was a part of her... and she loved him even more because he was a part of Ward.

She took the hand Ward extended and let him pull her up. For a moment, the three of them were linked. A feeling of infinite tenderness welled up inside her.

She had once thought she would never be a part of the closely knit circle between father and son, but at that moment she was.

She heaved a lonely sigh. For beyond these precious few days in her life, a family was the one thing the three of them could never be.

THE COMBINATION of fresh air, sunshine and Robbie's short nap made for a very sleepy little boy later that evening. It was shortly after seven when Jenna did up the final snap of his pajamas. Noting how short the sleeves were becoming, she glanced at Ward, who was busy gathering the discarded clothing. "He's going to need new pajamas soon," she said, lifting Robbie's sturdy body into bed. "It won't be long before these are outgrown."

Good-night kisses were given and Robbie was tucked into bed, and he was asleep almost before his head touched the pillow. "He's going to be tall," Ward said, drawing Jenna into the hall and quietly closing the door behind them. He lifted a hand and tucked a long strand of hair behind her ear. "Were your parents tall?"

Jenna had thought the same of Robbie many times before—between her and Ward, she didn't see how Robbie could avoid it. But the words, coming from Ward, as well as the pleasantly rough feel of his fingertips as they grazed her cheek, were strangely intimate. "My natural parents, you mean?" she asked softly. When he nodded, she shook her head. "I really couldn't say."

"I suppose not." A thoughtful frown creased his forehead. "You probably don't remember much about them."

Jenna nodded. "All I really remember is a man and a woman with dark hair and being held close in some-one's arms." She paused and added with a fleeting smile, "A feeling of being warm and cosseted, a feeling of belonging." *A feeling much like what she had felt today.*

"It's probably just as well," he murmured—a little absentmindedly, she thought, "that you remember only the good things."

They had moved toward the stairway, and he halted at the landing.

"It just occurred to me," he said slowly, "that I've never said thank-you for my son."

Jenna stood motionless, scarcely able to breathe from the lethargy that suddenly invaded her limbs. The last faint embers of the sun drifted in through the stained glass window above the stairs, subduing Ward's sharply angled features and making her achingly aware of the softness in his eyes. She was almost unbearably conscious of the warm weight of his hand resting on her shoulder.

She moistened her lips. "There's no need," she murmured breathlessly.

"There's every need." The quiet intensity of his voice stunned her. "I don't know how I'd have made it through this past year without him. And I'm begin-ning to wonder how I ever got along without you." There was something faintly alarming in his last state-ment, but for the life of her, she couldn't think what it was. All she could do was stare at him, at the oddly humble expression in his eyes. "Thank you, Jenna. From the bottom of my heart, thank you."

He bent his head and kissed her, a kiss as gentle as a light summer breeze on a warm moonlit night. Jenna was touched beyond words at the profound emotion in his voice. When he lifted his head, she looked up at him with shining eyes. A lump began to swell in her throat. "Oh, Ward," she whispered, "you make me feel so... so proud. And yet I almost feel as if I don't deserve this." Her voice trembled. She turned her head ever so slightly and pressed her lips against his palm where it lay cradled against her cheek.

At the feel of her lips against his skin, any thought of restraint that Ward might have entertained fled like dust before the wind. He simply wasn't capable of holding back any longer. He wanted to hold her, protect her, touch her and claim her for his own. He ached for her, ached with a longing he had never known before. His fingers wandered over her mouth and the curve of her cheek before he tipped her face to his. For an endless moment he held her gaze, unable to believe the emerald flame glowing in her eyes.

With a groan that was part joy, part relief, he folded her into his arms, glorying in the feel of her yielding softness, in the intoxicating scent of her hair and skin, the way she clung to him as if she would never let him go.

And that was exactly how Jenna felt. Her lips parted without any urging from his and she knew a moment of nearly uncontrollable joy at the tenderness of his touch. She couldn't hide from herself any longer; she couldn't hide her feelings from Ward, either, and she didn't want to. All her pent-up responses to him rose to the surface and blocked out all else. She had never felt closer to him, never felt more a part of him, than at this moment, and she longed to share herself completely and utterly.

Ward's arms dragged her closer yet, stroking the tender line of her back. Jenna gave herself up to the fiery urgency of his mouth, of his hands as they caressed her.

His breathing was as ragged as her own when he finally lifted his head. "Oh, Jenna—" he whispered her name "—I want you so much . . . I don't think I can stand much more of this."

His expression was so tortured she knew only that she had to find a way to erase it. "Then make love to me, Ward," she insisted recklessly. Her fingers smoothed the lines beside his mouth. "Make love to me now."

For a timeless moment their eyes locked. Wordless messages passed between them, communicating the depth of their need, the longing neither could contain any longer.

A feeling of heady excitement raced through her when he silently took her hand and led her down the hall. It wasn't until they were standing in the bedroom, Ward's room, that reality came crashing down around her. She couldn't help but remember that other painful night when they had almost . . . Meg had come between them then. Would it happen again? And if it didn't, would Ward be subconsciously thinking of her? Perhaps even pretending she was Meg?

Ward caught her by the shoulders just as she was ready to whirl and run from the room. In the shadow of the lamp that glowed dimly in the corner, he could see the fear in her eyes.

And he, better than anyone, knew what caused it.

Jenna's breath came jerkily. "Not here," she muttered, vaguely aware she probably wasn't making any sense. "Please not here."

Ward's arms slid down and pulled her taut unyielding body up against his. His hand slid soothingly up and down her back until he felt her relax against him. With a finger under her chin, he guided her eyes to his.

"It has to be here, Jenna," he said quietly. "Not just for me, not just for you, but for both of us. It's time to let go. You showed me that."

"I—I don't want any ghosts between us." Her eyes were cloudy, never wavering from his.

His fingers slid with lingering gentleness down her throat. "There won't be," he promised gently. "You were so right when you said that memories are precious," he said softly. "Let's make our own magic, Jenna. Let's make our own memories." His arms tightened around her. "I've brought you so much pain, Jenna. Let me bring you something else. Let me bring you pleasure."

Suddenly that was all that she wanted, too. Blindly her mouth sought his, and in seconds the kiss deepened to quench a ravenous thirst that consumed them both. Clothes were a barrier that neither would tolerate, yet Ward's touch was incredibly gentle as he undressed her. He seemed totally entranced when at last he gazed at her slender bared body in all its glory, and Jenna felt near to bursting with emotion. His eyes slid over her with heated intensity, kindling a warmth that spiraled like wildfire through her body.

Her fingers trembled as she slipped his shirt from his shoulders and undid the clasp of his belt. Her heart beat thunderously when he drew her to him on the bed with nothing between them but heated flesh. At first Ward only kissed her, but deeply, longingly, as if he couldn't get enough of her. The endless, drugging kisses sent her pulse spinning madly and she reached for him, digging her fingers into the taut muscles of his shoulders.

He seemed to know instinctively what would please her the most. Jenna moaned, gratified, when his mouth finally closed over the throbbing nipple of her breast, his tongue swirling hotly around first one aroused peak and then the other. A welter of excitement whirled inside her as his hands and mouth caressed and explored every inch of her skin until she was on fire for him.

It wasn't until she caught a glimpse of his eyes, dark and burning, that she realized how much he was holding back. Wanting desperately to drive him wild with the same searing pleasure he was giving her, her hands moved restlessly over his body. Her hands glided across the fluid contours of his back, and her fingers slid around to the lean planes of his abdomen, loving the silky feel of the dark hair that matted his chest.

But when his hands feathered over the inside of her thighs, the gnawing ache deep inside cried out for him to possess her. And somehow Ward knew it, too.

''Look at me, Jenna.''

His compelling tone blended with the mesmerizing touch of his hands. Helplessly she lifted her eyes to his, knowing her own reflected all the yearning and hunger she felt for him. The tenderness she saw there only intensified her longing to feel their bodies joined together as one.

''I've dreamed of seeing your face at this moment,'' he whispered raggedly against her cheek, then raised his head to look at her. ''Let me see you . . . now.''

And Jenna held nothing back as his legs parted hers. She cried out her joy when, with a surge of power, she at last received the bold strength of his essence, mindless of everything but him and knowing that nothing on

earth had ever seemed so right. Sensation after exquisite sensation rippled through her as she found herself
caught in a wave of spiraling delight that carried her
ever higher. Together in mind, body and spirit, they
soared, stealing out and away to a realm of glory that
knew no bounds.

Long minutes later, weak, satiated and overwhelmed by lethargy, Jenna was swept by a wave of
utter peace and she sighed. A pair of hard male arms
tightened around her, and warm lips brushed fleetingly against hers. Ward turned her on her side and
drew her back into the warmth and security of his embrace.

"I don't know why I fought against this so long,"
she murmured sleepily against his chest.

Ward pressed a fleeting kiss on her mouth. "Neither do I," he whispered, smoothing an idle pattern
down her spine.

Through half-closed eyes she gazed up at him. There
was a lazy half smile on his face, a glimmer in his eyes,
a glimmer she had never before seen. But Jenna was
simply too tired to be capable of analyzing either that
or the experience that had shaken her so deeply.

Tomorrow. There would be time tomorrow. For
now, all she wanted was sleep. With a sigh of contentment, she burrowed her face in Ward's shoulder and let
slumber overtake her.

CHAPTER THIRTEEN

JENNA AWOKE to the sound of a heartbeat drumming steadily beneath her ear and a sense of being uncommonly warm. Caught in a world halfway between sleep and wakefulness, she was for a moment incapable of orienting herself to her surroundings. She began to stretch, and found one slender leg intimately tangled between a pair of hard male thighs. Everything came back to her in a shattering rush of awareness. She had made love with Ward. *Ward.*

With absolutely no thought of Neil.

Her mind swam dizzily. She turned her head to where Ward still slept peacefully beside her, his hair dark and tousled against the pillowcase. A wave of guilt swept through her. How could she have been so foolish as to allow things to go so far? What had she done?

Ward chose that moment to finally waken. Stark surprise was registered in the sleepy brown gaze that met hers, and for an instant Jenna suspected he was just as confused, just as wary as she.

"Good morning," he murmured. His eyes flitted away, only to return again almost immediately. "Are you—okay?"

Almost unbearably conscious of the naked male body so near to hers, Jenna was feeling embarrassment enough for both of them. Yet at Ward's tentative question, a little of her shyness crept away, along with all thoughts of Neil.

She nodded faintly, unable to take her eyes from him. Ward's hair was mussed from sleep, and his jaw was dark with a night's growth of beard, but Jenna felt every nerve ending in her body quiver to life. "You need to shave," she finally blurted out.

Ward rubbed a hand over the bristly line of his jaw. "I know." His smile was a little sheepish as he propped himself on his elbows to look down at her. He seemed to hesitate. Then, as if compelled, he slowly leaned over to touch his lips ever so lightly to hers. When he lifted his head, he glanced over at the clock—the hands pointed to nearly eight-thirty—then back to her.

"You slept late." His words were accompanied by the gentle touch of his fingers brushing her cheek. "Big day yesterday?"

Jenna felt herself go weak from his kiss. She couldn't help but respond to the hint of amusement in his voice. "No." She paused, then added very softly, "Big night."

Ward's smile deepened. "I know the feeling." Leaning over, he kissed the tip of her nose, his expression warm and more tender than she'd ever seen it. "Jenna, last night . . . I can't tell you what it meant to me."

Her self-consciousness vanished at his declaration, and she whispered, "Oh, I think I do know." Her hand drifted up to cradle his lean cheek. Suddenly it seemed the most natural thing in the world to be lying there with him, reveling in the heat of his body next to her own. It seemed just as natural to lift her head and rain gentle kisses on his jaw and mouth. She felt something blossom and grow inside her when she sensed his lips smiling beneath hers. As she deepened the kiss, his mouth opened to accommodate the gentle glide of her tongue. Her heart jumped erratically, and she wanted nothing more than to lose herself to the heightened impatience already claiming them both.

"God, Jenna." Ward's breath came raggedly and his arms locked around her as he pulled her above him. Jenna's eyes grew smoky with passion as she felt the burgeoning heat of his arousal nudging her belly. She sighed with delight...and heard small feet hit the floor with a thud at the same instant.

"Robbie!" she gasped.

For an instant Ward's arms stayed tightly around her. Then, with a resigned sigh, he put her from him and sat up. "Much as I hate to say this," he muttered, running a hand through his tousled hair, "there are some definite disadvantages to having a three-year-old in the house on a lazy Sunday morning."

Jenna couldn't have agreed more, though she didn't say so aloud. The tiny voice of reason inside told her that Robbie's timing couldn't have been better. Clutching the sheet to her breasts, she sat up and swung her legs over the side of the bed, afraid that Robbie would soon make an appearance in Ward's bedroom.

"I—I think I'll head for the shower." To her utter embarrassment, her voice wobbled a little, and she felt a rare blush appearing at the sound of a soft masculine chuckle behind her.

She fled toward the bathroom while she still had the chance. It wasn't until she was safely in her own room again, a towel wrapped turban-style around her still damp hair, that she realized she had relegated Ward to yet another cold shower.

A slight grin edged her lips as she pulled the towel from her hair. She could still feel the imprint of his body on hers.

BOTH JENNA'S and Ward's warm, buoyant mood persisted throughout the day. She marveled that she had grown so close to him in so short a time, and knew a sense of sheer, unadulterated bliss that he seemed to feel the same. How many times he touched her that day, smoothed her hair away from her face, dropped a fleeting kiss on her cheek or lips, or simply sent a speaking glance across the room, she couldn't have said. She knew only that he made her feel giddy, alive and so full of joy she felt she would burst.

She should have known her newfound happiness was simply too good to be true.

With the evening dinner dishes done, she wiped her hands on a dish towel and gazed out the kitchen window. Robbie was busily playing in the sandbox, and Ward was in the barn, tinkering with the engine of the Cessna in preparation for his trip to Tulsa tomorrow. Her smile faded for the first time that day. She would miss him—miss him terribly, she knew—but to think about that would mean that she would also have to face up to what would come after his return home. And that was something she wasn't yet ready to do.

Squaring her shoulders, she pasted the smile firmly back in place and decided to check on Robbie and Ward. She had no sooner stepped out the back screen door than she heard the doorbell ring. The insistent peal was heard again just as she backtracked and reached the dining room.

"Coming!" she yelled, shaking her head and wondering who the impatient caller was. But her welcoming smile faded when she opened the door.

"Neil!" she gasped. "Wh-what are you doing here?"

"I could ask you the same thing!" he snapped. He brushed by her and closed the door, his eyes sweeping around the empty living room. "Are you alone?"

Still stunned by his appearance, she could only nod. He moved into the room, and Jenna eyed him, suddenly very uncomfortable. He looked tired, a little disheveled—and very angry.

She wet her lips nervously. "I had no idea you were coming. You haven't called—"

"Because all we do is argue," he cut in. "And I had the feeling I'd be waiting forever if I waited for you to call."

Jenna frowned. "That's not true, Neil."

"Isn't it? In case you've forgotten, we *are* engaged!"

His sharp tone made her wince, and she sat down heavily on the sofa. "No, I haven't forgotten," she said in a low voice. And she hadn't. She simply hadn't wanted to think about it, and now more than ever, she was beginning to realize why. She should have been elated at seeing him once more. Instead she felt nothing, no warmth, no responsiveness, just a niggling sense of unease.

"Do you have any idea how long you've been here?" he demanded. "It's been nearly a month. I thought you were only going to stay a few days—just long enough to see your son!"

"It just didn't work out that way." Her eyes dropped to where her hands were tightly clasped in her lap, then lifted. "Why have you come, Neil?" she asked again.

"Isn't it obvious? I think it's about time you came home."

His high-handed attitude was beginning to get to her. Her eyes narrowed speculatively as he paced to a halt in front of her. "I'm perfectly capable of coming home when I'm ready, Neil," she announced a trifle forcefully.

"Really?" His laugh was brittle. "And just when might that be? We're getting married in less than three weeks! Think you'll be back in time for the wedding?"

Her steady gaze faltered at his sarcastic tone. She opened her mouth, but to her horror, she had no ready answer. Her future was with Neil—not here. But she *was* here, and heaven help her, she didn't want to leave. She was with her son and she wanted it to go on forever. *Her son.* How could she disappear from his life once more with no regrets? But it wasn't only Robbie; it was Ward, a tiny voice reiterated firmly in her mind. Her feelings were just as deep—perhaps deeper, than those for her son.

Her heart in turmoil, she gazed at Neil. Was this the man she wanted to spend the rest of her life with? She'd met Neil within a year after Robbie was born. Could it be possible that when she and Neil had started dating and become engaged she had simply needed someone in her life? Needed someone to love who would love her in return? Someone to make up for the child she'd lost? She drew in a deep, quivering breath.

What she needed was here. What she needed was her son. And she needed Ward even more.

She could still feel Neil's eyes on her face, hard and accusing, when Robbie ran into the room. "See what I picked for you, Jenna? Flowers!" he cried proudly, and thrust a handful of bedraggled dandelions at her.

"Aren't they lovely?" contributed a dry voice. "I didn't have the heart to tell him not to bother."

Over Robbie's head Jenna saw Ward framed in the doorway. Her expression was unknowingly stricken, and two pairs of eyes focused sharply on her face, one in concern and the other in tight-lipped scrutiny.

Dimly Jenna saw Ward's eyes drift from her to where Neil stood in front of the fireplace. Recovering quickly, she made the necessary introductions.

"Robbie, why don't you go put the flowers in the kitchen sink and then play outside for a few more minutes? Jenna and I will find something to put them in later."

Ward's voice was very soft, but held an undercurrent that sent Jenna's eyes flying to his face. His expression was grim as he studied Neil, and there was a tightness about his mouth that sent a flutter of alarm racing up her spine. With a curious look at Neil, Robbie skipped happily from the room.

The words had no sooner left Ward's mouth than Neil pulled himself taller. "I'm afraid Jenna won't be around later," he said coolly, leveling a faintly challenging look at Ward. "She's coming back to Houston with me tonight."

Ward's gaze swung to Jenna. She saw a flicker of something that might have been disbelief in his eyes. "Is that true?" he asked her quietly.

His expression was questioning but steady, and somehow bolstered her courage. "No," she said firmly, then looked at Neil. "I'm staying, Neil."

"Like hell you are!" Neil's face contorted into a mask of rage. "Damn it, Jenna, I don't know what's gotten into you—"

"She said she's staying. Didn't you hear?"

At the crackling animosity that flared between the two men, Jenna felt like an unwelcome spectator at a three-ring circus.

Neil took a step forward and thrust out his chin belligerently. "This is between Jenna and me, so why don't you butt out?"

Jenna gasped at his rudeness, paling when she saw Ward's hands ball into fists at his sides. He seemed so big, all raw masculinity and hard muscles, and he towered at least four inches above Neil. She jumped to her feet and quickly moved to stand between them.

"Ward, please... Maybe you should go with Robbie. It really is best if Neil and I settle this alone." Her tone was pleading as she turned to him.

His eyes bored into her as he considered her request. "Are you sure?" he asked finally.

She nodded and he left the room, but not before sending another gritty look at Neil. Taking a deep breath, she met Neil's angry gaze unflinchingly. "I'd like to explain, Neil," she said quietly. "I've already told you about Robbie's chicken pox—"

"He didn't look sick to me."

"He isn't, not anymore. But Ward is going to Tulsa tomorrow, so he's asked me to stay with Robbie until he gets back later in the week."

"And then you're coming home?"

Her eyes faltered. "I—I'm not sure."

Neil snorted. "That's what I thought. You might as well tell me right now who it's going to be. Me or him?"

Her temper began to prickle at his sneer. "Would you deny me this time with my son? It's the only time I'll ever have to be with him—"

"I'm not talking about your son. I'm talking about his *father!*"

Shock held her motionless. Her heart almost stopped beating. "What do you mean?" she asked faintly.

"Oh, I think you know exactly what I mean!" he flung at her viciously. "Did you think I wouldn't notice the way he looked at you? There's something going on between you two, isn't there?"

The charged silence that followed threatened to choke her. "Yes," she whispered. She dropped down into the chair that was nudging her legs.

"Exactly how far has it gone? Has he ever touched you? Kissed you? Held you?"

Jenna nodded, feeling utterly miserable.

"I see," he said coldly. "Quite a little family affair you've had going here. No wonder you weren't anxious to return to me. Have you been to bed with him, too?"

She didn't answer. She couldn't. Neil was furious, as he had every reason to be. She had betrayed him, betrayed his love.

"Have you, Jenna?"

She closed her eyes against the drilling sound of his voice. But her heart remembered. Her heart knew. "Yes, I made love to him," she whispered, and knew with every ounce of her being that it was true.

Her eyes flicked open and she stared into Neil's blazing blue eyes. "Damn it, Jenna," he burst out. "I trusted you."

Her heart ached for him. "I'm sorry, Neil. It just—it just happened. Neither one of us planned it... I don't know what else to say."

"Don't say anything," he said bitterly. "Just so we understand each other this time—the wedding's off." He started toward the door, then changed his mind and turned back to her with a cutting look. "In fact, maybe I should be grateful. Your sudden attack of conscience doesn't say a lot for you, you know."

Sudden attack of conscience? He wasn't making any sense. "What do you mean?"

"Oh, come on, Jenna. You gave away your baby, your own flesh and blood. And then, when you finally decided to come back for another look, you were determined to walk away without a backward glance *a second time.* Who but a coldhearted bitch could do something like that?" His laughter was without mirth. "Like I said, maybe I should be grateful. I'd hate for you to do the same thing to a child of ours. Children aren't very tolerant about a mother's desertion, and let's face it, you don't exactly have a good track record."

Dimly she heard a car door slam, an engine roar, followed by squealing tires, and knew with a vague sense of relief that Neil had gone. Emptiness grew steadily around her and her head began to whirl. She was barely conscious of footsteps echoing hollowly across the kitchen floor.

She didn't realize she had covered her face with her hands until she felt Ward gently pry them away and clasp them tightly in one of his own. He was kneeling in front of her. "He doesn't understand," she muttered. "He doesn't understand!"

"Who doesn't understand?" he asked sharply. "Neil?"

"Yes." Her whisper was barely audible.

"Is he gone?" Ward searched her face as she nodded, noting how she looked. He took a deep breath. "What happened, Jenna?"

But Jenna wasn't paying any attention. She was still too numb with reaction. "I did it for love," she said in a whisper that tore into his heart. She lifted pleading eyes to his face. "I did it for love, Ward!"

"Jenna, for God's sake, tell me what happened!" This time there was a sharp edge of anxiety to his voice. "What did he say that upset you so much?"

"We're not getting married," she announced in a high, tight voice. "He—he broke it off." Her eyes were vague as they fixed briefly on his face.

Fear clutched at his insides. Was that what had sent her into this state? No! He refused to believe it.

Warm hands closed around her shoulders. "You don't love him, Jenna." The words were both a plea and a demand.

There was no response. She scarcely heard him, for Neil's words echoed through her mind, slicing into her heart like the lightning thrust of a rapier. *You gave away your baby, your own flesh and blood.* Her lips began to tremble and her face crumpled. "Oh, God," she whispered. "What have I done?" She buried her face in his neck as he pulled her forward into his arms.

"Jenna, please..." He smoothed her hair, feeling the tension coiled in her body as she drew long, shuddering breaths. "Will you tell me what's wrong?"

He felt a hand at his shoulder, and saw Robbie standing beside them, his small brow furrowed in concern, his green eyes wide with uncertainty as he sensed that all was not right. Jenna saw him, too, and with a ragged breath reached out and drew him to her, needing to hold him close to her as much as he needed to be reassured. He responded by throwing an arm around both Ward and her and smacking each of them wetly on the cheek.

Ward was relieved to note that the haunting vacancy in her eyes was gone and her smile, though shaky, was genuine. "Time for bed, young man." He stood up with Robbie in his arms and sent Jenna a look that seemed to say the subject wasn't closed yet.

She was in the kitchen making a pot of coffee, or trying to, when Ward came back downstairs. There were more grounds littered around the base of the percolator than in the paper filter lining the basket. He didn't say a word, merely came up behind her and stood ... waiting.

Jenna stiffened. Then her shoulders sagged defeatedly as she stared unblinkingly downward. "Will you look at this," she murmured. "I've made such a mess...."

The catch in her voice didn't go unnoticed by Ward, and he knew it wasn't the scattered coffee grounds on the counter she was talking about. He laid his hands on her shoulder, his thumbs kneading the tautness he found there. "You might have fooled Robbie," he said very gently, "but you don't fool me. I'm here if you want to talk about it. If not—" he hesitated "—then let it go."

"Let it go!" She felt hysteria rising in her and fought to battle it down. In its wake came a wealth of anger, frustration, disgust and, strongest of all, guilt.

"Don't you realize what I've done?" she whispered hoarsely. "I gave away my baby, my child, a part of me! And I planned it—*we* planned it! What kind of woman would give away her own flesh and blood and then walk away forever?'' She wanted to scream, to cry, but as always when she desperately needed the release, the tears refused to come. She turned then, naked heartache evident in her eyes.

Ward felt her anguish as if it were his own. It had been his selfish need, his and Meg's, for a child of their own, that was now tearing her apart. And just as surely, seeing her so distraught was tearing him apart. With trembling hands he reached out and cradled her against his chest.

Slowly, with jagged phrases and disjointed words, the accusations Neil had hurled at her came out. Ward closed his eyes and muttered harshly under his breath, and when she was finished, he lifted her chin and looked deeply into her pain-clouded eyes. ''You didn't walk away forever, Jenna.''

She shook her head. ''But I wanted to,'' she said miserably, her voice filled with self-loathing. She held herself stiffly away from him, as if by touching him she would somehow poison him, as well. The knowledge that her gift of life had made Megan and Ward the happiest people on earth was the only thing that had sustained her during the months following Robbie's birth. And though that hadn't changed, for the first time she couldn't forgive—or forget—what she had done. ''I tried to walk away. I really did. I just—I just couldn't.'' Her eyes darkened further. ''And you didn't want me here, Ward. You can't deny it.''

He was quiet for a moment. ''No, I can't,'' he said bleakly. Then his voice hardened. ''But I was wrong, and I can disagree with what that bastard said to you.'' With a gentle smile, he pressed a hand over her mouth to stifle her protest. "Through Robbie, you gave Meg and me so much, more than I can ever say. Please don't hate yourself for that. There's no shame in giving, and no shame in loving. You said it yourself, Jenna. You did it for love. Meg knew it, and I know it, now more than ever."

"Oh, Ward," she choked out, and flung herself against his chest. "I don't deserve this."

His fingers slid down her cheek to her chin, raising it until she was looking directly into his eyes. "What you don't deserve is the torture you're putting yourself through. You gave a part of yourself, Jenna, and I can't imagine a more loving gift. You are the most warm, sensitive, caring person I have ever known, and I pray to God with every day that passes that Robbie grows up to be like you."

An ache filled her throat. Did he realize how much that meant to her? The words were priceless, more precious than silver and gold. She slipped her arms around his neck and buried her face against his chest. "Oh, Ward." A hoarse cry rose from deep in her soul. "What will I do without you?"

Framing her face in his hands, he gazed down at her, his own expression a reflection of the joy and pain that filled her heart. "I've been asking myself that same question for days already," he whispered. "And I wish I had an answer."

His eyes revealed the depth of the emotional scars he carried, but there was also a faint light of hope there. With a sigh, their lips met in a passionate fusion of mind and body. Her senses were acutely attuned to his nearness, and the heat of his lips on hers drew from her a response that only he aroused. His hands skimmed her back as he swept her into his arms and held her as if he would never let her go.

Was it wrong of her to want this man so much that nothing else mattered, to long to share again the sweetness they had experienced last night? In his arms she could find forgetfulness, no matter how fleeting. In his arms she could find forgiveness . . . and love.

"Make love to me, Ward," she whispered pleadingly. "Please."

His arms crushed her against him. "You're so soft," he moaned into the dark cloud of her hair. As fiercely possessive as his hold was, his mouth grazing her cheek was unbearably tender. "I want you, Jenna. It makes me ache inside just to look at you, let alone touch you."

"Then make love to me," she begged again. She pulled his dark head down to hers, threading her fingers through the thick hair just above his nape. "Make love to me now."

Ward lifted her in his arms and carried her up the stairs. Jenna murmured a protest, saying she could walk, but he refused to let her go. Even when her body glided down the length of his as he lowered her to the floor, he kept one hand anchored on her waist as the other went to the buttons of his shirt.

It was exquisite torture to watch him undress with deft movements. With every inch of muscular flesh that was revealed to her, she ached for the moment she would be able to touch and caress him at will. When her own clothes had been disposed of, she stood in a soft circle of amber light.

His eyes roamed over her small firm breasts, lingering there before moving down over her flat abdomen, gently swelling hips and slender thighs.

Ward breached the distance between them with a single step and gazed down at her, his eyes lighted with desire. After spanning her waist with his hands, he trailed his fingers over the hollow of her abdomen, and commented softly, "You don't look as if you ever had a baby."

Jenna smiled rather shyly up at him. "Not just a baby," she whispered, "your baby." Her voice trembled as she added, "*Our* baby."

He smiled then, and Jenna felt her heart turn over at the tenderness in his eyes. He drew her to him, and she gasped at the feel of his male desire, bold with hunger for her as he laid her down on the bed. While his tongue probed the receptive caverns of her mouth, his palms slid coaxingly across the pink swelling tips of her breasts. Then he carved a pathway to one rosy nipple, taking it gently into his mouth. His tongue circled slowly, teasing the ripe peak to exquisite hardness and sending a current of desire racing through her. Gentle hands roamed over her hips and legs, tickling the soft skin of her inner thighs and sending waves of heat pouring through her veins.

Her hands stroked the muscles of his back, then slid to the taut hips pressed against her own, conveying her need to him with a subtle pressure of her fingertips.

For an instant Ward lay poised between her thighs, gazing down at her with a fevered intensity and a clear delight that left her breathless. "You're so beautiful," he whispered with awe.

Knowing that she gave him pleasure was far more important and precious to her than the fulfillment of her own desires, yet a sob of pure joy escaped her lips as he slid his hands beneath her and guided her to him. She arched upward, surrounding him with her warmth

and surrendering herself completely in her eagerness to
share herself.

Responsive to every slow, sure thrust, every endear-
ment murmured hoarsely in her mouth, every soothing caress of his hands on her aroused flesh, she felt
herself floating higher and higher in a glorious tide of
well-being. She loved this man, loved him as she would
never love another, and with each rousing motion of
love, her body expressed the overwhelming depth of
her feelings. Together they climbed to a pinnacle of
fulfillment, then floated gently as a feather back to
reality.

Later Jenna lay on her side, her head pillowed on
Ward's shoulder, her legs still entwined with his.
Overcome with a drowsy lethargy, she dimly heard him
chuckle as her lashes fluttered closed. Utterly exhausted, she fell asleep vowing that tomorrow she
would tell him . . . tell him that she loved him.

CHAPTER FOURTEEN

BUT TOMORROW CAME too soon, and with it, all the uncertainties of the days just passed. Jenna didn't doubt that she loved Ward; there was no question that he did. Yet there was no joy in the admission, no comfort in the truth, for theirs could never be a healing kind of love, a joyous kind of love. It was a love that could bring only hurt, a love that was tinged with sadness.

Morning crept in slowly, first in a hazy gray spear of light, then in errant shafts of golden radiance. Ward slept peacefully beside her, his dark hair tousled on the pillow next to hers, his breathing deep and even. He lay on his stomach, one arm curved over her slender waist. Awake since dawn, Jenna turned on her side to stare with vague fascination at the smooth expanse of his back, the tanned skin stretched across the vibrant muscles she had caressed and explored so eagerly.

They had made love again the previous night, and while it had taken only a single caress from him to set her on fire, the memory was bittersweet. Ward hadn't made love to a woman since Meg; despite the fact that he'd said the thought of making love with his head and not his heart left him cold, weren't there times when physical need overruled all else? No. *No.* Her mind rebelled at the thought. He felt something for her, she was sure . . . only was it enough?

She sighed, and when she did, Ward opened his eye
to gaze at her drowsily. "Good morning," he mu
mured. As he yawned, his arm tightened around he
and his fingers traced an idle pattern on the small of
her back. "Back to your old habits again, I see," h
observed dryly. "Awake at sunup again, weren't you?

Jenna made a halfhearted attempt at a smile. Wit
a pang, she realized just how much she loved him, an
her heart throbbed to know that her feelings weren
returned in full measure. But she could never be sati
fied with anything less.

And Ward would probably never be truly satisfie
with anyone but Meg.

"Jenna—" His fingers caught at her chin, cuppir
her face lightly in his hands. Her eyes dropped swift
against his gently probing gaze, and closing her eye
she buried her face in the hollow between his neck an
shoulder. She knew he was aware that something wa
wrong. But though Ward's eyes darkened at her odd
vulnerable expression, he said nothing. His fingers fe
away from her face to sift gently through the lor
strands of hair that spilled across his chest like a mi
night curtain of silk. "I like your hair," he said softl
"It's so long." He smiled rather crookedly. "Almo
as long as the rest of you."

Jenna felt her cheeks redden. Though neither h
tone nor his words implied any criticism, she wo
dered fleetingly if he was mentally comparing her
Megan. She had been so petite, with short blond ha
swirling softly around her face. Had he compared th
two of them last night when he held her in his arm
Had he enjoyed making love with Megan more th
her? Swiftly she put the brake on the disturbing esc
lation of such thoughts.

"I'll get the coffee on," she said hurriedly. Sitting up, she started to slide from the bed.

Ward wasn't yet ready to let her go. Moving with amazing speed for having awakened only moments before, he banded his arms around her waist and drew her back against the naked warmth of his chest. "There's no hurry," he said after glancing at the bedside clock. "It's barely seven." With unerring accuracy, his mouth nuzzled the acutely sensitized skin just below her ear.

"But—you're going to Tulsa this morning. And you have to pack yet."

"That won't take long." His gravelly whisper echoed in her ear. Her breathing quickened as he trailed a line of searing kisses across her shoulder. The feeling of his soft chest hairs pressing against her bare back kindled a fiery warmth inside her, and she ached to turn in his arms and lose herself in the hot desire already coursing through her.

The next moment she did exactly that. Currents of electricity raced through her as he stretched out beside her once again, the heat of his body a brand she sought to imprint fiercely upon her own. His mouth captured her breathless moan of passion, and when at last he released her lips, he gazed down at her with an elemental blaze in his eyes. Jenna shivered with pleasure, and reached for him.

At precisely that moment a cheerful voice demanded, "Are you guys gettin' married again?"

Startled, they both looked over to find Robbie at the side of the bed, his chin propped on his elbows and a pair of impish emerald eyes gazing at the two of them.

"Robbie…" There was an odd catch in Ward's voice as he stared at his son, but his lips twitched as he pulled the quilt higher over Jenna's bare shoulders. The horrified embarrassment he'd glimpsed in her face before she buried it against his shoulder was too precious for words. But somehow he made his voice sound suitably stern. "Robbie, it would be nice if you knocked before you came in."

Robbie's small black brows drew together in a frown. "Never had to before," he announced matter-of-factly, then looked at Jenna. "Will you fix pancakes for breakfast, Jenna?"

Ward smiled as Jenna's unintelligible mumble was lost somewhere in the vicinity of his chest. "Tell you what," he said, winking at Robbie. "If Jenna doesn't, I will."

When he finally scooted Robbie off in the direction of the kitchen, he tugged playfully at a strand of Jenna's hair. "It's safe to show your face again. He's gone."

"I suppose you think that was funny," she said, raising her head to glare at him.

"Funny?" Ward's lips quirked. "It wouldn't have been if he'd come in five minutes later." He laughed as her cheeks pinkened even more. "He's only three. He doesn't have any idea what was going on. And he associates kissing with marriage."

"Thank heaven for that," Jenna snapped, and began to gather up her clothes. With the sound of his laughter ringing in her ears, she stalked from the room.

When the time came for Ward to leave, however, she could only cling tightly to him. They were standing on the front porch, and Ward kissed the trembling lips she offered. "With this kind of a send-off," he murmured when he finally lifted his head, "I can't wait to see the kind of homecoming I get."

"When will you be back?" To her shame, she felt her eyes blur. She blinked rapidly, but she knew he saw the overbright shimmer of her eyes.

Ward tightened his arms around her and rested his chin on her shining head. "Wednesday evening," he answered absently. He drew back to look into her face. "You're not making it any easier for me to leave," he chided gently.

All she could manage was a tremulous smile. "I know." The smile faded. "I wish you didn't have to go," she whispered.

His breath caught at the depth of emotion reflected in her eyes. "So do I." The kiss he gave her was long and deep. His breathing was ragged when he finally raised his head. "I'll miss you." He pressed a last, lingering kiss on her parted lips, then reluctantly disengaged himself from her arms.

IT DIDN'T TAKE Jenna long to realize that the emptiness she'd felt that morning was only a prelude to what was to come in the days ahead. She tried telling herself that things would work out, but the little voice inside sounded just as uncertain as she felt.

When Ward returned, she knew she would have to leave, if for no other reason than to take care of the wearisome job of canceling the wedding. She was glad that an elaborate celebration hadn't been planned. Nevertheless, there were still numerous tasks to be taken care of. What she wasn't looking forward to were the inevitable questions about why the wedding was being canceled in the first place. She could only hope that people would be understanding enough not to pry unduly.

She knew now, more than ever, that she had never really loved Neil, not in the way she should have. She hated herself for hurting him, yet she knew she would never have been truly happy being married to him. While she was pregnant, she had tried so hard to suppress any maternal instincts she might have felt because she knew she would have to give up her baby. But she suspected it was the longing for a family of her own that had led her to believe she loved Neil in the first place, a need she had only fully realized during these past weeks with Robbie.

Early Monday evening Dr. Reynolds stopped by. Jenna was sitting on the porch with Robbie when he drove up, and Robbie promptly frowned at him, then took off in the direction of the swing set.

Steve Reynolds laughed as he sat down beside her on the top step. "Looks like I'm not exactly his favorite person."

"I guess not," she agreed, smiling at him.

He glanced toward the front door. "Is Ward around?"

Jenna shook her head. "He's in Tulsa for a few days. He'll be back Wednesday."

"That's just as well." The look he gave her was piercingly direct. "Actually, it's you I wanted to talk to." He cleared his throat. "You see, I've finally figured out why you've looked so familiar to me all along."

"Oh?" She smoothed a strand of hair away from her face and smiled. "I'm sure we haven't met before."

"No. We haven't."

Something in his tone brought her eyes to his in a flash. She found him gazing at Robbie. "Plains City is a small town and—well, people do talk. Surrogate motherhood is still the exception rather than the rule when it comes to a woman's infertility.'' There was a brief pause. "Most of the people in town don't know that Robbie is really Ward's son."

"I'm not surprised,'' she said quickly—perhaps a little too quickly. His eyes traveled from Robbie to her, and remained fixed on her face unwaveringly. Her heart began to beat with thick, uneven strokes. "You know, don't you?'' she whispered.

Steve Reynolds nodded. "I'm only surprised it took me so long to figure it out. The resemblance is really amazing."

Jenna swallowed. "And I suppose you think I shouldn't have come."

He hesitated for a moment. "It's not my place to judge. I'll admit that as a physician I'd have advised against it—'' he shook his head, then smiled a little wryly "—but if Ward hasn't minded letting you stay with him all this time, then that's good enough for me."

A grateful smile spread across her face. "Thank you,'' she said softly. She reached out and squeezed his hand. "That means a lot to me."

Steve Reynolds looked a little embarrassed, but then he grinned. "It would mean a lot to me,'' he said emphatically, "if you would seriously consider coming to work for me. I still haven't found an office nurse. An old country doctor like me can't afford to pay big city wages.'' He raised an eyebrow. "I have a feeling we'll be seeing a lot of you around here."

She smiled rather wistfully. "I doubt it. I'll probably be heading back to Galveston when Ward returns."

He studied her gravely before rising to his feet. "If you change your mind, you know where to find me." He extended his hand, and they exchanged goodbyes a minute later.

It wasn't until after he'd left that she realized just how tempting the offer was. Her mind began to race. Now that the wedding to Neil was off, was there really any reason she couldn't stay here—permanently? Mentally she ticked off the advantages. She suspected she wouldn't mind working with Steve Reynolds; it would be a change from the hectic pace in E.R. She liked the quiet, small-town atmosphere and found the wide-open plains soothing and restful. She would be only too happy to call this sleepy little town home. And of course there were two very obvious attractions—Robbie and Ward.

Ward. Her shoulders slumped as she climbed the stairs to ready the tub for Robbie's bedtime bath. What would he say when he came home from Tulsa and she told him she'd found a job here, that she was set on moving lock, stock and barrel to Plains City? Would he think it was to be near Robbie? It was, partially. But her mind suddenly froze. Perhaps he would think she had an ulterior motive—to inspire his trust and then someday run off with his child. Considering his conduct since her arrival, and even very recently, all the signs pointed in that direction. For that matter, could she watch Robbie grow up, and remain uninvolved, a spectator on the sidelines?

She was far too involved already, she realized sadly.

And yet there wasn't only Robbie to consider; there were her feelings for Ward, her love for him. Even if he approved of her moving to Plains City right now, what about tomorrow? Next month? Next year? Even if

Ward's feelings for her did indeed blossom and grow,
would they ever be enough for her? He had loved Meg
all his life, *still* loved her, in fact. Her thoughts grew
bitter. How could she, the mere mother of his child,
ever hope to compete with fifteen years of marriage
and love everlasting?

She was immediately ashamed of the thought. It
wasn't fair to any of them; nor was it fair that for the
first time in her life she felt utterly out of control. Her
future held nothing but a series of question marks.

The only thing that Jenna was certain of was that
nothing would ever be the same without Ward. Nor did
she want to jeopardize or tarnish the memory of what
little happiness they had shared together.

THOSE BLEAKLY distressing thoughts stayed with her
throughout the night and much of the next morning.
She had only to look at her son or pass by Ward's bedroom to be reminded of her problems. She felt as if she
were caught in a whirlpool, being pulled inevitably
downward, with no hope of ever surfacing.

The weather matched her mood. The sunshine of the
past week had disappeared, and the sky was a dark,
leaden gray as gloomy storm clouds swirled and
churned their way north. Her one small reprieve came
when Eileen burst in the back door shortly after lunch
that day, her face wreathed in smiles. "Guess what?"
She threw her arms around Jenna, who was just
emerging from the dining room. "I did it!" she cried
gleefully. "I actually did it!"

Jenna couldn't help but smile at her air of infec-
tious excitement. "You actually did what?"

"I got a job!" Eileen's voice rang out exuberantly. "And not just any old job, the *perfect* job! I'm the newest staff photographer for the *Abilene Herald!*"

Jenna's eyes widened. "That's wonderful!" She hugged the older woman. "Didn't I tell you not to give up hope?"

"You certainly did!" Eileen laughed. "In fact, I owe it all to you. It was your idea in the first place, you know. Remember the day you said it was too bad I didn't live in New York or Los Angeles, because then I could work for one of the scandal sheets?" Jenna nodded, and Eileen added triumphantly, "Well, that's when I decided to check with some of the newspapers in the area. Although I think the reason I got the job is because the editor got tired of taking my calls every day."

"Oh, I think you deserve a little credit, too," Jenna teased. "A little persistence never hurt anyone, and after all, you're the lady with all the talent, you know." She moved to the cupboard to remove two cups, as well as a glass for Robbie, who had scampered in to give his aunt an enthusiastically sloppy kiss. Jenna smiled at the sight and asked over her shoulder, "When do you start?"

"Next Monday." Eileen sat down at the table, only to get up the next minute, too excited to sit still. "Although I'm not sure how I'll ever get through the next week." She laughingly groaned. "I'm not sure I can wait that long."

"What did Frank have to say?" Jenna placed a steaming mug of coffee in front of her and joined her at the table.

"He was nearly as excited as I was." She grinned happily. "As I *am*," she corrected.

They chatted for a few more minutes before Eileen suddenly jumped up. "I almost forgot. I left something in the car." She returned a moment later with a huge leather-bound album in her hands. Placing it on the table in front of Jenna, she smiled. "This is for you."

Frowning, Jenna reached out to trace the gold binding, but the look changed to one of budding delight when she opened it. "Oh, Eileen," she exclaimed. "I can't believe you did this." The album was filled with dozens and dozens of pictures of Robbie.

"I found most of them in a box in the linen closet," Eileen said. She shrugged, looking a little embarrassed. "And I thought you might like to keep them."

Jenna smiled and flipped back to the first page, where she saw that one was of her and Robbie, the first day Eileen had visited during his bout with chicken pox. His arms were thrown around her neck and she was smiling radiantly down at him. In it, Eileen had captured all the love she felt for her son.

"This is precious," she whispered, genuinely touched. "Thank you, Eileen. I'll treasure it always." She leaned across the table and hugged Eileen once more. When they finally drew back there was moisture shining in both their eyes.

"Sentimental old me." Eileen laughed shakily, taking a handkerchief and wiping her eyes. "Frank always says he dreads the day Katie or Tim gets married, because anyone looking at me will likely think it's a funeral, instead."

Eileen was still visiting when the phone rang a short time later. Jenna heard it as she was descending the staircase after putting Robbie to bed for his nap, and

Eileen held out the receiver when she returned to the kitchen. "It's for you," she said. "Long distance."

Neil. Jenna's heart sank, but she took the receiver and spoke into it cautiously. "Hello?"

"Jenna, thank God I reached you!"

It wasn't Neil at all, but her mother. Recognizing the unfamiliar sound of strain in her voice, Jenna instinctively tensed. "Mom! What is it? What's wrong?"

"It's your father, Jenna." Her mother sounded terribly distraught. "He's been hurt...."

"Hurt! How?" she gasped.

"The hurricane... he was in the shed this morning...a branch of the cottonwood tree crashed through the roof."

Stricken, Jenna looked through the window over the sink. Even this far north, the wind was blowing gustily. As she watched, several large raindrops splattered the window. She should have known there was a storm raging on the Gulf Coast. "How is he, Mom?" she asked hurriedly.

The line crackled and it was a moment before Marie Bradford's voice could be heard. "Not good, Jenna. He's in the hospital. They'll be taking him into surgery in just a few minutes." Marie's voice broke treacherously. "He—he's in critical condition."

"I'll be home as soon as I can." With that urgent promise, she hung up the phone. Dazed and ashen, she buried her face in her hands.

"Jenna?" Eileen touched her shoulder anxiously. "Jenna, what's wrong?"

Jenna looked up into Eileen's concerned face and shook her head to clear it. "My father," she muttered hoarsely. "The hurricane on the coast...he's been hurt. I have to go. I have to pack." On leaden feet she began to move toward the stairway, gathering momentum as she took the steps two at a time. Eileen followed and watched Jenna heave the suitcase onto the bed, as if she were scarcely aware of what she was doing. But suddenly Jenna stopped and pressed hot hands to her cheeks. "Oh, Lord," she muttered. "I completely forgot about Robbie. What will I do with him? Ward won't be back until tomorrow...."

"Don't worry about Robbie. I'll stay here with him until Ward gets back." Eileen's voice came from directly beside her, and Jenna saw that she had already scooped up some underwear from the dresser drawer and was folding it neatly into the suitcase.

Jenna opened her mouth. "But your job—"

"Doesn't start until Monday, remember?" She guided her firmly onto a chair and directed Jenna to stay put and gather herself together. In an amazingly short time, Eileen had her suitcase packed and sitting by the door. "The only thing that bothers me," she said with a deep frown, "is how you're going to get home. If Ward didn't have the plane—"

"I'll be fine," Jenna said with a valiant attempt at a smile.

"I don't like the idea of your driving all that way by yourself," Eileen said quietly. "If I didn't have to stay with Robbie, I'd go with you myself." Her eyes brightened. "Maybe Frank—"

"Eileen, really, I'll be okay." She held her hands out, palms downward, and gave a forced laugh. "See? Steady as she goes."

Ward's sister glanced skeptically toward the window. "But what if the weather worsens?"

Jenna squared her shoulders. "A little rain and wind won't stop me." Eileen's face still wore a worried expression, and with a sigh, Jenna moved toward her. "Eileen, the best thing you can do for me is to stay here and take care of Robbie. He'll likely be upset when he wakes up and I'm not here." She smiled a little wistfully. "Or maybe that's just wishful thinking." She couldn't help but think of Ward, as well. What would his reaction be when he arrived home and found she wasn't there?

Eileen's smile was halfhearted. "No. It's not. He'll miss you, Jenna. We'll all miss you." The smile faded. "This is goodbye, isn't it?"

Jenna nodded, her throat suddenly tight. There was no need to lie, to pretend she would be back. She wouldn't. She couldn't. It would be much too painful. Perhaps what she regretted most of all was not having the opportunity to say goodbye to Ward, to see his face just once more....

Eileen made Jenna promise to call and let her know when she'd arrived safely back in Galveston, no matter what the hour, and to let her know how her father was doing, as well. Jenna was surprised to see tears sparkling in Eileen's soft brown eyes, and she hugged her one last time.

"Thank you again for the album," Jenna said softly. She squeezed Eileen's hand. "I think I'll look in on Robbie before I leave."

In his room, Jenna's eyes rested quietly on her sleeping son. How she loved him—loved him because he was a part of her, but more because he was so much his father's son. He possessed the same square chin, the same straight nose. His lashes fanned out like dark crescents on his face, and she lovingly traced her fingers over the soft curve of his cheek, knowing that never again would she touch her son. Never again would she hold him in her arms or listen to the bubbly sound of his laughter. Her fingers memorized the silkiness of his hair. Then she bent slightly and pressed a whisper-soft kiss on his mouth.

There was so much pain swirling inside her that she wasn't sure which was worse—the agony of leaving Robbie and Ward or the desperate fear that clutched at her heart in knowing that her father lay weak and ill in a hospital bed so far away.

Finally she drew back to look down at him one last time. The tears slipped unheeded down her cheeks as she said a last goodbye to her son. "Think of me sometimes, Robbie," she whispered to the sleeping little boy. "Think of me and remember that I love you, that I'll never stop loving you though I can't be with you."

CHAPTER FIFTEEN

THE WEATHER JENNA had so blithely dismissed to Ei
leen had her nerves stretched tautly by the time she was
even halfway home. The wind howled eerily through
the cracks in the car windows. The highway was wet
and slippery, and she passed more cars than she cared
to count that had careered out of control and lay
abandoned in the ditch.

It was the middle of the night when she finally pulled
into the hospital parking lot. It was nearly deserted
and she dodged the puddles pooled on the asphalt as
she ran through the entrance. Her steps never wavered
until she passed through the double doors of the in
tensive care unit.

In her father's room, her legs threatened to buckle
beneath her when she first glimpsed him. Her fingers
curled tightly around the metal side rails of the bed for
support. The hospital setting was her work environ
ment, one she was well used to, but unaccountably the
antiseptic smell, the tangle of IV tubes and monitors
attached to her father's inert form almost gagged her.
His skin appeared lifeless, almost as pale as the stark
white of the sheets and pillowcase, and an array of
mottled bruises darkened the left side of his face and
one arm.

Her hand trembled as she touched the shock of tan
gled gray hair that lay on his forehead. He didn't stir

idn't move a muscle. He just lay there, his breathing eep and labored beneath the oxygen mask clamped to is nose and mouth.

One of the night nurses came in then. Jenna recogized her and nodded abstractedly, all her attention ocused on her father's gaunt form. The nurse gave her brief rundown of his condition, but all Jenna really aught were snatches of phrases—"internal injues...punctured lung..."

Her head was whirling as she stumbled toward the CU waiting room off the hallway. Her mother's voice s she rose from a cramped position on the sofa rought Jenna out of her trance.

"Jenna. Thank God you're here! Have you seen our father yet?"

She nodded, and mother and daughter embraced. enna took a deep breath. Then her eyes moved over e worry lines etched in her mother's forehead. Mom," she said in some concern. "You shouldn't be ere. You should be home in bed!"

Marie shook her head. "I couldn't leave him. I idn't want him to be alone in case..." Her lips tremled and she broke off.

"He'll be all right," Jenna said with a surety she idn't feel. Her heart ached for her mother, and she ished she had been there to comfort Marie during the ong, lonely hours that day. "He has to be," she said ervently. "He just has to!"

"It doesn't look good," Marie said sadly. "He's eak and frail and...he's just not as young as he used o be. He's been out of surgery for hours already and e still hasn't regained consciousness. The surgeon—" er voice faltered "—he says it's touch and go."

But Jenna refused to give up hope. She couldn't convince her mother to go home and snatch a few hours rest, but with morning's first light, she was relieved to note that a little of the strain had left her mother's expression. Jenna's heart was heavy, but she was glad she was there to lighten the burden on her mother's shoulders.

Nonetheless, the next twenty-four hours were a nightmare she cared never to repeat in her life as both she and her mother silently prayed for a miracle.

WHEN WARD ARRIVED HOME Wednesday evening, he had no idea that Jenna was in Galveston, standing vigil at her father's bedside. He could hardly wait to see her. Two days away from her had made him realize what he'd already begun to suspect. Since Meg had died, even though he had Robbie, there were so many times when he'd felt alone and so empty. But he knew now, beyond any doubt, just how much Jenna had given to him, how much she meant to him.

She meant the world to him.

His stride was light as he took the porch steps two at a time. He grinned as he remembered Jenna's parting kiss, thinking of the welcome he knew was only seconds away, impatient to feel her soft lips beneath his once more.

He stopped short when he found Eileen in the kitchen instead. Seeing his father, Robbie flung himself at his legs. Ward lifted him and kissed the chubby cheek his son offered. Then his eyes sought Eileen's. "Where's Jenna?"

The anxious look on Eileen's face when she saw him in the doorway sent a cold shaft of fear through him. His arm tightened around his son.

Eileen made a helpless gesture with one hand. "She's gone, Ward—"

"Gone? Gone where?"

Eileen darted him a tentative glance. "Back to Galveston." He looked so wounded that for an instant she felt they'd both been hurtled backward to another time, not so very long before.

"Ward, she had to leave," she said. She moved closer and laid a hand on his arm, looking up into his taut features. Shooing Robbie into the living room, she hurriedly explained what had happened to Jenna's father.

"Have you heard from her?" he asked tersely when she was finished.

Eileen nodded.

"How is her father?"

She shook her head. "Not good, from the sound of it."

"Jenna," he said abruptly. "How is she? How did she sound?"

Eileen hesitated. "A little tense," she said in a low voice. "Though she told me she was fine and not to worry about her."

A grim little smile curved Ward's lips. That sounded like Jenna. She was probably scared as hell, even while stubbornly insisting she was fine. She would be brave even while her heart was breaking. She was so strong, so independent—and so damned vulnerable. He cursed softly beneath his breath. The smile faded. "I guess it's a good thing I didn't bring my suitcase in. Looks as if I'll be needing it tomorrow." At his sister's puzzled gaze, he said quietly, "I don't want her to be alone, Eileen."

She looked up at him. "You're going to Galveston?" When he nodded, she reminded him, "She does have her mother with her." She hesitated. "And her fiancé."

"I want to be with her. I have to know that she's all right." His voice hardened. "And she no longer has a fiancé."

He ignored Eileen's soft gasp of surprise and brushed by her into the other room. "Ward, wait!" She practically ran after him. "I...I understand, really," she said breathlessly when he stopped. "You see...Robbie said something today...." She glanced away when Ward's eyes narrowed questioningly. "He mentioned seeing you and Jenna in bed together. And at first I thought I must have misunderstood. But I didn't, did I?"

"No," he stated baldly.

She met his gaze levelly. "I'm glad," she said quietly. "I loved Meg, but I've always hated the thought of your spending the rest of your life alone."

"I don't intend to." His voice was very low, but his meaning was clear. Eileen smiled as their eyes met in silent understanding.

TWO DAYS without sleep had left Jenna feeling numb and weary to the bone. She had finally persuaded her mother to go home and rest Wednesday night, but only by issuing strict orders that she was not to show her face at the hospital until at least eight o'clock in the morning. Jenna had also assured her mother that she wouldn't leave until she returned the next day.

It was getting harder and harder to sit by her father's bed, watching his still form. She hated the feeling of helplessness that plagued her, knowing there was nothing she could to help him. If there was consolation to be found, it was in the fact that while he was no better, neither was he any worse.

"Jenna." She looked up to find Neil in front of her, holding a cafeteria cup and saucer. His smile was tentative. "I thought you could use some hot tea."

"Thanks, Neil." She had been lying on the narrow couch in the waiting room. Family members of patients in the intensive care unit had been filtering in and out all morning and well into the afternoon, but she'd been alone for the past fifteen minutes. Straightening up, she accepted the cup appreciatively.

"Any change?" Neil shoved his hands into his trouser pockets and looked at her.

"No," she said quietly. "He's still unconscious."

"Where's your mother?"

"In with Dad." Jenna took a sip of the clear amber liquid and leaned her head back. Only one visitor at a time was allowed, and then only for a short time.

Neil glanced around the small room, then took the armchair across from her. She was too tired to notice the uncomfortable look that flitted across his face, but after a time he cleared his throat and said, "Jenna, we need to talk."

She sighed and turned her head to look at him. Neil had stopped in to check on her father several times since her arrival, but neither Jenna nor Neil had mentioned their last disastrous meeting. Jenna had been too worried about her father to give it much thought. Neil had offered kindness and a shoulder to lean on, and she had accepted it gratefully, if not lovingly. In reality, it was Ward she longed for, Ward she ached to confide in, Ward's arms she wished would hold her and soothe away her fears.

"Neil, please." She gestured vaguely. "This isn't the time or the place."

"I know," he said. "But with your father ill, we haven't had much time to ourselves." He hesitated. "I suppose we should postpone the wedding."

Jenna looked at him numbly. "The wedding?" she repeated. "There isn't going to be a wedding."

"I was angry and upset when I said that," he told her quickly. "I said a lot of things I didn't really mean."

"Neil—"

"No, please, hear me out." He ran a hand over his smooth brown hair, obviously speaking with difficulty. "I won't pretend it will be easy," he said finally. "I hate the thought of you with another man, but I think the best thing for both of us is to forgive and forget."

Forgive and forget? Did he really think she could dismiss either Ward or her son that easily? She shook her head. "It's not that simple, Neil."

His mouth tightened. "Why not? It was hard for me to accept that you had another man's child, but I've come to terms with it. As for Ward Garrison, I know you well enough to accept that it won't happen again after we're married."

Jenna clasped her fingers tightly in her lap. She didn't want to hurt Neil any more than she already had, yet what could she say? That she didn't love him—that she never had, not really? Compassion stirred in her.

"There's no use pretending anymore, Neil," she finally said heavily. "You and I—we're just not right for each other. Our marriage would never stand a chance. Don't you see that?"

"No, I don't. You said you loved me!"

"I thought I did." Helplessly she lifted her eyes to him. "Only I know now that what I felt wasn't love. That's not to say that I don't care for you, because I do. Only—only I can't marry you," she concluded miserably.

A muscle worked angrily in his jaw. "Damn it, Jenna! You can't possibly have changed that much in the few weeks you were away!"

"No, I haven't," she agreed quietly. "I'm simply seeing things differently, more clearly. My feelings for you aren't what I thought they were—they were what I *wanted* them to be.... It's over, Neil. Accept it. Please." Her eyes pleaded with him.

"Accept it!" He jumped to his feet. "Damn it, Jenna, I won't let you do this! It's not going to end like this, do you hear? It isn't!"

He strode angrily from the room, and Jenna stared after him silently. It had ended a long time ago, she acknowledged wearily. She was exhausted, both physically and mentally. The interminable hours of waiting were finally exacting their toll on both body and mind. She thought of her father, lying still and unresponsive, though both she and her mother willed him to live. But as she did so, the lingering thread of hope she had clung to so stubbornly these past two days began to fray at the ends, and she felt herself coming apart.

The walls of the small room, whose neutral blue-and-gray color scheme was meant to be soothing, suddenly began closing in on her. She stumbled into the hallway, but even there, as she took deep gulps of air, a wave of despondency swept over her. She had never felt so alone. And she was tired, so tired of trying to pretend that everything was going to be fine, when in reality, *nothing* would ever be right again.

If only Ward were here, she thought desperately, sagging against the pale green walls of the hallway. He would know what to say, what to do. God, how she needed him! Her throat felt raw with the effort to keep from sobbing.

Her head jerked up at the sound of footsteps echoing in the long, dismal hallway. A man had just stepped off the elevator and was walking straight toward her, his steps firm and purposeful. He was dressed in dark slacks that clung to powerful thighs. The pale gray shirt he wore emphasized the muscled width of his shoulders. Her eyes widened as the tall spare figure drew closer.

Finally the man drew to a halt, an odd half smile lifting his lips as he stopped and stared directly at her. Her heart fluttered as she stared back, unable to believe her eyes.

"Aren't you even going to say hello?"

It was that deep, gentle voice that finally prodded her into action. With a strangled half sob, she threw herself straight into Ward's arms.

"How did you know?" she murmured shakily. "How did you know I needed you?" She rubbed her cheek against his shoulder, reveling in the feel of his arms around her, strong and secure, and of his heart beating steadily beneath her ear.

He didn't answer at first, at least not directly. His fingertips glided over her face as if to memorize her every feature. Then he bent his head, and the roughness of his cheek grazed hers as he gathered her closer in his arms. "I wanted to be with you," he said softly.

Jenna drew back to gaze up at him through shining emerald eyes, her hands still linked with his. Somehow those few, simple words meant more to her than anything else he could have said.

Ward noticed with concern the faint mauve shadows beneath her eyes. "Are you all right?"

"I am now." She smiled up at him.

"And your father?"

Jenna sighed and briefly described her father's condition. Ward slid his arm around her shoulders and brought her gently up against his lean strength. "When was the last time you ate?" he asked with a frown. "Or slept?"

She flushed a little. "I had some tea a little while ago," she said quickly.

They had been walking toward the waiting room as they spoke, and now they stopped in the doorway. "And I suppose you've been sleeping on that." His tone was stern as he waved a hand at the narrow couch along the wall.

Jenna sighed and looked away.

"That's what I thought," he said grimly. "The first thing I'm going to do is get some food inside you and get you home and into bed."

"Ward, wait!" she protested as he took her firmly by the shoulders and began to march her into the hall once more. The idea of going home and snuggling into the warm comfort of her bed sounded heavenly. But she bit her lip guiltily and glanced toward the imposing double doors that led into ICU. "I hate to leave my mother alone here. It's been so hard on her...."

His face immediately softened. He lifted a thumb to stroke the curve of her cheek. "What if I take you home and then come back here to be with her? I won't be able to stay very late, though. I'll need to pick up Robbie in Houston before nine tonight."

"Houston?" Her eyes widened. "Robbie's in Houston?"

"He's with an old college buddy of mine," Ward explained. "He and his wife have a little girl about Robbie's age, so he's in good hands." He smiled a little at her stunned expression. "I brought him along because I didn't want to burden Eileen, not with her starting her new job. I also thought your mother might want to see him. Do you think she'll mind?"

In answer she stood on tiptoe and lifted her lips to graze his cheek. At the last minute he turned so that her mouth met his instead. The kiss they shared was brief, but Jenna felt herself drawing strength from the warm touch of his mouth on hers. "I'm glad you came," she whispered shakily. "And I'm glad you brought Robbie."

Ward's hand on her waist guided her gently back to the tiled floor. "There's no place I'd rather be." His tone was grave, but his eyes were lighted with an oddly tender expression.

Shyly, softly, she kissed him once more. With that fleeting caress, she felt the knot of pain inside her begin to uncoil. "I'll let Mom know I'm leaving," she said, then disappeared through the double doors.

Inside the intensive care unit, she beckoned to her mother. They spoke in hushed whispers near the doorway.

"Oh, Jenna, I think he's better." Marie's eyes were shining. "He opened his eyes once, only for a second, and he squeezed my hand while I was talking to him."

They clasped each other tightly. "He's going to be all right, Mom," Jenna said in a choked whisper. "I know he is."

Marie squeezed her hands and stepped back. "I think you're right." Her eyes scanned her daughter's face. "Why don't you go back to your place for a while? If there's any change, I'll call you."

Jenna nodded. "That's what I came in to tell you." She paused, then said softly, "Mom, Ward's here. And Robbie is with him."

A look of surprise flitted across Marie's face. Then she smiled. Jenna had few secrets from her mother, and she had confessed her feelings—and her fears—about Ward, and her doubts about Neil, as well.

"On second thought, why don't you plan on staying at home with me for a few days?" Marie suggested. "There's plenty of room for all of us. It will be less cramped than your apartment and it's closer to the hospital."

"That's a good idea," Jenna agreed, then frowned. "Though I'll have to check with Ward to see if he's made other arrangements. I think he's planning on staying tonight, but after that I'm not sure."

He would, he assured her a few minutes later, be staying as long as he was needed. *I'll need you forever,* she told him silently. The only thing that prevented her from blurting it out was the realization that he might not want to hear that from her.

"How did you get here?" she asked curiously as they began walking down the dimly lighted corridor.

"I flew." He reached out in front of her to press the Down button on the elevator.

Jenna gasped. "You flew? With Robbie? In this weather?"

Ward shook his head and sent her an admonishing glance. "You haven't been outside the hospital at all in the past two days, have you?"

"No." Her tone was a little sheepish as they stepped into the elevator. A moment later she saw what he meant. The autumn sky was a brilliant blue, and white puffy clouds floated high above. It seemed almost indecorous to come from the stifling atmosphere of the hospital to the freshness of outdoors, where a warm scented breeze blew in from the Gulf on such an achingly beautiful day.

Still, the signs of violence from the recent hurricane were readily apparent. Crews were still hard at work cleaning up the downed tree limbs that lay scattered throughout the city as Ward and Jenna drove to her apartment, where she picked up some clean clothes. When they finally pulled into her parents' driveway, she couldn't prevent her heart from leaping into her throat. It took a conscious effort to prevent her eyes from lingering on the pile of faded bricks and torn shingles that had been the shed.

Ward saw the look and wasted no time in pulling her into the house. Less than an hour later, she had been briskly and efficiently fed, showered and dressed in a white linen nightgown.

Drawing the covers back on the wide double bed in the room Jenna had occupied throughout her years at home, Ward motioned her into it. "Remember the time you said I was always trying to put you to bed like a child?" His grin was a trifle wicked.

"This is your big chance, then." She smiled as she obediently slid into bed.

Ward laughed and plumped the pillow under her head. "I remember thinking there wasn't a chance I'd put *you* to bed like a kid."

"And I've always thought you were a very capable man." When he pulled the covers over her, an impish smile curved her lips. "Do you tell bedtime stories, too?"

"Not at three o'clock in the afternoon," he said promptly. His eyes ran appreciatively over her slender curves, outlined beneath the lightweight blanket. He placed his hands on either side of her body and looked down at her. "Right now bedtime stories are the last thing on my mind."

Jenna smiled her satisfaction. Despite her fatigue, her body responded to the dark flame in his eyes. So she sighed when he straightened and briskly tucked the loose ends of the sheet and blanket snugly beneath the mattress. "Just like my mother," she grumbled good-naturedly. But her eyes lighted up as she turned on her side and snuggled beneath the blankets. "Except she always kissed me good-night," she murmured, looking up at him from beneath her lashes.

Ward's eyes darkened as they ran over the silken tangle of her hair, fanned out behind her on the pristine whiteness of the pillowcase. "I think that could be arranged," he said, and bent down to give her a deep, lingering kiss that had Jenna smothering a frustrated groan when he finally lifted his head.

"That wasn't a very motherly kiss—or a fatherly one, either." The protest was made as she looped her arms around his neck. "Maybe we should try it again till you get it right," she suggested throatily.

"If I do, you'll be getting more than just a kiss. You don't exactly inspire maternal *or* paternal feelings where I'm concerned."

Ward smiled down at her and shook his head. He was indeed sorely tempted to sink down beside her and love the breath from her. "You need to rest right now," he decided. "And I need to get back to the hospital and your mother, and then pick up Robbie later this evening.''

''Then I suppose I'd better sleep now while I'm able to.'' Her eyes sparkled rather mischievously. ''Maybe we should have stayed at my apartment, instead. Because I doubt I'll sleep tonight, knowing you're in the next room with Robbie instead of me.''

Ward smiled and pressed a kiss on her mouth. ''There will be other times,'' he said softly, then gently disentangled himself from her arms.

CHAPTER SIXTEEN

IT WAS NEARLY NOON when Jenna finally made it downstairs the next day. The memories of the previous night—her father, Ward, Robbie—rushed into her mind, and she hurriedly showered and dressed.

She wasn't quite prepared for the sight that met her eyes in the kitchen. Ward was at the sink, his forearms plunged into soapy dishwater, while Robbie was sitting in her mother's lap, contentedly stuffing his mouth full of homemade chocolate chip cookies.

It was Ward who finally looked up and saw her wavering in the doorway. "Well, well," he said lightly. "Look who the wind blew in."

Marie and Robbie glanced up at the sound of his voice. Robbie wasted no time in scrambling off Marie's lap and hurtling himself at Jenna. Scooping him up in her arms, Jenna received a damp kiss on the mouth and returned an equally warm one of her own.

Jenna's smile encompassed all three of them, but it was Ward she spoke to. "So," she said, eyeing the sinkful of dirty dishes, "my mother's put you to work already."

"Oh, I'm not complaining." His eyes were affectionate as he glanced over his shoulder at her, then traveled to her mother. "At least not yet," he added dryly.

Marie laughed, and Jenna couldn't help but notice the look of shared amusement that passed between them. The thought flitted through her mind that it was almost hard to believe they had met for the first time just last night. It wasn't until Jenna moved toward the table that a slight frown found its way between her dark brows. "How's Dad today?"

"Well—" Marie paused, then broke into a wide smile "—why don't you ask him yourself? He's been waiting for you all morning."

Jenna stood stock-still. Her arms tightened around Robbie. "Do you mean it?" she breathed.

Marie nodded, her eyes lighted with the same vibrant delight as her daughter's.

"Well, then." Jenna set Robbie on his feet, her face transformed by a brilliant smile. "What am I doing here?"

"I was wondering the same thing myself," her mother said, laughing as Jenna moved toward the door. Robbie grinned as Marie tweaked his nose and lifted him into her lap once more. "You can tell him I'll be up shortly," she called after Jenna. "Right now I think I'll get acquainted with this young man."

JENNA WAS MORE than pleased that her mother, Robbie and Ward took to one another so well. Ward took over the household chores in his typically capable manner, leaving both Jenna and Marie free to visit the hospital whenever they wanted.

The next evening after dinner, Ward and Marie lingered at the kitchen table over their coffee. Jenna had darted over to her apartment to check on things and had taken Robbie with her.

Marie placed her spoon on the table and gazed across at Ward, her expression rather speculative. "You and Jenna have grown very close, haven't you?"

The corners of Ward's mouth turned up in a fleeting half smile. "I certainly hope so. Jenna means a great deal to me." He hesitated. "Has she . . . said anything to you?"

"Yes, she has." Marie's look grew thoughtful. "But even if she hadn't, there are times when Jenna doesn't have to say a word for me to know exactly what she's feeling." Her brows lifted. "You know she's adopted, don't you?"

Ward nodded.

"Losing her parents was very hard on her," Marie went on to say. "Her first year with us wasn't easy for any of us. She scarcely uttered a word, but those huge green eyes said it all, and I don't think she was even aware of how much she was communicating." She sighed and shook her head in remembrance. "I used to think she would never open up, never let us help her. It used to break my heart to watch her, knowing she was hurting inside and not letting any of it out. It sounds crazy, but Jerry and I used to pray that she would cry or scream—anything to let go of her grief."

Ward's eyes darkened. His heart ached for the child his sweet, loving Jenna had been. So scared. So alone. And so damnably brave. "She was lucky to have you," he said very gently.

Marie's smile was pensive. "Jenna was an extremely quiet, sensitive child. Even once she began to warm toward us, there was still so much she kept bottled up inside herself." She paused. "Do you know that to this day I have never seen her cry?" she added quietly. "She had the usual scrapes and bumps, just like any other child, but I never once saw her shed a single tear."

Ward's throat tightened, remembering the night he'd surprised her going through the picture album, and the ensuing flood of tears. Tears shed not for herself, but for Meg. And then later, she'd been just as confused and afraid as he was of the tumultuous feelings that had sprung up between them. But despite her fears, she was so strong, so giving, so alive to the feelings of everyone around her.

He loved her. With all that he possessed, with every ounce of feeling in his soul, he loved her.

"I'm glad you've been here for Jenna." Marie's quiet voice broke into his thoughts. He looked up at her, his expression rather dazed. Then he smiled.

"Jenna is one very strong woman," he said softly. "Like her mother."

AFTER THOSE CRITICAL first days, Jerry Bradford's condition improved daily, though the doctors anticipated he would be hospitalized at least another week. He was moved from intensive care to a regular room Sunday morning, so both Jenna and Marie wore radiant smiles when they returned home Sunday afternoon.

Ward grabbed Jenna by the shoulders and seemed just as heartened as she by the news. It wasn't until her mother and Robbie withdrew from the room that a shadow passed over his face. When he drew her quietly toward the sofa, her heart began to pump fearfully.

"What is it?" Her eyes anxiously scanned his face.

"Jenna—" he squeezed her hands "—I have to head back home soon."

"Wh-when?"

"I should leave tomorrow. Tuesday at the latest," he said quietly. "My partner called while you were gone. Something's come up and I'm needed back at the office as soon as possible." He paused, his dark eyes gauging her reaction.

"I—it's all right." She spoke hurriedly at his guilty look. He'd said there would be other times, and she had to believe that. Her eyes lifted to his as she took a deep, steadying breath. "Ward, we—we need to talk before you leave."

"Yes," he said slowly, "we do." His eyes roved over her pale face. "Jenna..."

But whatever he was about to say was cut off abruptly by the sound of the doorbell.

It was Neil.

She heard Ward's indrawn breath behind her and saw Neil's face tighten at the same time, and half turned to see the two men sizing each other up. She knew a fleeting sense of déjà vu and quickly positioned herself squarely between them.

"Hello, Neil," she said quietly.

He nodded in response to her greeting and stepped inside. An uncomfortable look flashed across his face as his eyes swung between Ward and Jenna before he finally addressed her. "Do you think we could go for a walk or something? I'd like to talk to you," he added hastily on seeing Ward's frown.

Jenna stilled Ward's displeasure with a pleading look as their eyes met and communicated. Then, to her relief, Ward's eyes softened. He silently retreated, leaving Jenna alone with Neil.

The atmosphere was strained as Jenna pulled a windbreaker on over her pale blue blouse. The temperature wasn't all that cold, but the day was cloudy and there was a cool nip to the breeze. Neither she nor Neil spoke as their steps carried them down the sidewalk edging the wide, tree-lined street.

Finally Neil pulled her down onto a bench in a nearby park where Jenna had played as a child. For a long time he just looked at her. Then at last he spoke.

"It really is over, isn't it?"

It was more a statement than a question, yet Jenna found herself searching for an answer. She jammed her hands into the pocket of her coat and looked straight ahead. "Yes, Neil," she said quietly. "It is."

"It's him, isn't it?"

She turned to look at Neil then. She had no trouble discerning his meaning, but surprisingly, there was no trace of anger on his handsome features, only an oddly pained resignation lurking in his eyes. "You mean Ward?"

He nodded.

"It would have happened, anyway," she told him very gently. "Even before I left for Plains City, I'd begun to have doubts." In the tumult of the past few days, she hadn't realized she still wore his ring. Now she removed it and very gently pressed it into his hand. "Let's not lie to ourselves, Neil. We weren't right for each other. And it's better that we discovered it now, before we made each other miserable."

Neil gave a short laugh. "You think I'm not miserable now?"

"Neil, please." Her eyes were shadowed. "This is hard enough as it is. Don't make it worse."

"I suppose you're right." He sighed and stretched his long legs in front of him. "I didn't take the job at Bates-McKinnon," he said after a moment.

"Because of me?" Her eyes widened.

"Partly," he admitted. "But then I started thinking... Maybe you were right, after all. It would have been like going over to the enemy camp."

She touched his arm gently. "I'm proud of you, Neil," she told him softly. "I think you did the right thing."

"I hope so." A grim smile curved his lips as he stood up. "I hope it works out." His blue eyes flickered as his smile faded. "And I hope things work out for you, as well."

The sound of children's laughter drifted to her ears as they retraced their steps. In the driveway of her parents' house, Neil gently touched her cheek, his eyes roaming over her face. On impulse, Jenna reached up and touched her lips gently to his, then murmured a last goodbye, unaware of a watchful pair of brown eyes glued to her every movement from inside the house.

She should have been relieved, she realized as she watched him drive off, that he had finally accepted the end of their engagement so calmly. She was free, as free as she had once proclaimed Ward to be, free to love whomever she chose.

But there was a part of her that was almost afraid to believe...

Her mind was suddenly filled with Ward. His laughter. His smile. The feel of his arms, strong and secure as he held her against his chest. Those dark brown eyes soft with love...

For his son. For Meg. For her? Yes. Yes! He did love her! She clung to the thought before a fleeting despair nipped at her. But was it enough? She wanted all that he had to give, all his love—as he had given Meg. Was that so selfish of her?

Suddenly the front door opened and Ward stood there. For a long time they stared at each other. Ward's face was somber, his eyes dark and unreadable. His taut stance in front of her only served to further her apprehension, to tighten her stomach into a cold hard knot as she moved inside.

The tense atmosphere increased when he finally stepped inside and closed the door behind her.

It was Ward who finally broke the brittle silence between them. "Which is it?" he asked in a very low voice. "Congratulations or condolences?"

She sent him a deep, searching look. "Why? Are you waiting to pick up the pieces?"

"As a matter of fact, I am," he returned very quietly. "If it comes to that."

If it comes to that? She was almost afraid to read too much into his words. Her eyes were dark with uncertainty, the color of jade as she tipped her head to the side.

Ward approached her. His fingers encircled her wrist and he lifted her hand to stare at it, his eyes on the bare spot where she had so recently worn Neil's ring. "Does this mean what I think it does?"

His tone was hushed, his eyes guarded as they met hers. She felt a flicker of awareness that Ward was just as uncertain as she. "It means," she said in a voice that wasn't entirely steady, "that I have a wedding to cancel. But—you already knew that."

His look grew more intense. "Are you sure you want to do that?"

Jenna shook her head, her eyes glued to his. "I—I don't love Neil, not in the way I should, not in the way he deserves. I could never be happy with him."

"And what about me, Jenna? Could you be happy with me?"

The moment stretched out endlessly as Jenna stared at him. "Ward," she whispered, "what are you trying to say?"

"I think you know." There was a heartbeat of silence. "Don't you, Jenna?"

The tenderness in his eyes did not disguise the hint of anxiety in his voice. The combination sent Jenna's mind racing and her heart thudding wildly. The flame of hope burning faintly in her heart began to grow stronger.

Ward could hold back no longer. With a shuddering breath, he started to reach for her, but her sudden gasp brought him up short. Jenna was staring intently at his hand.

"Your wedding ring!" Her eyes flew upward to his. The flame burned brighter yet. "It's gone—"

"I should have stopped wearing it a long time ago," he said quietly, his expression reflective. "It belongs to another time." He paused, and then continued. "You brought light into my life, Jenna. You showed me that I've been living in the shadows, and for that I'm grateful."

"I—" Her hair swirled around her face as she shook her head. Gratitude? She didn't want his gratitude; she wanted his love—all that he had to give and more! "Ward, please—what do you want from me?" Her hands lifted in an almost pleading gesture.

The next thing she knew she was caught in a rough embrace that was all the more precious because of its urgency. Ward took her mouth in a scorching kiss that was both tender and demanding, sending a torrent of desire rushing through her veins. She sagged against him weakly when he finally tore his mouth from hers and drew back from her.

"Oh, Ward, I wish you didn't have to leave tomorrow! I wish—'' The words came from deep inside her, but suddenly she stopped, aware of his eyes boring into hers.

"What, Jenna? What do you wish?" His fingers tangled into her thick hair and brought her face to his.

Under that intent, scorching gaze, she felt as if he were reaching into her soul. And she could no longer deny to him what she had never denied to herself since she had first discovered it. "I wish..." She struggled for breath, her heart thundering painfully in her ears. "I wish we could be together forever." Her voice caught painfully. "I—I love you, Ward."

His eyes searched the dark green depths of hers. Then his arms tightened around her in a fierce embrace that nearly crushed the breath from her. Yet Jenna reveled in the contact, the heat of his body, the strength of his arms around her. She buried her face against his chest.

"Oh, God, Jenna." He drew in a harsh, rasping breath and rested his chin on her bent head. "I didn't realize how desperately I needed to hear you say that until I actually heard the words." He tugged her head back so he could look directly into her eyes. "I love you, Jenna," he said very softly. "I love you."

Her heart melted beneath the velvet of his voice. She felt herself being slowly drawn into the warmth of his eyes and she knew a moment of brief spiraling joy, but suddenly her eyes were filled with torment.

"Oh, Ward." She pulled away from his arms and sank onto the sofa, weak-kneed and shaken. "How can you be sure?'' she whispered. She focused her vision on her hands, willing them not to shake.

He sat down beside her and took her hands in his. His hands were warm, comforting, immeasurably gentle despite their strength. "Don't you think I know what I feel?" he asked very quietly.

"I think you know what you *think* you feel." Still she refused to look at him. She desperately yearned to believe him, and yet she was afraid.... "You just said you were grateful. And maybe—" her voice was a halting whisper "—maybe you're mistaking gratitude for love. Maybe it's because of Robbie! And not only that, you've been alone for so long—"

"No." There was no mistaking the firm conviction in the voice that cut through hers. "I was in love for years, Jenna. Believe me, I know the feeling."

"Oh, Ward!" His name was a cry of pure agony on her lips. "You're still in love with Meg! Don't you think I know that? Maybe it's selfish of me, but I want to be loved for myself. I—I don't want to play second fiddle to Meg!"

She started to lurch to her feet, but Ward's relentless grip on her hands wouldn't let her. The seconds ticked by. The room was steeped in silence. The pressure on her hands increased until she felt her bones would be crushed. Then, abruptly, he released his hold and his hands came up to cradle her face. Gently he turned her toward him. "A part of me will always love Meg. I can't deny it," he told her quietly.

A raw pain throbbed in her breast as she felt the words clear to her soul. She opened her mouth to speak, but he stilled the sound with a finger on her lips.

"But that doesn't lessen what I feel for you. That doesn't mean there isn't room in my heart for you. You fill my heart, you fill my soul, in a way I've never even dreamed of, in a way that's never happened before, even with Meg." His voice dropped, and his eyes moved over her face tenderly. "As for Robbie, he's only one of the reasons—not the only reason—that I love you. He looks like you, he has the same sweet, loving nature, and nothing could please me more. Looking at him and knowing that he is a part of you fills me with so much pride, so much love, I can't begin to describe it."

His hand feathered over her cheeks, her eyes, her trembling mouth. "Oh, Ward," she whispered. "I can't believe this is happening. I'm afraid that if I close my eyes I'll open them and find it's all a dream."

With infinite gentleness, he bent and pressed his mouth to hers. "Never doubt that I want you," he whispered against her mouth. "Never doubt that I need you. And *never* doubt that I love you."

Jenna's eyes clung to his, but she could not speak. All the uncertainties, the doubts, all the anguish of the past weeks were banished as she slipped her arms around his neck and held him with all the love she felt in her heart. Ward gathered her close and took her lips with a kiss that spoke of need, of passion, of boundless love that sent a surge of aching sweetness through her veins.

It wasn't until Jenna felt herself being lifted, cradled in strong, tender arms and borne toward the stairway that she realized his intentions. "Ward," she murmured weakly, "my mother...and Robbie..."

"Have gone out for ice cream." He flashed a triumphant smile. "I very politely requested that they not hurry home too soon."

He carried her with surprising ease straight toward her bedroom. She hid her smile in his shoulder. "And what did she say to that?"

His eyes glinted as he set her on her feet and very deliberately closed the door behind them. "Your mother," he said, pretending a thoughtful air, "is a very wise and obliging woman." Then he grinned. "She said she would be more than happy to see that Robbie doesn't disturb us until morning."

"Rather sure of yourself, weren't you?" Jenna retorted, a sparkle lighting her eyes.

Ward's eyes sobered, and Jenna realized in that instant how very uncertain of her he had been. "You scared the hell out of me when I saw you kiss Neil," he admitted.

"I never really loved him," she told him gently.

His hands settled possessively on her waist. "It doesn't matter anymore." He drew her to him once more and kissed her lightly, then more deeply, with ever increasing ardor.

And then there was no more time for words. His hands shook as he slowly removed her clothing, and allowed Jenna to do the same for him. Her fingers moved over his skin with the same lingering tenderness, the same caressing touch that he had used on her, arousing a flame of passion in both of them. Ward moaned his compliance as they stretched out on the bed, his body molded against her curves.

His hands traveled a searing path, grazing her throbbing nipples, wandering over her stomach, and lower. His mouth followed, warm and tormenting, as he paid homage to first one ripe peak and then the other. Weak and yearning, Jenna clutched at his shoulders and, with a breathless moan, began to incite him to the same fevered pitch she had reached, stroking and sliding her fingers over his back, reveling in the smooth texture of his skin beneath her fingertips.

And then they were one, fused in throbbing delight that carried them ever higher, ever upward, to the heavens and beyond. Jenna breathed his name as waves of heat poured through her, and she reached her quivering release as Ward took his own with a driving compulsion that was all the more precious for the pleasure she knew she gave him.

The shadows of early evening found their way through the narrow opening in the curtains. His tender arms held her gently as she floated back to earth, basking in a warm cocoon of contentment. She snuggled drowsily against Ward, a smile of serenity curving her lips as she ran a lazy hand over the dark mat of fur on his chest.

Ward stilled the motion of her hand, lifting it and planting a warm kiss in the palm before he settled it on his stomach once more. His eyes were lighted with affection as he turned his head slightly to gaze down at her.

"I suppose it will mean going to the expense of a new and bigger water heater," he whispered, a smile on his lips that sent a warm glow radiating through her, "but can we finally tell Robbie we *are* getting married?"

Her hand ceased its restless exploration of his flesh, still warm and faintly damp from their fervent lovemaking. Jenna propped herself on an elbow and stared down at him. A tinge of uncertainty crept into her voice. "Are you sure that's what you want?"

His eyes, warm and glowing, captured hers. Jenna waited, almost without breathing, for his answer.

"Oh, Jenna." Her name was half laugh, half groan s he threaded his hands in her hair and brought her nouth down to his. "That is what I want, more than nything in this world. I love you, and I want you beide me, as my wife, for the rest of our lives."

The heartfelt emotion, the raw conviction in his oice, touched her deeply. Joyously she cried his name, nd was rewarded as his lips took hers in a deep, soulrenching kiss that had them both breathing heavily vhen he reluctantly drew away to look at her.

He sighed as he saw that her cheeks glistened. Overhelmed with happiness, Jenna was helpless as her eyes illed and tears slid unchecked down her face.

Softly he kissed away the lingering traces of dampess from her face, then pressed her back on the pilows and gazed down at her with loving eyes. "Just romise me one thing," he requested.

"Anything," she told him tremulously. "Anyhing."

She smiled through her tears, and Ward felt his heart urn over. He framed her face with his hands and ran is thumb beneath her misty green eyes. "Please, enna. It breaks my heart to see you cry. No more ears. Ever."

Her eyes once again burned, her throat ached, but he was so full of joy she felt she would burst with it. I can't promise," she whispered against his mouth. hen she smiled, a beautiful, brilliant smile, and kissed im with every ounce of feeling she possessed. "But I'll y...."

HE HAD NO TROUBLE keeping her word—until a glorious day the following autumn. That was the day Christina Marie Garrison was born. Wasting no time

in letting the world know of her arrival, she let out
loud wail and was promptly handed first to her ra
diantly smiling mother and then to her beaming fa
ther, who was garbed in drab green surgical attire. Th
sight of her husband, so big, dark and strong-lookin;
tenderly cradling his tiny daughter with love and prio
shining from his eyes, filled Jenna with such profoun
emotion that she promptly burst into tears.

The days sped by, filled with love and laughter an
a wealth of happiness. At the tender age of nearly for
months, Christina still occasionally woke her mothe
for a midnight feeding, and a particular night a wee
before Christmas was one of those times.

Jenna sat in the rocker near the fireplace whi
Christina nursed contentedly. She had carefully cre
downstairs with the baby so as not to awaken Robb
and Ward. Outside the world was crisp and cold an
dark, but inside the gaily decorated house the atm
sphere was warm and welcoming, despite the midnig
hour. A lamp burned dimly in the corner, casting ju
enough light in the room that Jenna was able to se
both the tiny figures of the Nativity scene spread out o
a silky blanket of angel hair across the mantel and th
huge Christmas tree in the corner.

She brushed her fingers lovingly across the fine da
fuzz that covered the baby's head, noting that her lor
feathery lashes were beginning to droop. Already h
eyes were beginning to darken to the same warm, go
den brown as her father's.

A rustle of movement caught her attention, and sh
looked up to see Ward standing at her side, his ha
tousled from sleep. Her breath caught in her throat
the tenderness in his eyes, resting hungrily on her u
turned face. She would never cease to be moved by th

love and warmth that filled his eyes whenever he looked at her.

Yawning, he rubbed a hand across his chest. "You're spoiling her rotten," he said, dropping down beside her. Leaning over the arm of the chair, he brushed his lips across the baby's chubby cheek.

"Feeding her is spoiling her?" Jenna wrinkled her nose at him. "Now if you said that her grandma and grandpa and Aunt Eileen and Uncle Frank spoiled her, I might be inclined to agree."

He grinned a little ruefully. "Guess I'm just jealous." His expression was indulgent as he touched the tiny dimpled fist that lay curled against her breast, and his eyes feasted on the expanse of bare skin that lay open to his gaze. Glancing down, Jenna noticed that the baby's small mouth had dropped away from her nipple.

"I hope you didn't do that on my account." Ward laughed as she frowned good-naturedly and modestly covered her bare breast with her nightgown once more.

He followed along behind her as she silently padded up the stairs. When she bent to lay Christina in her crib, he brushed aside her hair to drop a warm kiss on her nape.

Once they were cozily ensconced in their own bed, Ward wrapped his arms around her and tucked her head into the hollow of his shoulder. "By the way, I forgot to tell you. I saw Steve Reynolds this afternoon. He wanted me to ask if you would be interested in filling in for Marianne this summer. She's taking a two-week vacation in August."

Jenna smiled. Dr. Reynolds, who had delivered the latest addition to the Garrison family, had lamented long and loudly when he was forced once again to hunt for an office nurse, his latest having abdicated in favor of her husband, son and newborn daughter. He had hired Marianne only the day before Christina was born.

"I don't see why not." She pressed a kiss on Ward's beard-roughened chin. "Unless you have something planned."

She felt him smile against the soft skin of her temple. "I don't have anything planned for August," he murmured. His hand drifted below the hem of her nightgown to trespass on the satiny skin of one bare thigh. "But I do have something planned for the next few minutes."

She playfully slapped away his hand as he started to mold her tightly against one lean hip. "You've already had your fun for the night," she reprimanded tartly.

He laughed softly. "I wouldn't count on it."

Before she knew it her nightgown had been whisked neatly over her head and dropped in a heap next to the bed.

"Again?" She laughed a little breathlessly, then shivered as his hands traced a lazy, erotic pattern on her full breasts. "This is beginning to become a habit—and not at all in keeping with the image of a forty-year-old man." They had celebrated his birthday last May.

Tender fingers traced the outline of her lips. "It's funny you should say that," he answered thoughtfully. "Because I feel as if my life is just beginning."

Then he took her lips in a long, drugging kiss that sent a feverish excitement swirling throughout her body, and Jenna's last thought before she was drawn into a whirling vortex of love and passion was that he was right.

The best was yet to come.

Available now from

Harlequin Superromance®

Bridge to Yesterday
by Muriel Jensen
(title #468)

If you'd grown up believing your parents cared so
little about you that they'd given you up for
adoption, how would you feel? Then, if you found
out that they'd only let you go because they loved
you more than life itself, what would you do?

For Leah Alden, there was only one answer—she
had to find her birth parents. And although she'd
been separated from him for a year, there was only
one person Leah considered asking for help—her
husband, Jeff.

As their search went on, Leah began to have a new
hope. If she could build a bridge to yeaterday, then
she and Jeff might also find a future.

**Bridge to Yesterday
(title #468)**

A story about life and love that will touch your
heart and leave you feeling good about being
alive.

FASH-S

NEW FROM

Harlequin Superromance®

Coming in October:
THY HEART IN MINE (title #471) by Cara West

At age forty, Elizabeth Waite has resigned herself to the fa
that she will never have a family of her own.
Then, miraculously, Mac Reynolds comes into her life.
Handsome, successful, Mac can promise Elizabeth
everything she wants—except the one thing she wants
most desperately of all....

Meanwhile, Elizabeth has sensed a presence in the buildi
where she works, an old Confederate widows' home.
A woman from the past is reaching out to her. Could it be
that she has a message for Elizabeth, one that is crucial t
the dilemma she faces with Mac?

THY HEART IN MINE—a story about
the enduring power of love.

Coming in January 1992:
Lynn Leslie's dramatic new Superromance novel
DEFY THE NIGHT (title #485)

DEFY THE NIGHT is a ground-breaking novel by a writi
team new to Superromance. This poignant romance is
guaranteed to touch the hearts and minds of all who read

Heidi Allan has always looked after her sister, Faith. And
when Faith's illegitimate newborn is stricken with a fata
disease, Heidi knows it is up to her to help Timmy, too.
Heidi decides to end his pain, even at the cost of her owr
freedom. But it's a choice that is hard for others to acce
particularly Luke, a lawyer and Timmy's paternal uncle.
Can he learn to live with that choice and to defend and l
the woman who made it?

Available wherever Harlequin books are sold.

SON-R

Fall in love with

Harlequin Superromance®

Passionate.
Love that strikes like lightning. Drama that will
touch your heart.

Provocative.
As new and exciting as today's headlines.

Poignant.
Stories of men and women like you. People who
affirm the values of loving, caring and
commitment in today's complex world.

At 300 pages, Superromance novels will give you
even more hours of enjoyment.

Look for four new titles every month.

Harlequin Superromance
"Books that will make you laugh and cry."

SUPER

This October, Harlequin offers you a second
two-in-one collection of romances

A SPECIAL
SOMETHING

THE FOREVER
INSTINCT

by the award-winning author,

Barbara Delinsky

Now, two of Barbara Delinsky's most loved books are
available together in this special edition that new and
longtime fans will want to add to their bookshelves.

Let Barbara Delinsky double your reading pleasure with
her memorable love stories, A SPECIAL SOMETHING and
THE FOREVER INSTINCT.

Available wherever Harlequin books are sold.   TWO-D

HARLEQUIN®
OFFICIAL SWEEPSTAKES
RULES

NO PURCHASE NECESSARY

1. To enter, complete an Official Entry Form or 3"× 5" index card by hand-printing, in plain block letters, your complete name, address, phone number and age, and mailing it to: Harlequin Fashion A Whole New You Sweepstakes, P.O. Box 9056, Buffalo, NY 14269-9056.

   No responsibility is assumed for lost, late or misdirected mail. Entries must be sent separately with first class postage affixed, and be received no later than December 31, 1991 for eligibility.

2. Winners will be selected by D.L. Blair, Inc., an independent judging organization whose decisions are final, in random drawings to be held on January 30, 1992 in Blair, NE at 10:00 a.m. from among all eligible entries received.

3. The prizes to be awarded and their approximate retail values are as follows: Grand Prize — A brand-new Mercury Sable LS plus a trip for two (2) to Paris, including round-trip air transportation, six (6) nights hotel accommodation, a $1,400 meal/spending money stipend and $2,000 cash toward a new fashion wardrobe (approximate value: $28,000) or $15,000 cash; two (2) Second Prizes — A trip to Paris, including round-trip air transportation, six (6) nights hotel accommodation, a $1,400 meal/spending money stipend and $2,000 cash toward a new fashion wardrobe (approximate value: $11,000) or $5,000 cash; three (3) Third Prizes — $2,000 cash toward a new fashion wardrobe. All prizes are valued in U.S. currency. Travel award air transportation is from the commercial airport nearest winner's home. Travel is subject to space and accommodation availability, and must be completed by June 30, 1993. Sweepstakes offer is open to residents of the U.S. and Canada who are 21 years of age or older as of December 31, 1991, except residents of Puerto Rico, employees and immediate family members of Torstar Corp., its affiliates, subsidiaries, and all agencies, entities and persons connected with the use, marketing, or conduct of this sweepstakes. All federal, state, provincial, municipal and local laws apply. Offer void wherever prohibited by law. Taxes and/or duties, applicable registration and licensing fees, are the sole responsibility of the winners. Any litigation within the province of Quebec respecting the conduct and awarding of a prize may be submitted to the Régie des loteries et courses du Québec. All prizes will be awarded; winners will be notified by mail. No substitution of prizes is permitted.

4. Potential winners must sign and return any required Affidavit of Eligibility/Release of Liability within 30 days of notification. In the event of noncompliance within this time period, the prize may be awarded to an alternate winner. Any prize or prize notification returned as undeliverable may result in the awarding of that prize to an alternate winner. By acceptance of their prize, winners consent to use of their names, photographs or their likenesses for purposes of advertising, trade and promotion on behalf of Torstar Corp. without further compensation. Canadian winners must correctly answer a time-limited arithmetical question in order to be awarded a prize.

5. For a list of winners (available after 3/31/92), send a separate stamped, self-addressed envelope to: Harlequin Fashion A Whole New You Sweepstakes, P.O. Box 4694, Blair, NE 68009.

PREMIUM OFFER TERMS

To receive your gift, complete the Offer Certificate according to directions. Be certain to enclose the required number of "Fashion A Whole New You" proofs of product purchase (which are found on the last page of every specially marked "Fashion A Whole New You" Harlequin or Silhouette romance novel). Requests must be received no later than December 31, 1991. Limit: four (4) gifts per name, family, group, organization or address. Items depicted are for illustrative purposes only and may not be exactly as shown. Please allow 6 to 8 weeks for receipt of order. Offer good while quantities of gifts last. In the event an ordered gift is no longer available, you will receive a free, previously unpublished Harlequin or Silhouette book for every proof of purchase you have submitted with your request, plus a refund of the postage and handling charge you have included. Offer good in the U.S. and Canada only.

HQFW-SWPR

HARLEQUIN® OFFICIAL SWEEPSTAKES ENTRY FORM

4-FWHSS-1

Complete and return this Entry Form immediately – the more entries you submit, the better your chances of winning!

- Entries must be received by **December 31, 1991.**
- A Random draw will take place on **January 30, 1992.**
- No purchase necessary.

Yes, I want to win a FASHION A WHOLE NEW YOU Classic and Romantic prize from Harlequin:

Name _____ Telephone _____ Age _____

Address _____

City _____ State _____ Zip _____

Return Entries to: Harlequin **FASHION A WHOLE NEW YOU,**
P.O. Box 9056, Buffalo, NY 14269-9056   © 1991 Harlequin Enterprises Limited

PREMIUM OFFER

To receive your free gift, send us the required number of proofs-of-purchase from any specially marked FASHION A WHOLE NEW YOU Harlequin or Silhouette Book with the Offer Certificate properly completed, plus a check or money order (do not send cash) to cover postage and handling payable to Harlequin FASHION A WHOLE NEW YOU Offer. We will send you the specified gift.

OFFER CERTIFICATE

Item	A. ROMANTIC COLLECTOR'S DOLL (Suggested Retail Price $60.00)	B. CLASSIC PICTURE FRAME (Suggested Retail Price $25.00)
# of proofs-of-purchase	18	12
Postage and Handling	$3.50	$2.95
Check one	☐	☐

Name _____

Address _____

City _____ State _____ Zip _____

Mail this certificate, designated number of proofs-of-purchase and check or money order for postage and handling to: Harlequin **FASHION A WHOLE NEW YOU Gift Offer, P.O. Box 9057,** Buffalo, NY 14269-9057. Requests must be received by December 31, 1991.

ONE PROOF-OF-PURCHASE

4-FWHSP-1

To collect your fabulous free gift you must include the necessary number of proofs-of-purchase with a properly completed Offer Certificate.

© 1991 Harlequin Enterprises Limited

See previous page for details.